Snipe Hunt

Also by Susan Hasler

The Truth Mines Trilogy
Intelligence (Book One)
The Flat Bureaucrat (Book Two)

Other Books

Project HALFSHEEP

KRILL

Drawing on Cave Walls

TRUTH
3
MINES

Snipe Hunt

Susan Hasler

Bear Page Press • Asheville

SNIPE HUNT

Copyright © 2025 by Susan Hasler.

Printed in the United States of America.

Snipe Hunt is a work of fiction. The story, all names, characters, and incidents portrayed in this production are fictitious. No identification with actual persons (living or deceased), places, buildings, and products is intended or should be inferred.

Cover and artwork by Susan Hasler.

www.SusanHasler.com

ISBN: 979-8-9990626-1-1

Published by Bear Page Press, Asheville, North Carolina.

Bear Page Press and the Bear Page Press logo are trademarks of Zreil Global Marketing, Inc., or its affiliates.

In Memory of Judi Hill

Acknowledgments

The accomplishments of women in intelligence are being erased as I write. Their photos are being removed from walls of honor and their careers dismissed. So first and foremost, I would like to thank the remarkable CIA sisterhood of counterterrorism officers who inspired this series. I will only mention the ones who have been most public and whom I knew best—Cindy Storer, Barbara Sude, Gina Bennett, and Margaret Hennock. They are just a few of the female powerhouses I came across in my work. They stuck their necks out and held the line no matter the cost to their careers. I salute them.

I owe so much to my writer friends who have offered comments, support, and commiseration over the years. Special thanks go to the three women who served at one time or another as my "writing partners." Linda Erday, Janice Lierz, and the late Martha Woodroof contributed so much to my work and my spirit. Carolyn Elkins and Bill Spencer have been unceasingly fabulous. Bill has also served as my editor, and a better and more thorough editor you will not find anywhere. I would like to thank my agent, Liza Dawson, for her extensive comments on this work. My husband, Stephen White, has provided constant love and support. Finally, I have dedicated this book to Judi Hill, who started the Wildacres Writers group and gave me and so many others a community of voices and a place where we could find love, joy, and support as we learned to write loud and well.

Author's Note

This work is set in an intelligence agency akin to the Central Intelligence Agency, where I worked for 21 years. For the purposes of my novels, I put the CIA under light metaphorical cover and called it "the Mines." Like other examples of "light cover," this device does not so much conceal the subject as lend it a sheen of plausible deniability. It also serves to remind the reader that this is a fictional institution built atop surface and subterranean memories of a real agency. The terminology is my own, taken from mining vocabulary and whimsy. I wanted to give the sense of an insider language full of acronyms and cant without using the real terms.

The Attack Maddie Remembered

What did I know, and when did I know it? You would think that question would be easy to answer, but the verb *to know* is tricky. The mind isn't a brightly lit conference room where facts gather around the table awaiting executive decisions. It's a haunted hoarder's house crossed with a crumbling metropolitan sewer system. The lights are flickering. There's stuff in there you don't know about, disorganized and covered in muck. Decision making works like a child's paper fortune teller. Answers depend on your favorite color today and which numbered flap you lift.

So random.

What did I know, and when did I know it? To clarify here, I am referring to the "what" and "when" of the Screamer Attack on the Mines, our nation's premier intelligence agency. I remember nothing about the more recent attack. Nothing. No "what," no "when," and certainly no "why." So, I have to start with the Screamers, because the response to that attack is what led to that event I can't remember, the one that left visible scars on the surface of my head, and invisible scars buried so deep inside I can't begin to reach them.

I was at my desk when the Screamers went off, trying to discern the outlines of an attack I knew was coming. When the sound burst from amplifiers hidden in the lights, I felt something click into place in my mind. A click imbedded in a fraction of a second. Then I launched myself backwards, upending my chair. The rhythmic, unrelenting waves of sound swamped my body, rolled it, and shook loose connections in my brain that still spark and dangle. I fought the shakes to right my chair and climb back into it. We were under terrorist attack. Why didn't I leave?

That click told me that I could have averted the attack if only the right puzzle piece had fallen into place in time. A silver fish surfaced in my mind holding the puzzle piece in its mouth. I had to stay put and catch the fish before it darted back into the depths of my subconscious.

I popped a couple of gummy bears in my mouth but didn't chew. The vibrations got stronger as the building took up the rhythmic beat. A term shook loose in my head—*harmonic vibration*. It makes structures collapse. Dust drifted down from the ceiling in pulsing clouds and caught in the morning light. The heartbeat of a dying institutional beast. How many years did my bureaucratic soul lust after a window? Now cracks snaked across that window and advanced with each pulse.

The noise was coming from the new full-spectrum lights, a so-called "morale-boosting initiative" hatched by our idiot Boss of Mines. Another contractor boondoggle. Money must be spent by the end of the fiscal year, or it would vanish. Nothing was worse than losing money. Except for what was happening all around me.

"Money!" I yelled at the ceiling. It gushed into the system in the years after the towers fell. Contractors collected like flies. They promised the moon if only we would give them a piece of that money.

Who had time for properly vetting those contractors? Who would get richer if rules were overlooked?

The day they installed the lights in my office, I opened one of the boxes, slid the tube out, and examined it. I didn't know what I was looking for. I should have walked the thing to the techies and had them take it apart. The workman scowled and reminded me that the bomb-sniffing dogs had gone over everything. I handed the light back like a nice girl.

That workman's face was sour and contemptuous. We later determined that not all the installers knew what those lights contained, but this one did. I saw the glint of murder in his eyes but didn't recognize it in time.

Glint of murder. Silver fish. Flash. Click. I could have stopped this attack if I had kept hold of that light.

Why did I choose that moment to be compliant when I had a well-documented reputation for poor interpersonal skills? *Bitch* was the unofficial term. When you're working for assholes, you have to be a bitch every single day, because the assholes are assholes every single day. They do it with a natural, enviable ease. It's almost like it leaves them refreshed. It's hard work maintaining the bitch edge necessary to be heard. And while you're being bitchy enough to be heard, you must take care you're not so bitchy as to torpedo your own career and be silenced completely.

As it says in the Upanishads, "Sharp like a razor's edge is the path."

I ruffled too many feathers. I watched one train wreck after another and saw the sort of person who walked away and the sort who didn't. My spirit sagged. I lost my bitch edge long enough to hand that damned light back.

And now we were in the middle of a terror attack—an attack of such odd shape that no one anticipated it in all brainstorming sessions conducted by all the experts in all the gray conference rooms across all the countries participating in the "War on Terror."

I took the softened gummy bears out of my mouth and jammed them in my aching ears. I climbed on top of my desk and stood on tiptoe to remove the translucent ceiling panel covering the screaming tubes. They were hot. I plucked my sweater from the chair back and used it to remove a tube that was so much heavier than the old fluorescent tubes. That's what I should have noticed. I threw the tube at the window and the cracked glass disintegrated, leaving an opening to sanity and silence.

I connected to the minds of the tower jumpers. They were years and miles away, gone under rubble and history, but across that distance, our minds melded. I felt the sound as searing heat. I smelled burning jet fuel. The vibrations turned into an echo, echo, echo of every attack I had been unable to stop in my career. If only I could reach that window, I could find sanity and silence and atonement.

A security guard appeared at the open door checking for stragglers. I ran for the window. He tackled me as we passed through it. We fell together on the narrow strip of decorative stone that covered the seventh floor setback. My head and left arm came down first and hard. I briefly lost consciousness; then the bite of broken glass brought me round. I struggled to get away, to find escape over the edge, but he lifted me up. I fought, but he was huge.

He dragged me out of my office and into the hallway. He put me down in a river of terrified humanity. It carried me toward a stairway. Larger bodies pushed against me from all sides. I started to fall, but the man behind me grabbed me under the armpits, lifted me up, and pushed me through the door ahead of him. I wish I knew his name. In the stairwell it was slow, hot, and close. The farther down we went, the more people pushed in from lower floors. It got slower, hotter, and closer. I longed for that window as I struggled to find pockets of air to breathe.

My shoes came off. Stray shoes were everywhere, like small animals tripping us up. The stairs vibrated and threatened to liquefy beneath our feet. I smelled my own blood and felt the warm moisture down my left side. My head swam. The only thing that kept me moving was a desperate yearning to walk on solid ground again.

When we finally arrived in the basement, security guards were there to point us in the right direction. The nature of the noise changed, or rather the ability of my ears to hear it changed. The cilia, the tiny hairs inside the ear canal, lost their resiliency. Wind rushed through the hollow space of my brain. Then the screamers went silent, and the lights went out.

We were blind, deaf, and packed into a confined space. If people found an exit blocked, they would panic and surge backward against the oncoming crowd. Compression asphyxiation—yet another echo of an earlier attack. I smelled smoke. I could feel something about to tip. I had been fine with dying by defenestration, but I was terrified of being crushed to death in the darkness.

Small flashlights carried by the guards popped on. I remembered the combination whistle/flashlight I carried on a chain around my neck. They handed them out after the Strikes. I turned my light on, as did others. Tiny points of light, but enough to keep us from falling into a fatal panic.

We finally emerged from the ground-floor entrance at the northeast side of the building and stumbled into the sun, blinking. The ground should have been solid, but I could still feel a sickening shift in the universe. I looked down at my arm and saw layers of fat and muscle spread open. I passed out.

"Until you get your feet back on solid ground," was what Carlos said when he sent me here for "therapy." But here, in these ancient stone mountains, is where I discovered that solid ground is nothing but a cruel illusion.

2

The Dead, the Deaf, and the Bewildered

I s anything ever truly laid to rest at the Mines? Every day, miners labor under the delusion that secrets can be kept, delete buttons permanently delete, and corpses never rise to the surface of the water. But the fundamental paradox of the intelligence world is that while the truth may be irretrievable, it is never entirely lost. The men and women who succeed are the ones who work creatively with its debris.

As they gathered for the second senior-level funeral of the week, the surviving officials of the Mines were up to their necks in debris, bad trouble, and opportunity. Funerals removed obstacles, freed up headspace, and suggested new paths. Yesterday's services had laid to rest Dashiell Aspling, the late Boss of Mines or BOM. Aspling had succumbed to a coronary during the Screamer Attack. His seventh-floor office was now available.

The bad trouble was blame, hovering over them like an Acme safe over Wile E. Coyote. The president, the Esteemed Legislative Body, and the public demanded a scapegoat to be held accountable for the humiliating attack on the Mines. Someone had to be savaged, mocked, and pilloried until justice was served. The person or persons who had dropped the ball and failed their country. Outrage must be stoked. Pathos magnified. Television ratings depended upon it.

The top officials of the Mines had abandoned the word "scapegoat." It was tainted. They coined a new term, "snipe." They needed to offer up a snipe to save themselves and the institution. Dashiell Aspling would have been the obvious choice, as he was guilty, although unwittingly so. "Unwitting" was the operative word. It should have been carved on his tombstone. "Here lies Dashiell Aspling, Continuously Unwitting from 1956 to 2009." The problem with a guilty snipe was that guilt rarely belonged to one person alone. It rubbed off on those in proximity. Inquiring into Dashiell's sins would bring investigators too close to certain irregularities committed by some of the very people in attendance at this funeral.

They needed another snipe.

The Reverend Brown stood, and all eyes focused on the closed casket containing the compressed remains of Shelby Isherwood Wexler. Shelby was the late Boss of the White Mines—one of the four horsemen, as the leaders of the four divisions of the Mines were called. He was killed in the Screamer Attack when the concrete portico over the main entrance of the headquarters building collapsed.

The White Mines is the analytical branch of the Mines. Its mission is to illuminate the future in a way that will allow the busy policymaker to manipulate it. It should have provided intelligence to prevent the attack.

It failed.

Shelby failed. Could they pin the blame on Shelby? He wasn't directly involved in any of the worrisome irregularities, although he had learned of them after the fact. Digging into his story would only unearth sins of omission. It was plausible that sins of omission alone could have allowed a terror attack to happen. The assembled mourners frowned as they considered this question, along with the question of how Shelby's flattened and obese body had fit into that casket. Did they fold him like an omelet?

Greyson Earl was the Boss of Black Mines, in charge of clandestine operations, the spy work people associate with the Mines. He stood at the back edge of the funeral canopy, half-hidden by a spray of butter-yellow gladiolas. Suspicion had drawn his shoulders into a vulturous hunch, but he was still a towering figure. The other mourners glanced over their shoulders and looked away with a shiver. More than one entertained the thought that Greyson was gloating over the body of his old bureaucratic foe.

But no, Greyson genuinely regretted Shelby's death. It complicated his plans. With great forethought, he had taken steps to implicate Shelby the moment the Screamers went off. Sitting at his desk, he immediately recognized the sound as a terror attack and realized that it had something to do with intercepts he had suppressed. The only extant copies of those intercepts were in the bottom drawer of his personal safe. They must not be found there, or they would bring the blame for the attack down on his own head.

As sound tore through the building, Greyson's executive assistant tried to hustle him out the door. Greyson pulled away and made a move to punch him, and the man fled. Greyson stayed in his office even as he felt the rhythmic vibrations and guessed that the building might fall. He'd rather die than have those documents found in his possession. He opened the bottom drawer of his safe, grabbed the file folder, closed the safe, and spun the lock. He went into the outer office. It was a joint office suite, shared with the Boss of White Mines. Greyson went into Shelby's office and opened the desk drawer where the man had kept his booze before AA got hold of him. Now the drawer contained nothing but an old pair of gym shorts. Greyson slipped the file folder under the shorts, secured the suite, and joined the mass of people moving down the stairs.

This delay in evacuating led to severe damage to the delicate structure of Greyson's inner ear, which had already sustained damage early in his life, back when nobody realized you should wear ear protection during live-fire training. Now the ears were beyond repair. The only thing he could hear was high, ceaseless ringing.

The ringing disturbed Greyson's concentration as he weighed the pros and cons of a dead snipe. Dead Shelby couldn't fight back, so theoretically any number of crimes could be pinned on his carcass, but dead Shelby wouldn't satisfy the public hunger for fresh blood. A live snipe would have been better.

To further complicate things, Shelby had been a generous and charitable man, which would make it more difficult to malign him. Looking around, Greyson saw uniformed Boy Scouts everywhere. Shelby had been a scoutmaster. Even with all that, perhaps fatal errors could be laid at his door if done carefully and respectfully. Greyson couldn't appear to enjoy trashing the man's reputation. A tone of pained regret was the key. He should probably try to shed a tear now, but his ducts had dried up in the early eighties.

Greyson's mind turned from trouble to opportunity. The empty seat on the seventh floor beckoned. The consensus was that it should be filled quickly with someone with deep intelligence experience. The president had summoned Greyson to the Oval. The appointment was set for the next day at 11 a.m. He had no doubt that he was about to be nominated for the job. How could there be any other choice? He was born and bred to be top dog, to raise his leg and shoot a steaming arc of piss over the lesser dogs.

Greyson checked his watch and silently cursed the pastor for delivering prayer after prayer. Shelby had made no secret of his aversion to religion. If it had been up to him, he would have been cremated without ceremony and had his ashes scattered in his bottom left desk drawer where he kept his booze. But Shelby had neglected to write down his final wishes, so his funeral was planned by Esther, his pious widow. Greyson didn't like her. She was a hugger. He had allowed her one hug in deference to her loss, but he had stayed out of her range after that. She had that powdery, floral, well-maintained old lady smell that he hated.

When yet another prayer was over, Thelma Madison, Shelby's long-time secretary, stood. Greyson brightened. He loved looking at her. She was tall and arresting, dressed today in a perfectly tailored, aubergine suit set off with a yellow and lavender silk scarf. During the Screamer Attack, she had used one of her signature scarves to make a tourniquet for a bleeding victim, turning herself into a media heroine. She didn't like the attention, but she was too photogenic to be ignored. Her luminous eyes appeared both alert and peaceful, and the paradox added greatly to her beauty. She was upright and unattainable, and the subject of endless male fantasies in the Mines.

It occurred to Greyson that Thelma might be attainable, as a secretary at least, now that Shelby was gone. A stunning secretary was an enviable accessory to power. As Thelma made her way to the front, Greyson's eyes wandered to his own well-worn accessory, Karen Dasch, who was parked on a folding chair with her legs planted wide. Between her feet sat an oversized Care Bears tote bag full of used tissues. She bent over it, rooting around for a clean one. Not for tears, for snot. She had allergies from April to November. She had a toothy smile for Greyson and her fellow Black Mines secretaries, and a scowl that could freeze hot coffee for everyone else. She decorated her desk with stuffed toys and motivational decor. With each passing year, she dyed her frizzy cap of curls a brighter shade of magenta so that now it glowed. She wore short, snug skirts and flashed the office whenever she turned in her chair to pull a page from the printer.

As tempting as it was, however, Greyson dismissed the idea of replacing Karen with Thelma. For all her shortcomings, he trusted Karen. She was fierce, effective, and as loyal as a bulldog. She would have fought terrorists, alligators, or Martian invaders to protect him.

Most importantly, she was an excellent liar, which was an indispensable skill in the Black Mines. Thelma, on the other hand, was honest, outspoken, and lacked a self-censoring mechanism. The woman said what she thought—a terrible habit.

Greyson wished that this funeral had been closed-captioned. He needed to know what Thelma had to say. Not to worry. She had thoughtfully xeroxed her remarks for the hearing impaired. Her son was passing them out. Greyson leaned forward and snatched a copy as the boy was handing it to another mourner.

Thelma dabbed at her eye with a tissue and took a moment to compose herself. She began. "Now we all know that Shelby had his faults. He drank too much and he was grumpy and hard to be around like most men get at that age."

The Reverend Thomas looked up with a frown, and Thelma's son made a downward pressing gesture with his flattened hand, indicating that his mother was shouting. Her hearing was returning, but she still had trouble modulating her voice.

Thelma continued in a lower tone. "But Shelby was a good man, and I know that because I worked for him for a long time. He was generous and smart. He remembered everything I ever told him about my family. He didn't just pretend to listen. He loaned me money when my husband lost his job and told me I didn't need to pay it back. I did, but he refused to take interest. He wasn't sneaky and mean, like some people get when they reach the seventh floor." Thelma directed a significant look at Greyson. Her face softened as she turned to Shelby's widow. "Esther, you shouldn't feel bad about being hard on him at the end. It was for his own good. You made him quit drinking and that would have saved him if the concrete hadn't smashed him. And how could you guess that something like that was going to happen? Shelby loved you. That's the thing you should remember.

"I have one last thing to say. I've been in the Mines a long time, and I know what you people are like. I know you're going to try to put the blame for the attack on Shelby because he's dead and can't defend himself. It is partly his fault, but there are a lot of people sitting"—Thelma glanced again at Greyson—"and standing here who are to blame, too. So, if you attack Shelby, you can count on me fighting back. I already found something in his desk drawer I know he didn't put there." Greyson looked up sharply from his xerox page, and Thelma met his eye. "That's all. Think about what I said."

Thelma returned to her seat. Greyson crumpled his xerox sheet and was about to toss it on the ground, but he changed his mind, straightened it, folded it several times, and put it in his pocket.

Birdie, the maid, heard Mr. Earl bellowing. "Ol' bull full o' bull," she muttered. He was swearing, not commanding, so she needn't respond. She'd worked for him for thirty years, so she was used to his foul language. She said a quick prayer for his soul. Not that she thought it would help and not because she really wanted him to end up in heaven. Frankly, if Mr. Greyson Earl ascended, her whole life was a joke. No, she prayed for him because she felt obligated as a Christian. Another burden God had dumped upon her shoulders.

Birdie jammed a narrow brush into one of the bottles the kefir came in. Kefir. It was the stuff that had replaced gin and tonics after the Mines made Mr. Earl dry up. Sour milk for a sour man. Alcohol had made him erratic, angry, and violent more often than not. She'd lost count of the Waterford glasses he'd broken throwing them up against the wall like they was cheap as Solo cups. Now he was sour, angry, and only violent now and then. She soaped around the wire that held the ceramic stopper to the foolish ceramic bottle, all the while snorting like an agitated horse. It was tiresome and probably unnecessary. The fancy shmancy bottles would be washed again by the kefir man, but it went against her grain to leave the dregs of fermented milk to harden and attract fruit flies. They sold kefir in plastic bottles in the store, but store-bought kefir was not good enough for Mr. Earl. Oh no. Vanity of vanities. He had to buy the stuff made by an actual O'Session, Obsession, Assertion, whatever the guy was. Some crazy brand of Russian. Called him a former "business associate." *Business associate my foot*, Birdie thought. She knew what her boss did for a living. He was thick with every rapscallion from here to Siberia. She finished and put the bottle with the others in a box by the door. Tomorrow morning, the Ossetian would pick up the empties and replace them with full ones.

Birdie longed for the days when Mr. Earl spent years at a time overseas and her only job was to dust his mansion while he was away.

More bellowing. Mr. Earl had been at it almost nonstop since yesterday. He had been acting strangely since the Screamer Attack, but now he was truly unhinged. Birdie chuckled. Lord forgive her, but it served the Mines right to get attacked. God's punishment. She felt a thrill of satisfaction every time she saw someone's sin being rightfully punished. Birdie turned on her radio to the Christian AM station. The chords of an organ rose loud enough to penetrate the walls of her boss's study, but he wouldn't hear. A choir sang "What a Friend We Have in Jesus," and Birdie joined in with her reedy, off-key soprano. Now she could play her music and sing her hymns any old time she wanted to. That was her reward for virtue. She'd had a good time since the attack, and a good time was a rare and blessed thing when you worked for Mr. Earl.

"Fuck the fuck-ass, fucking president," Greyson screamed as he paced the length of his home office. His throat was raw from screaming, but he heard nothing of his own voice over the maddening ringing. Worse, he couldn't hear his footsteps. This rattled him. And it pissed him off because, damn it, nothing rattled him. Except this. He could feel the vibration in his feet, but the resulting sound was too faint to capture.

Greyson had loved the sound of his outsize hooves pounding the hardwood. He designed this room to amplify it. He bought this house, an ill-proportioned McLean McMansion, solely because of this long, narrow room, which had once housed an indoor lap pool. In it he saw a sounding chamber for his footsteps and the outlines of a study perfect for a long-legged man who plotted and paced for a living. Now an exorbitantly expensive Brazilian walnut floor covered the hollow space of the old pool. A standing desk occupied the north end of the room. Greyson rarely sat and he paced more often than he stood still. Sometimes he would stop at the desk to drum his knuckles against the wood. All the surfaces of the room were hard, to allow his noise to reverberate.

But now a hollow, whiny ringing had replaced that noise and destroyed his equilibrium. He could not feel his connection to the ground.

Greyson screamed, "Fuck the president!" He strained his voice. "Fuck the damn fucking, fuck-a-roni president! Fuck him to hell and back!" Nothing. His throat ached, but all he heard was ringing.

Then he heard something else, a screeching return of the screamers. Greyson's eyes bulged and fixed on the ceiling, his body went rigid, and he crashed to the floor. Eventually, the screaming subsided and the ringing resumed, louder than ever. Greyson went limp. After a minute, he gathered himself up and staggered to his feet.

The instances of phantom sound were less frequent than in the first few days after the attack, but they were still strong. Greyson stood until his breath and heart rate returned to normal. Then he yelled, "Fuck the mother-fucking, fuckmeister, fuck-o-maniac president!"

Yesterday, Greyson had suffered a devastating blow. When he first walked into the Oval, all signs indicated that the news would be good. The president greeted him with a beneficent smile and a firm handshake. The coffee table held the good pastries, the kind offered for a celebration. But then the meeting went badly. So badly. To communicate, the president scribbled notes on a pad. Greyson bellowed his responses. Then something in his brain short circuited, sparks appeared before his eyes, and the screamers exploded in his head. The president watched with alarm as Greyson leaped to his feet, clapped his hands over his ears, and prostrated himself atop the eagle on the carpet, panting. The president called for a doctor and cut the meeting short without offering him the position of BOM. In a press conference later that day, he announced the nomination of a Mines official who had not been in the attack—Alberta Bennet-Mason.

Alberta was a smart cookie toughened by decades in the Black Mines. She was currently getting out-of-agency experience by serving as deputy director of the nation's audio collection agency, popularly known as "the Ear." Anyone else would have recognized that she was being groomed for the top spot, but Greyson was old school. He could only imagine a woman serving under him. Indeed, Alberta had literally served under him for years. They had been engaged in a long-running affair which, had continued even when Alberta's late husband, Brick Mason, became BOM.

Time to dump the bitch without ceremony, Greyson thought.

Just then, a vibration in his pocket announced the arrival of a text. Greyson took out the phone in the hope that it was all a mistake and the president had changed his mind. But no, it was from Alberta. He read it in disbelief. "Ex-ops are over, in light of my new position. Regards, A." Ex-ops were extracurricular operations, code for their affair.

The bitch had dumped him.

Greyson stared mutely at the phone. Then he texted a response. "This is war!"

"Always has been," Alberta responded.

What did she mean by that? Greyson hurled the phone against the wall. This could not happen. He had to stop it. Could he stop it?

"Yes, I can!" Greyson screamed. If he moved quickly enough, he could discredit Alberta before her confirmation hearings. She was tough, but vulnerable. In fact, Alberta herself could be blamed for the Screamer Attack. She was the one who kept key intercepts from being disseminated. None of the Mines counterterrorism experts ever saw them. If this information got out, Alberta would never become BOM.

But neither would Greyson, because he was the one who had persuaded her to suppress the intercepts because they had picked up the voice of a senior senator—the then-Chairman of the Mines Oversight Committee, Harrison Westerly. That could only end badly for the Mines. Perhaps Greyson could claim that she did it on her own and it would be a case of "he said, she said." Could she have any proof that he had made the request? They were in bed at the time, but what were the chances that Alberta—an ex-sharper, a deputy chief of the Ear, and a profoundly manipulative woman with a killer instinct for self-preservation—would not have bugged the pillow? Zero to none.

Alberta had wiped that intercept from the computer system, but Greyson had kept hard copies—the copies he had hidden in Shelby's desk drawer. Except that they weren't in Shelby's drawer anymore. Thelma had them. Greyson's head hurt. He needed to pay a visit to her, and he should have done it already, but he had spent the time preparing for that presidential interview, which had gone so badly.

Greyson upped the ferocity of his pacing. He reached the end of the room and glanced at the "power wall" behind the desk. Photos of Greyson with various dignitaries crowded the space but it had been a long time since he'd added anything new. At some point he had realized that the thing wasn't to have pictures of yourself with important men on your walls. The thing was to have important men collect pictures of you on their walls.

Greyson grabbed a half-finished bottle of kefir from the desk, took a swig, and pivoted. The pool-room-turned-study ran windowless down the center of the house and jutted out into the tiny back garden, where the walls turned to thick glass, tinted for the sake of privacy in a neighborhood where brassy mansions elbowed each other like Russian women on the metro. The room was decorated with polished slices of exotic hardwoods. Framed descriptions of these woods, cut from rare dendrological tomes, accompanied each specimen. An elaborately framed and illuminated copy of the Janka Hardness Scale occupied the center of the east wall. Greyson was a collector of fine woods, the harder the better, preferably harvested illegally.

Greyson didn't glance up. He watched his feet pierce the reflected pools of light from the Moroccan pendants, which hung at intervals along the ceiling. His stride cut long, even slices through space until he reached the white board that sat on an easel at the far end of the room. He stopped before the board, took a swallow of kefir, and picked up a red marker.

He needed a narrative to satisfy the public, disgrace Alberta, and secure the executive suite. The marker hovered over the white board, but nothing came to Greyson's head but ringing. He'd never had trouble coming up with a story before. Seeing his talent early on, his mother had hoped he might become a great novelist. Her eyes misted over as she called her son's pathological lying "an emergent genius for fiction." Now genius had evaporated.

Maybe he should kill Alberta. He knew people.

Greyson stepped back, wheeled and threw the marker down the length of the room. It hit the floor, slid, and came to rest five feet from his desk. A silent, useless gesture. Greyson wanted—needed—to make noise. He emptied the kefir bottle in one long swallow, gripped it by the neck, and slammed it against the wall. The thick bottle didn't break. The only noise Greyson heard was a light tap all but lost in incessant, high-pitched ringing. He hauled back and hit it again. This time the bottle shattered noiselessly. He looked down at the jagged neck still in his hand. At first, he didn't recognize what he saw. Or rather, he did and didn't recognize it. He knew what it was, but his mind wouldn't accept it. His mind tried to turn it into something innocent, but there was nothing innocent this thing could be. His hand shook as he jiggered the wire and pried the bottle neck apart along a crack. He extracted the small listening device buried in the ceramic.

He could hear nothing, but someone else was hearing everything. Someone else had stolen all the words he had spoken in this room, all the muttered plans and schemes. Greyson had never been able to drop the habit of muttering in places he assumed to be safe. He should never assume anything.

Paranoia swelled. This was a threat to everything Greyson was and everything he'd ever done. He lowered himself into a crouch and looked up, as if the danger came from the Moroccan pendants. His breath grew shallow. He pressed a hand to his pounding chest. He stayed in that position until his heart quit thrashing and his knees were on the verge of seizing up. Then he hauled himself up, a twitch away from face planting. What had he given away and who was paying the Ossetian?

A better question might have been "Who wasn't paying the Ossetian?" An old sharper like Greyson should have known that exclusive contracts are rare in espionage.

Greyson threw the neck of the bottle against the wall. That bit of violence restored some of his equilibrium. He knocked over the easel with the white board. Yes, he was feeling better. He could stay ahead of this. He picked up the easel, stomped on one leg to break it off, and gripped it like a Louisville Slugger. He took a vicious swing at the frosted glass, and his slick-soled shoes went from under him. Greyson crashed to the floor. His full weight came down on the coccyx.

Brazilian walnut is one of the hardest woods on the Janka scale, which measures the amount of force required to drive a .444-inch steel ball into a piece of wood to half its diameter. Brazilian walnut requires 3,684 pounds of force. The coccyx shattered.

An inhuman yowl brought Birdie scurrying to the scene. She found her boss sprawled awkwardly on his side, wild-eyed, with his hand hovering over his tailbone, not touching it. She prayed to the good Lord to give her the fortitude not to laugh.

3

The Perpetrators

As Shelby's coffin settled into the hard clay subsoil of Northern Virginia, the men behind the Screamer Attack paused in their flight to eat a good meal. Fahad followed Akil as they moved along a table covered with a white cloth and stacked with the makings of a continental breakfast. Other guests, budget travelers gearing up for Sound of Music tours, grumbled at their manners. The men reached over shoulders to snag croissants and packets of jelly. They piled these onto small plates and topped them off with slices of mild cheese. Triumph made them ravenous.

The men took pains not to stand out from the multiethnic crowd in the Salzburg pension. Fahad had grown a mustache. Akil had shaved his beard. Both wore comfortable, generic clothing. No brand logos to be remembered later. They could not resist cock strutting, however. Conceit rippled under their skin and sparked in their eyes. They needed an end zone, a ball to spike, and a gallon of Gatorade dumped over their heads.

Fahad struggled to steady his hands as he poured his tea. He wanted to lecture the tourists on their meanness, to let them know that they were in the presence of something greater than themselves, to spray them with bullets, and see the tablecloths blossom with their blood. He had a gun in the backpack slung over his shoulder. Akil was similarly armed. Fahad had always been the brains behind murders committed by other, more expendable brothers. Two of his men had earned paradise in the Screamer Attack. Fahad envied the immediacy of their sacrifice. The urge to risk everything, to pull the weapon out and use it was overwhelming.

"You're spilling it," Akil said.

Fahad looked down and saw a pool of tea staining the cloth. He put the teapot down.

"There's a table over there," Akil said.

"We can't eat here. I've got to get away from these people."

"How will we get this stuff up to the room?" Akil pointed to the food. They had filled up two plates each, and now there was the tea to consider.

Fahad looked around and focused on a wall of decorative plates. He walked over and reached up to take a large, engraved pewter charger off the wall.

An elderly American lady tourist shook her finger. "You can't do that."

Akil turned to her. "Shut up."

Someone else said, "Someone should get the proprietor."

The two men turned to stare at him with cold eyes. Akil had exclamation points of scar tissue bisecting each brow. He was missing fingers on his right hand. Fahad had a scar across his cheek. The room got quiet. The generic clothing didn't matter. They would remember these men.

Fahad placed the small plates of food and cups of tea on the charger and added a stack of paper napkins. Once out of the room, they began to laugh. The tourists exchanged glances. This was the laugh that had led to numerous complaints the night before. The men had laughed until the wee hours. They couldn't stop. They were in an elevated, numinous mood, like a bride on her wedding day or a student giving a valedictory address. Reality bent, time warped, and the hour promised to stay golden forever.

They were still laughing as they entered their room. Through luck they had the best and biggest room in the pension. It had a corner table and banquette of carved wood. More plates, pewter-rimmed and painted with artless flowers, hung on the wall.

Fahad set the charger on the table, sat, and spread a napkin over his lap. The muscles on one side of his face tensed. The other side, the side that had been slashed with a glass bottle, remained slack.

"The lopsided frown," Akil said. "You're thinking too much."

"I shouldn't have done that," Fahad said.

"No shit. Let's pack this stuff up and get out of Austria."

"Agreed."

They gulped tea as they sliced open rolls and added cheese or jelly.

"I wish this place had a TV," Akil said. "I can't get enough of watching it. Their ears will be ringing for the next decade."

Fahad wrapped his sandwiches in napkins with neat, precise movements. "We need to follow it up. Their pants are down, their arses shining in the sunlight."

"Savor the victory. Laugh."

"We've been laughing like hyenas since the screamers went off," Fahad said. "It's time to get serious. They're more vulnerable than they've ever been."

"Thanks to us," Akil said. "You want to push our luck?"

"Yes. What's our purpose? To plan for a cozy retirement? Look at them now. They're scattered in rented buildings, deaf and half out of their minds. They're scared and making bad decisions. We can't let this opportunity pass."

Akil drained his tea and wiped his mouth with his sleeve. "Impatience is their downfall. Don't make it ours."

"We have Hamid there."

"The slow chap? I'd forgotten. You pulled him off the attack. You didn't trust him."

"I trusted him. Still do. That's why I put him in reserve and separated him from the others. And he's not slow, just shy."

"Why is he still in the country?" Akil asked.

"I asked him to stay."

"Why would you do that? He could give us away."

"It's an opportunity," Fajad said. "A simple suicide operation. An explosion and some bloody shots for the nightly news."

"Why something so crude after what we just did? That was a symphony and now you want to bleat on a kazoo?"

"Big impact for small effort. Look at what's going on over there now—anti-Muslim riots. In this atmosphere, the impact of anything we do will be magnified. It won't take much to push them over the edge. Hamid will blow something up. He'll leave his passport where the authorities will find it. The press will put his dark face in front of every American. More fuel for the fire."

Akil considered this as Fahad wedged his sandwiches into a plastic bag and tucked it into his backpack. "What about support? Who's there to support him and supply him with what he needs? We pulled everyone else out. This is a bad idea. Besides, he's slow. He would probably run in the wrong direction."

Fahad decided there was no need to tell Akil about the arrangements he had made with the American. Akil had never approved of the odd alliance, although it had been critical in pulling off the Screamer Attack. It was a huge risk, but Fahad was willing to take it. He would like to have Akil's approval, but he would keep him in the dark for now.

"You're right." Fahad shouldered his backpack. "Let's get out of here."

✦✦✦

Hamid heard about the Screamer Attack on the news, like someone who meant nothing to Fahad. He was to have died securing the control room to make sure the electricity stayed on to power the screamers. It should have been his face on the news, his blood spattered on the walls of the Mines, his honor, his ticket into paradise, and an end to his misery.

Hamid ached for a glorious death to balance out a pathetic life. This was not the first time death had overlooked him as if he were too insignificant to notice.

He was nothing. Hamid was not even his own name; it was the one he had taken from his cousin. As children, some people mistook them for twins they were so similar in appearance. In personality, they were not the same. The real Hamid was outgoing, funny, and resourceful. He was only older by weeks, but he still played the part of protector for the younger boy. He was so good at inventing games he served as recreational director for the whole neighborhood. It was fine to live in Hamid's reflected glory. It was a haven for an introverted child, who otherwise would have struggled at the bottom of the pecking order.

They should have been together on the day Hamid died, but the younger cousin was home sick when a misguided bomb hit their school. Collateral damage. Perhaps there should be no period after *collateral damage*. An ellipsis would be more appropriate. Collateral damage . . . dot dot dot. Because it echoes.

How could recruiters not target that younger cousin after that? The pain and anger were plain to read on his face. He no longer had a place in his world. He was lost, wandering, grieving. His parents understood the danger he was in. They had some family in the UK. They managed to get to Manchester, where they let their guard down and other recruiters found their son.

The younger cousin took on the name and identity of Hamid as he moved away from his family and into this new group of brothers. He resolved to forget that he had ever had any other name. He became especially attached to Fahad, an important man in this new world. He was a natural acolyte. Devotion was his greatest virtue.

But Fahad had abandoned him. Glory had evaded him. Once again, he hadn't died when he should have died.

Hamid waited for a signal from Fahad to move forward with a new attack. On the fifth of every month, he walked to the nearest chain bookstore. The cashier recognized him now and smiled. "I have it right here." She reached under the counter and pulled out a puzzle magazine with the name GRIDZ in big black letters on the front.

Hamid never smiled back. The woman's buzz cut offended him. His hands didn't tremble as he paid for the magazine. He bought himself a tea and sat down in a corner booth of the adjoining coffee shop to work the nonogram.

To solve a nonogram, one either blacks in a square of a grid or leaves it blank, according to the numbers arrayed along the X and Y axes. When the puzzle is complete, the blackened-in squares form an image. Hamid approached the task with reverence, working carefully. Fahad himself had taught him how to solve the puzzles. Hamid had a knack for it. He was proud that these puzzles were Fahad's special way of communicating with him. The other operatives got their messages in a different way. He had been separated from them because Fahad promised he might have a special role to play, but he had heard nothing.

Hamid tried not to cry when the squares resolved into an hourglass. Wait. He walked back to his small apartment on the sixth floor of a vinyl-sided block of identical units. He was disappointed but not despairing. If Fahad demanded patience, then that was what he would give.

4

Maddie's Loaded Assignment

The Screamer Attack spawned hundreds of cases of noise-induced hearing loss. The damage might be temporary or permanent. In the early days, none of us knew if the silence had an end or not.

For me, going deaf was like clinging to a board and drifting away from the shore. It was not so much the feeling of distance or separation that threatened me, but lack of desire to do anything but drift. Lethargy took over. I curled into a ball with a down comforter on top and featherbed underneath. They were gifts from Mom. She had come back as soon as she heard about the Screamer Attack. All was forgiven. She had had an affair with and married my ex-boss, Harry Esterhaus, but that was over now. She had finally recognized what I had tried to tell her all along—that he was a lying, scum-sucking gerbil fucker. Now that I no longer had to imagine her in bed with Harry, I could accept her as my mom again. I didn't even mind that she had moved back into my house and had begun to repopulate it with bunny-themed tchotchkes. She took care of everything and made it easier for me to drift.

It was probably hot outside, but Mom had turned the air conditioner to Arctic to counteract her vicious hot flashes. I imagined snow blanketing the world. All I wanted was softness and silence to drift on my ice floe to nowhere. Softness to block out the sharp light and the odd, hollow fragments of sound that reached my cilia. My pet rabbit, Abu Bunny, burrowed under the covers with me. Mom brought us Rice Krispies treats as we drifted in mid-blizzard. I thought I heard the wind howl.

I broke my own rule against taking muscle relaxants for my back spasms. I had never liked feeling loopy, but now it hardly made a difference. If I moved my head the wrong way, the world rolled. A worm of pain chewed through my frontal lobes.

Mom tried to tempt my appetite with Southern comfort food rich with salt and butter. I took three bites of whatever was offered. That was the rule from my childhood. Three bites, and Mom would stop nagging and I could go back under the covers. The food tasted like it had been processed through oily machinery. Not Mom's fault: she was an excellent cook. My tastebuds were malfunctioning as if in sympathy with my cilia. My senses were off. It left me feeling as vulnerable as a turtle without its shell. All tender tissue. No armor.

Mom was doing everything in her power to turn me back into a child—a fetus, almost, but I was fine with that. In the past, her efforts to infantilize me had run up against rigid resistance. With that gone, she worked herself into a maternal frenzy. In addition to the girly bedding, she bought pints of my favorite butter pecan ice cream and an odd-looking appliance that made s'mores. For my birthday, she baked me a bunny cake with coconut icing and a maraschino cherry for a nose. She got me markers to decorate my bright yellow fiberglass cast. I wore new pink polka-dot pajamas and fuzzy bunny sleep socks. Being an adult sucked. I was over it. I decorated my cast with ballerinas. I took a full swan dive back into the fifth grade. Only this time I was much more compliant than I had been the first time around.

My mind wandered far and wide, refusing to settle in any one spot long enough for rational thought. A phrase mutated and got caught in a loop. The worst happens and then more worst happens and then more worst really fucking happens again. I made no attempt to sort my feelings, although I was aware of gratitude, not gratitude that I had survived the attack but gratitude for having been inside that building. Suppose I had been outside taking a walk? I would be working now, shouldering my share of the blame and worrying what was coming next. For a second, the thought of the Mines' vulnerability almost jogged my brain awake, but I resisted it. No, the concussion, broken arm, and damaged ears were not only my just desserts, but they were also lovely excuses. How long had my mind been caught up in impending doom? Long enough to warp it completely.

It wasn't enough, though. Sometimes I ached for the quiet space outside my office window, for the voices that had called to me from the towers. Anger against the officer who had saved my life surfaced from time to time.

Days could have been years or seconds. I couldn't hear the ticking of the clock. Then I began to feel a small, rhythmic vibration in the small bones of my ear. I didn't associate it with sound at first.

My ability to recognize voices returned before my ability to recognize words. Mom and I communicated through the Lil' Princess Magnetic Doodlebug Boards she'd bought at a toy store. They were pink and glittery with a feather-topped stylus, but they did the job. I could write in big letters and not have to squint to read tiny blurry words.

One day a familiar but strange voice made its way through my fluffy bedding. My brain registered it slowly. Someone I liked, no loved, the way you can only love someone who understands everything you've been through because she went through it with you—Vivi.

I peeked out from under my covers. Time bobbled and jumped. While I had been dabbling in childhood, Vivi had fallen into age and exhaustion. Her eyes were bloodshot, and the skin below them pouchy and purplish. Her hair needed brushing. She evidently hadn't had a full night of sleep since the attack. Every attack had taken a chunk of flesh out of her. The African Embassy bombings, the Strikes, the Stadium Attack, and now the Screamers. How much more flesh could she lose?

What right did I have to drift while my fellow bomb dissectors were pulling double and triple shifts? Guilt mixed with panic. I sprang out of bed, stumbled, and face-planted on the carpet. Pain shot through my head. Vivi rushed to help me up.

"Really, I'm fine," I said.

Vivi tried to lead me back to bed, but I resisted. "No. I've been lying down too much." I pushed Vivi toward the bed. "You lie down." I was shouting. I kept forgetting that everyone wasn't deaf. Vivi and the other bomb dissectors worked in an off-compound building unaffected by the attack. "Take a nap," I told her. "Then we'll talk."

She protested, but with my one good arm, I gave her another push that sent her sprawling backwards. When she hit the feather bed, the expression on her face changed to bliss. I slipped her shoes off and covered her with the comforter. I pulled the blinds and left the room, shutting the door softly behind me.

I stumbled out into the living room. How many days—or weeks or months or years—had it been since the attack? I turned on the television. They were still covering it. A camera focused on a reporter standing in the median strip on route 123 near the stoplight where employees turned left into the Mines compound. This was where a terrorist had gunned down several Mines employees. Vivi and I were at work that day and all that night. We were young enough then that pulling an all-nighter barely left a mark on our faces.

I read the words in the caption at the bottom of the screen. "Agency officials are still denying our news teams access to the damaged campus."

"Why would we let you in?" I asked the screen. I switched to CNN. An anchorman stood next to a hologram of the late BOM, Dashiell Aspling. What the creepy fuck? I remembered then that Dashiell had done a hologram interview shortly after he was sworn in as BOM. They must be replaying it. Thank God they hadn't figured out how to reanimate the fool. I jabbed the remote. This time I landed on another 24-hour cable channel. A sharply dressed man strolled through a computer simulation of the damaged Mines headquarters. The screen said the man was a terrorism expert, but the name, Howard Bettelheim, wasn't familiar.

Bettelheim tapped a pointer on the collapsed portico at the main entrance, and his words appeared on the screen. "Here is where Shelby Wexler died. He was one of the Mines' most senior officials. He was walking toward the entrance with Arthur White, another senior official, when the screamers went off. White escaped. Was it coincidence that the attack began just as these two officials passed under the portico? Wexler and White had reserved parking spaces and drove very distinctive vehicles. Wexler drove a green '92 Ford truck. On the morning of the attack, he was carrying a load of fertilizer similar to the kind used in the bombing of the Mariah federal building." Bettelheim walked around to the back of the truck as the digital tarpaulin disappeared to reveal a stack of fertilizer bags.

I spoke back to the screen. "Shit, you idiot. He was carrying manure, organic fertilizer, shit. He never covered it with a tarp. He left it on display where everyone on the east side of the building including the BOM could see it from their windows. Everyone knew he hauled shit in that truck. The man didn't believe in commercial fertilizer. He gave me a lecture on it once."

Bettelheim continued. "Experts speculate that terrorists planted those bags in the truck during the night before the attack."

"Experts? What experts? You cooked that up in your own pointy head. Do you think Shelby wouldn't have noticed?"

Bettelheim droned on. "I believe a terrorist may have been hiding under the tarpaulin when the truck entered the Mines that morning. It is well known that the guards at the entrance don't search the vehicles of senior officials. I believe that the terrorist was watching from under the tarp and so knew exactly when to begin the attack. He may have been planning to drive the truck full of fertilizer into the building in a suicide-style attack after the screamers went off."

"Shit doesn't explode unless it hits the fan." I switched the channel to an interview with a victim's family. I shut the TV off, not because such a thing would upset me, but because it would leave me deadly cold. The coping mechanisms I had developed early in my career had become too effective. Avoidance of pathos became a deep aversion to any effort to manipulate my feelings. Then the feelings themselves atrophied from being stored too long.

I looked around for newspapers even though I would only be able to read the largest headlines. I subscribed to the *Washington Post* and the *New York Times*, so there should have been some lying around. I went into the kitchen and checked the recycle bin. Nothing. Mom probably tossed them out in an ironic effort to shield me from unpleasantness.

Where was Mom, anyway? Shouldn't she be hovering? I went back to the living room and peeked through the front curtain to see that her car was gone. She had probably gone out to buy me more stuff.

Vivi woke up after an hour's nap. She came out of my room with her phone in her hand, thinking we could text. I shook my head. "I can't deal with tiny text. Too blurry. Wait." I went back to my bedroom to fetch a Doodlebug for Vivi.

"I'm coming back to work tomorrow," I said with a conviction I didn't feel.

"No." Vivi wrote on the Doodlebug. "You can't."

"I will."

"The MOC wants to talk to you." She slid the big purple button on the tablet to clean the slate. "I had to promise not to talk about attack." Button. "Before they would let me come."

"I'm being isolated like a virus?"

Vivi gave me a sheepish nod.

"Why haven't I heard anything?" I asked.

Vivi scribbled her answer. "Brand came 2 days ago. Your mom wouldn't let her in."

"Senator Brand was here?"

Vivi nodded.

Brand had replaced Harrison Westerly as the chair of the Mines Oversight Committee after the last election. I could not imagine her designer heels on the mildewed concrete of my front door stoop.

After Vivi left, I made myself a pot of strong coffee and determined to snap myself out of my lethargy. No more drugs. When Mom came home, I wouldn't let her put me back to bed. I wandered the house until it was no longer strange to be on my feet. The next day I got up early. I got on the Internet, zoomed the view until I could read the screen, and emailed Senator Brand's office to set up an appointment.

Three days later, my blurry vision had cleared. I put on my best briefing and funeral ensemble for my trip to the Hill. Vivi drove me. She told me I looked fine, but I bitterly regretted the decorations on my cast. I covered it as best I could with long sleeves, even though the weather was warm. I still had a big scab on my chin, but I was as close as I could get to looking presentable.

Constance Brand was standing at the window when I arrived. She could have been posing for a magazine shoot or a campaign ad. Her posture was perfect and her gaze distant and thoughtful. She turned and smiled. She was, of course, the quintessential polished professional woman. Not the typical, government-type, buys-her-suits-on-sale-at-Lord-and-Taylor professional woman, but the high-price, big-business type. Her hair was what mom called "rich girl blond," which was twenty degrees classier than your average double-process bleach job. It was a darker blond shot with subtle gold highlights. She even smelled pricey. I got a good whiff of her perfume when she shook my hand. I wondered if she could smell the grapefruit-scented lotion I was wearing. I had bought a half-gallon bottle of it for nine dollars at Costco in 2004 and had been using it ever since.

I steeled myself and determined that I was not going to be intimidated by her.

Brand said something. I thought she was asking about my hearing.

"My hearing is getting better," I said.

The look on her face told me the response didn't match her question.

"My hearing is fine, so you don't need to shout."

"I'm sorry."

Senator Brand smiled and pointed me to a leather wing chair. When she had settled herself behind her desk, she handed me a typed note.

"Dr. James, the committee has an assignment for you."

I tried not to show my surprise as I continued reading. "You are in a unique position. As Chief of Alternative Analysis, you were untainted by the 'group think' of other counterterrorism experts. And we don't want you to be exposed to it now. You'll get to question them later, but no contact until then. We want you independent because you are going to draft the intelligence section of the committee report on this attack. She paused to watch a play of conflicting emotions cross my face.

It was a plum. I liked nothing better than drafting a humongous, monstrously complex, mother fucker of a paper. I liked nothing better than to be able to request any piece of information I needed. Call me strange, but it was my specialty, and I was damn good at it. But was it a poison plum? Would they politicize it? Would they expect me to write an indictment of my colleagues? My colleagues were dedicated people doing an incredibly hard job—a job that could never be done perfectly due to a variety of factors, most of them outside of their control.

"I don't know if I can accept this assignment," I said.

Brand wrote something on a legal pad and handed it to me. I read. "We're only asking you to get to the truth of the situation. Don't you want to do that?"

"Of course." I wanted nothing more than to figure out why intelligence had missed the attack. I had my theories. I was convinced that Shelby Wexler knew something he wasn't telling me. He could never tell me now but someone else must have known what he did. With the weight of the MOC behind me I could ask anyone any question I wanted to. But ...

"I don't want my words to be twisted," I said. "I want editorial control over the final product."

Brand wrote, "Done" on a sheet in big letters. She handed it to me with a flourish. Her response was too quick, too easy, too automatic. It was undoubtedly a lie. I hesitated.

She quickly scribbled on the pad. "You need these answers as much as we do, and this is the only way you'll get them. Think of it this way: someone will write this report; wouldn't it be best if it were you?"

Could I beat them at their own game? I supposed I had to try.

I grasped her hand. It was soft and powdery.

"Where will I be working?" I asked.

This time Brand handed me another typed note. She must have been pretty sure I would take the job. "You'll get further instructions later. You will have committee staffers assigned to help you. In the meantime, don't tell anyone about this meeting. Not your mother. Not your closest friend. Not anyone."

"Why?"

Brand scribbled out a note. "If they know what you're looking for, they'll put something there for you to find. And it won't be the truth. Am I wrong?"

She was not wrong. I didn't trust her, but I accepted the job.

I regretted losing the opportunity to question Shelby. Shortly before the attack, he had suddenly agreed to give me the funds and personnel I had requested for the Alternative Analysis Unit. This after months of stonewalling. When I asked him why, he was evasive. I came right out and asked him if he had some threat information he wasn't sharing with me. He fled my office. That was the last time I saw him alive.

If Shelby had seen some information that I didn't, it meant that something that should have been disseminated wasn't. That had to be the work of a senior official, probably not Shelby. He was more a sins-of-omission type of guy. I could see him covering up for someone else, but I didn't see him as the perpetrator.

Suddenly I was happy and excited about the job in front of me. It might be an opportunity to place some senior official's pale, dimpled ass in a sling. God's work, if ever there was such a thing.

Mom talked nonstop as she shoveled food onto my plate. I nibbled at some eggs and made no effort to understand her words. She was probably making the same argument she had made since my meeting with Brand: that it was too early for me to return to work.

But I was eager and ready to hit the ground—stumbling if not running. I didn't know yet where I would be working. Senator Brand had insisted on sending a car for me since I wasn't cleared by my doctor to drive. She had been mysterious, however, about my destination.

I didn't hear the knock on the door, but Mom did. I followed her out to the foyer. She opened the door to a man in white coveralls. He was an older gentleman with a kind, handsome face. He couldn't be my driver, not dressed like that.

He smiled at my confusion and handed me a card explaining that his name was Joseph Beal and that he was a Mines driver who would be at my disposal for the duration.

I grabbed my briefcase and followed Joseph out the door. Mom had gifted me the briefcase when I got my job at the Mines, but I had never used it since I couldn't take classified work home. Now, however, I was starting an important new job on the Hill, and I needed the extra shot of professional oomph a briefcase would provide. No one had to know that the case contained my lunch, a large bag of gummy bears, and two of the pink magnetic Doodlebugs Mom had bought. They might come in handy for interviews.

If I say so myself, I looked like a damned sharp career woman in my dark blue suit. The cut of this suit did a better job of hiding my cast, which I had gone over with a thick black Sharpie to cover the ballerina drawings. The scab had fallen off my chin. I felt important. I should have gotten a clue from Joseph's white coveralls, but I still expected to be led to a dark government car. Instead, he led me to a white panel truck with the words "Pass Waterworks" emblazoned on the side in foot-tall letters. Underneath, in smaller print: "Plumbing, Bathroom Renovation, and Tile Work."

I gave Joseph a questioning look. He shrugged a wordless apology. He led me to the back of the truck and opened the door. He offered me a steadying arm and averted his eyes as I scrambled in, showing my upper thigh to the neighborhood. He pointed to a small, hard seat up against one side of the van. I sat down, and Joseph indicated that I was to buckle up. Then he slammed the back doors closed and climbed into the driver's side.

I sat in the company of toolboxes, tubs of thinset, and six-foot lengths of PVC pipe as we drove through Northern Virginia traffic. I sniffed and smelled something vaguely sewery. A row of coveralls hanging behind the driver obscured my view of the road, but I was sure we weren't crossing any bridges into D.C. After a while, I had the strange feeling we were taking the same path I usually took to work. I felt the van go through the familiar serpentine tire-slasher-and-yellow-cone obstacle course at the route 123 entrance. I was going back to the Mines.

My stomach turned over as I contemplated re-entering the building it had taken me so long to exit. Joseph stopped to show security his Mines tag and then continued around the perimeter road. I wondered where he would stop. Why would he be taking me here? I was working for the committee now, not the Mines. The people I would need to interview were working in buildings scattered around the D.C. area.

The van didn't pull into a close-in parking lot, so we weren't going to the Old Shafts Building. Certainly, we weren't going to the New Shafts Building? That thing was in even worse shape. I had heard that it was going to need millions of dollars in structural work before anyone could return. The van made a left turn, slowed, and then came to a stop. Joseph got out and came around to the back.

When the doors opened, two men stood in front of me: Joseph and Slinky Nardovino, the Boss of Paper Mines. The Paper Mines was responsible for administration, security, and logistics. I knew who Slinky was, but I had never had a reason to speak to him. He wore jeans and a T-shirt smudged with soot. He looked askance at my suit and heels. Then he and Joseph helped me out of the van, half lifting me to the ground. I was surprised to find myself in front of a low brick structure, the Print and Photography Building. Slinky waved me inside. He snapped his fingers at the napping guard at the entrance with no effect, then gently nudged the man's arm with the Hosmer hook. I wondered if anyone else was using the building. Slinky led me down first one narrow corridor and then another. The lighting was fluorescent, and the building was undamaged. Apparently the "Illuminating the Mines" initiative had not reached this backwater. We stopped in front of a gray door. Slinky consulted a slip of paper from his pocket. As he worked the combination, I read the small sign next to the door: B/P&PD/B&PG. Slinky handed me the slip of paper with the combination and cipher. I had been assigned the former office of the Boss of the Bindings and Packaging Group of the Print and Photography Division.

Ever since my meeting with Senator Brand, I had fantasized about working in the worn elegance of a Senate office building with high ceilings and stately cornices—a cubicle dweller's fantasy. Yet here I was back in a cramped, low-ceilinged, windowless room with metal furniture and photographs of someone else's family attached to the side of a filing cabinet with beer-themed refrigerator magnets. According to the nameplate on the desk, the former occupant was Norman "Buddy" Burns. I gave Slinky a questioning look.

He reached over, grabbed the nameplate, and dropped it in the trash. He asked a question in a loud voice. I thought he was asking me how well I could hear, but I didn't want to guess wrong again, so I stared blankly. I knew from the newspapers that Slinky was completely deaf. He shut the door and pointed to a sheet of paper on my new desk. It was a heavy, cream-colored note with Senator Brand's letterhead. I slid into my new seat, snagging my nine-dollar pantyhose on a jagged edge of metal. I read with irritation.

Dear Dr. James,

You must be wondering about the curious arrangements I have made. I wanted you to be on-site during the investigation. With the invaluable help of Salvador Nardovino—the only Mines official I trust—I have obtained the documentation and passes necessary for you to go into any restricted area or question any one of the on-site investigators. Mr. Nardovino will arrange for you to search the offices of other senior officials and any other office necessary. I do not want any of them to know that you are on the compound or that you are working for the MOC. Therefore, you will work under the name "Jennifer Morris" and wear light disguise. Your assistants will work out of my office. From now on, please wear disguise on any trips to the Hill.

Sincerely,

Constance J. Brand

I gave Slinky a quizzical look. The idea of searching senior offices appealed to me, but in disguise? Slinky said something to me, but I couldn't make out his words. He reached for the clipboard that hung from his left hip. It was attached to his belt by a clever, quick-release clasp. It had a mechanism on the back that clipped onto his hook so that he could hold the board steady while he wrote with his good right hand. I waited while he scribbled out a message. He handed it to me.

I read, "Officially, you'll be on medical leave from the Mines. You'll draw your regular salary. BTW, shred and burn bag my notes and Brand's letter." I opened my briefcase and got out my Lil' Princess Magnetic Doodlebug Board. I wrote, "I don't need a disguise!" and turned the board around.

Instead of responding to my protest, Slinky dropped his clipboard and reached for my Doodlebug. He examined it closely, put it down on the desk and wrote. "Light, no electronic emissions." He slid the button to erase it. "Quick fix 4 face-to-face comms. Where'd u get it?"

Sheepishly, I took the board and wrote down the name of the store where Mom bought it —Toyz Toyz Toyz. Slinky nodded, turned the board over on the desk, and copied the brand and model number onto the top sheet of his clipboard. I assumed that the diaspora of hearing-impaired Mines employees would soon be receiving bright pink Lil' Princess Magnetic Doodlebug Boards.

"Do I have to wear disguise?" I wrote.

"Yes!" he wrote and underlined it twice. "Horsemen come here. They distrust u. Would kick u out." He cleared the Doodlebug, thought a second, and wrote, "Dress down. Soot everywhere."

The next day, the Pass Waterworks truck showed up again, but it didn't take me to the Mines. Instead, the truck headed south and spent some time crawling through rush-hour traffic. Eventually it came to a halt, and Joseph opened the back doors. He was about to help me out, but I was wearing jeans and sneakers, so I jumped, landing on oil-stained pavement. I almost did a face plant because I was still unsteady on my feet. Joseph caught me in time and righted me. Looking around, I saw dumpsters, stained cinder block, and metal doors. The smell of something rotten emanated from the trash. Cigarette butts covered the pavement. We were behind a small strip mall. Joseph led me to a door labeled "Brown's Barber Shop" and opened it to a cluttered back room.

I stepped inside, and he left me alone, or so I thought. A purple curtain opened to my left. I recoiled at the face that appeared—stark white skin, slashing brows, bow mouth, eyes staring from pools of red. It took me a moment to register that this was a Caucasian girl in full Kabuki makeup and black wig. She wore a man's undershirt and black tights. She had a tattoo of the Dr. Who Tardis on her left bicep. The right bicep had a blue M&M man. She wore an overpowering fragrance that called to mind a plug-in air freshener.

She began to talk, but I yelled, "I can't hear a thing. Use this." I got a Doodlebug out of my briefcase and handed it to her.

"Cool," she wrote, then, "Can I keep it?"

I shook my head, and the Kabuki face distorted into a frown. "Please," she wrote.

"This is mine, not government issue. I can't afford to hand them out like business cards," I said.

That mollified her somewhat. "I'm Jade," she wrote.

"Why the Kabuki drag?" I asked.

"Don't want to look like gov't drone," she wrote. She eyed me and wrote, "No offense." She grabbed my arm and pulled me behind the curtain.

I found myself in a small alcove with a barber chair and mirrors on three walls. A table pushed up against one wall held bottles, bowls, brushes, and other tools of her trade. I glanced under the table and recoiled at the sight of bags of hair.

Jade nudged me toward the chair. "You allergic to anything?" she wrote on the board and put it down on the counter in front of me.

"No," I said.

She leaned over me to write, "Have to test. Stick out arm."

I did so reluctantly. She dabbed patches of various substances on my inner arm: adhesives, liquid latex, other things I couldn't identify. "While you dry, I'll evaluate face."

"I don't want my face evaluated," I said. I was fast approaching what my mother termed "Maddie's wet cat mood."

Heedless of the danger, Jade grabbed my chin and turned my face this way and that while I suppressed the urge to bite her. The creepy Kabuki face was too close. I need extensive personal space, and I do not like to be touched without permission. My right hand involuntarily clenched into a fist.

"Relax!" she wrote, then slid the big purple button to erase it. "Think of this as day spa." Button. "You need massage." Button. "Uptight!!"

"I hate spas. It would not relax me to have complete strangers groping me and applying smelly crap to my body."

She wrote on the board, underlined what she had written with two swift strokes and turned it around. "I don't care!" Jade gave me a grotesque smile. She dropped the board on the counter in front of me and went back to staring at me. She poked at my face with her fingers. Her nails were short—probably a requirement of the job—and painted a glossy TARDIS blue.

My eyes were beginning to water from Jade's fragrance. A tear slipped down my cheek and I swiftly wiped it away as she wrote on the Doodlebug.

"Sharp little fish bones," I read from the board. "Pointy chin. Pointy nose. Will need prosthetics."

I jerked around to look her in the face. "That is not light disguise! No fake parts. Absolutely not!"

Jade rolled her eyes. The effect was chilling with the Kabuki makeup. "Bone structure too recognizable," she scrawled.

"No."

"Tough!!" she wrote. "Thin nose. Won't need a honker to cover it." She slid the button. "I'll give you pretty nose. Soft chin." Button. "Pinken sallow skin."

"I don't fucking want to be pinkened," I said.

"Don't fucking care," Jade wrote and underlined it three times.

I was starting to hate this woman. "How long is this going to take?" I asked. "I need to get to work."

She shrugged.

I shut up and let her rub her finger up and down my nose. I wondered how well and often she washed her hands. Asking would only slow the process down.

Jade pulled the hair bag out from under the table and began to rummage through it. Presently she extracted long platinum blond locks.

"Absolutely not," I said. "That's hooker hair."

Jade ignored me, put down the wig, and started to tuck my hair under a cap. When she finished, she studied me and made a face. "Corpse of Paris Hilton," she wrote on the Doodlebug. "Need warmer color." She ripped the wig off and went back to her big bag-O-hair. She pulled out a strawberry blond, not too bad. Too curly for my taste, but it wasn't supposed to be my taste. When Jade put it on me, it wasn't me, but it wasn't horrible. Jade gave a thumbs up signal in the mirror.

Getting custom-made prosthetics involved two things I hate: sitting completely still and having gooey stuff on my body.

"I'll make you perky!!" Jade wrote on the Doodlebug. I wanted to protest, but my face was already stiffening under mesh and silicone rubber. I got the feeling that Jade had decided to give me an appearance that I would find completely repulsive.

I spent most of the day with Jade; then Joseph took me straight home. I didn't even get to start my work.

The next day, Joseph took me back to Brown's Barber Shop. The face that greeted me at the purple curtain made my heart jump, even though I had told myself to be ready for anything. Jade had made herself up to look like a Day of the Dead skeleton. She grinned at the expression on my face and waved me toward the chair. On the counter I saw my new nose and chin laid out like parts about to be breaded and deep fried.

Jade gestured at my briefcase and eagerly took the Doodlebug I dug out of it. "You'll be pretty!!" She opened a tackle box full of small bottles and chose a half dozen. Despite myself, I was impressed as I watched her mix, check the paint against my face, and adjust the color. She painted the prosthetics, then showed me how to apply the adhesive and blend the prosthetic to my face. Jade was appalled that I had no skill with the makeup brush. "You never wear makeup?" she wrote on the Doodlebug. "Insane!"

"It's perfectly sane. I would have to set the alarm clock fifteen minutes earlier. That would be 4:45 a.m. Seriously, do you think I'm going to do that to improve someone else's view?"

"You and me from different planets," Jade wrote.

Thank God, I thought to myself.

When she was done, Jade slipped the wig over my head and made a thumbs up gesture.

I considered my reflection as she brushed the curls into place. I was surprised to feel a thrill running up my spine. The woman in the mirror wasn't me. She was someone else, someone who didn't carry Maddie James' baggage. The circles under her eyes had been concealed, and her frown lines smoothed. I laughed and watched the carefree sprite in the mirror laugh. Her nose was fleshier than mine, up-turned, more frivolous than severe. She looked happier than I've ever been. I glanced at Jade. She was grinning broadly and holding up a set of fake boobs.

Why not? I thought.

5

The XX-BOM

They already called Alberta the XX-BOM, after her chromosomes. She would be the first homogametic Boss of Mines. There was a time when even the heterogametic BOMS would not have dared to let their X chromosome sashay freely about the executive suite of the nation's premier spy service. But times had changed. The Mines had made tolerable strides in moving women up through the ranks. The younger generations didn't bat an eyelash at the idea of a female at the helm. But not all the old boys had died off. A few lodged in senior positions like calcium deposits in arteries. They were bitter. They whispered that her tenure would be more damaging than the Screamer Attack. The president did it to spite them. He had nominated Alberta Bennet-Mason to be BOM and the Esteemed Legislative Body had confirmed the nomination in record time. Done and done. Unreal. She would be sworn in only weeks after the Screamer Attack.

It wasn't entirely that she was a woman. They could have accepted a woman of their own choosing—they even had a name or two they could have offered up. The problem was that Alberta was the last woman on Earth they would have picked. They had treated her badly, very badly, in those early days of her career. Rumor had it she had been raped and had not taken it like a trooper.

Their chagrin—and their inability to hide it—made Alberta want to laugh. Not a carefree laugh. She was no fool. Her laughter was more darkness than light, more calculation than humor. It had a chilling, old-girl sexiness. She stifled it, though, before she climbed out of the dark government car. The car and driver had been at her disposal since she passed muster at her hasty confirmation hearings. For once both parties agreed on something: it would be dangerous to let the Mines go rudderless for any length of time.

Alberta ignored the line of officials waiting to greet her. She turned toward the Old Shafts Building. Her face betrayed nothing but the grim determination appropriate to a widow who was about to take over what was once her deceased husband's job, a woman returning to the place where she had worked for decades to find it shaken by a terror attack.

Alberta glanced towards the seventh-floor office her late husband Brick Mason once occupied. Their marriage had been complicated, unconventional, and sometimes rocky, but he had been her best friend and staunchest supporter. In her mind, she could hear the noise he would have made at the news that she had beaten out Greyson Earl for the job. She heard that exultant expulsion of air—"Ha!"— accompanied by a raised fist and followed by a bear hug smelling of Faberge Brut. Because Elvis wore Brut. She felt a flash of anger against Brick for committing suicide and robbing this moment of the one thing that would make it most meaningful for her—his pride and joy.

But she would not shed a tear. Conscious of the camera, she made sure that her expression had the right combination of sadness and determination. No trace of salt-water weakness must appear at the corner of her eye. When the shutter clicked, she moved on.

The Bubble, as the detached, semi-spherical auditorium was called, was undamaged in the attacks. The "screamers" were in the main structures: the Old and New Shafts Buildings. Alberta insisted that the swearing-in ceremony take place in the Bubble, even though the miners had not returned to the damaged complex. Only senior Mines officials would be present today, along with the president and a few other dignitaries from outside the Mines, and a Mines photographer to record the moment. His bulb flashed in Alberta's face as she climbed the steps.

He will not catch me smiling today, she thought, *but it won't be easy to suppress.* Even amid the destruction and the sadness of missing Brick, she was happy. She glanced to her left to gauge the progress of efforts to remove the crumpled concrete portico in front of the Old Shafts Building. She never liked the design—those pillars that tapered as they approached the ground. No wonder the thing fell over. Yes, it was time to give the Mines a facelift. She took in a lung full of air still peppered with char and thought of the creative possibilities inherent in destruction.

Another flash, and the camera caught Alberta's face looking suitably thoughtful. There was something of an alien insect queen in the slant of the eyes and the set of the cheekbones. Something mantis like. Her shapely head was slightly bowed, her body clothed in a faux-modest, faux-black suit. Faux-modest because it was a superbly tailored and ridiculously expensive designer ensemble. Faux-black because the rough silk was a hand-dyed hue called "Brushed Iguana," the deepest of greens, chosen to set off her eyes. They were a bare shade lighter than the iguana, with an aureole of steel blue.

Alberta's outfit was bought with some of the payoff from Brick's life insurance. It was an in-joke. When Brick was filling out the paperwork for the policy, he had said, "You'll probably blow the whole sum on a pair of shoes." He had laughed. He wore discount suits, while her tastes ran to raw silk and cashmere. The running argument was amiable, but it would have pissed him off to see money frittered away. Yes, Alberta missed him, but she couldn't pass up the opportunity to have the last word. She almost smiled but turned that smile into a grimace of pain at the last instant, lest the photographer catch her in an inappropriate mood.

Greyson Earl waited at the top of the stairs, his long body hunched and tense. Alberta speculated that her ascension to the job he had always coveted had finally broken him but then banished the thought. It could be a fatal mistake to underestimate him, especially today. He was moving like an old man, but a dangerous old man. A bony ridge of brow left his eyes in shadow as he watched her. He transferred his cigarette from his right hand to his left and greeted her with a handshake. She could feel the electric spark of tension in his enormous paw with its copious mid-digital hair. She knew he wanted to squeeze her hand until the bones snapped.

Alberta lowered her eyes to the cigarette dangling from his left hand. She let them rest there. It was a small sign of disrespect that he didn't toss the thing when she got out of the car. Small, but not insignificant, not something to be overlooked. Nothing could be overlooked with Greyson. Bent though he was, he was still a circus tiger. The whip must always be in sight. She raised her eyes to his and locked them in a gaze calculated to shrivel the testicles. After an uncomfortable moment, he flung the cigarette in the direction of the ash receptacles at the entrance to the auditorium.

Alberta felt no regret over the end of the long affair. There was never anything resembling love on her side. Only expedience, desperation, calculation—such a long, old, bitter story. A story now nearing its denouement.

The new deputy BOM, Carlos Hernandez, waited for her inside the building. He was her own choice for the position. She had long been his mentor. He was smart, loyal, and level-headed. He wasn't a rule breaker. He had been overseas during the Screamer Attack, so he had no issues with hearing or PTSD. His Latino heritage would help with the Mines' efforts to recruit minorities. He was the perfect, no-skeletons, no-drama choice for the number two position. Greyson had even given him the nickname "Mr. Boring Normal." Alberta hoped that he would succeed her whenever her tenure was over. She thought that boring and normal would be good for the Mines for a change. Carlos was clean-cut, good-looking, and had a particularly engaging smile complete with dimples. She planned to send him out to do any press interviews and speeches that she did not have time for herself. He would be a great public face for the Mines.

Carlos would have given her a hug if this had been a private gathering, but in public, he confined himself to a handshake and a wink. Alberta congratulated herself on choosing a man with good judgment on even the smallest matters of protocol.

Leaving Carlos, Alberta turned to the other surviving horsemen, Slinky Nardovino and Arthur White. Slinky was one of the few men in the crowd, other than Carlos, who appeared completely calm and self-possessed. Calmer than Alberta had ever seen him before. It made her uncomfortable, but she couldn't put her finger on why. Arthur, on the other hand, was as edgy as Greyson. Alberta could feel a light tremble in his body as he shook her hand. Alberta noticed that Arthur's cold blue eyes were rimmed with pink. Evidently, he hadn't been sleeping well.

Looking around at stifled yawns and blue circles under the eyes, it appeared that none of the occupants of the executive suites on the seventh floor had gotten a good night's sleep since her nomination. No wonder. There were men here who had harassed her a quarter of a century earlier, grabbed her in intimate places, whispered obscenities and threats, spread rumors to bring her down. Now she saw their noses ripple. They smelled her.

What did Alberta smell like? Dior Poison, which she chose as much for the appealing name as for the hints of coriander, tuberose, and sweet myrrh. But there was something else that was not perfume. Something smoky, although she did not smoke. Something alcoholic, although she did not drink. It was as if she had absorbed the scent of the old boys and transmuted it into something else that they felt like they should recognize but could not. She smelled like a predator, like someone who was planning massive personnel changes.

She was, but not yet.

Above the low grumbling of discontent, Alberta could detect a trill of fear. An intense hum. It sounded like bees had invaded the Bubble. The walls vibrated. It almost brought her to orgasm.

"Exceptionally capable" the president called her in his speech. *Capable of anything*, people thought.

She had added a touch of extra eyeliner in deference to the cameras, which would provide the diaspora of miners with live video of the ceremony. Closed-captioned, of course. She wanted her employees to feel like she was staring straight into their souls. "I'm going to change you," she told them as she accepted the mantle of Boss of Mines. Not "I'm going to change the Mines," but "I'm going to change you." She knew better than to waste energy on the superficial reorganizations so popular with her predecessors. She was going for something deeper.

After the ceremony came the customary stiff poses in front of the auditorium. The photographer was careful to keep signs of the attack out of the frame. With a small, respectful gesture he directed Alberta and the president to the right to avoid the shadow of a crane on the pale skin of the bubble. He rejected the Memorial Pond as a backdrop because fleeing miners trampled its iris and ornamental grasses.

"Enough of this," Alberta said. "I want a picture in front of the building, damage and all. Give this moment in history its due."

The photographer looked doubtful. It went against his instinct to record this sort of thing. On his first day on this job, they gave him a long lecture on what not to photograph—Mines tags, classified documents, under-cover employees, security installations, and anything that might bring embarrassment to the Mines. Certainly, a terrorist attack on the Mines' headquarters fell into the last category. Besides, he loved symmetry and grand symbols. He preferred to center his subjects between flags, or Agency seals, or marble columns. The damage to the Old Shafts Building was disturbingly asymmetrical. The concrete awning pitched to one side when it fell. Tacky orange police tape zigged and zagged across the scene at crazy angles.

Alberta turned to the president, who looked doubtful as to whether rubble was always a good backdrop for a chief of state. It had been in the past, but somehow this particular rubble was charged with ambiguous meaning.

One of his staffers stepped forward. "The president has to be back at the White House for a meeting; we're going to have to cut this off."

After the president and his security detail sped away, Alberta motioned to the photographer to follow her. She walked along the front edge of the collapsed awning, next to the orange police tape writhing and snapping in the wind. Alberta had sprayed her hair into place. Gusts could not ruffle her fitted jacket and pencil skirt. Meanwhile, the photographer struggled with flapping tie and coattails and a comb-over that kept flipping back like a lid. Alberta arranged herself at a flattering angle from the camera, raising her face so that the light accentuated her cheekbones.

"Get down," she told the photographer. "I want the building and some sky."

He stiffly lowered himself to his knees after combing through the damp grass with his fingers, checking for shards of glass or metal.

"Lower!" Alberta yelled into the wind. "That angle won't get you anything above the third floor. Most members of your profession would happily bend themselves into pretzels to get a good shot. What kind of photographer is afraid to get his elbows dirty?"

Answer: a photographer who operated a Mines front company in Africa until Security uncovered significant irregularities in his accounting. Brick chose not to fire him and gave him this job. He assumed it was a place where the man could do no damage. Alberta, however, was acutely aware of how much damage a bad photographer could do.

Reluctantly, the photographer stretched out and planted his elbows on the ground. His posterior stuck up awkwardly as he squinted into the viewfinder. He would have grass and blood stains on the knees of his trousers. To show for it, he would have a photograph with a tilting horizon and a slightly out-of-focus BOM—nothing like the majestic image Alberta envisioned. By next week, he would be working in the motor pool.

Greyson Earl stood in the back during the swearing-in, while Thelma Madison sat near the front. When the ceremony was over, he fixed his eye on her red-flowered scarf as she moved up the aisle toward the exit. He intercepted her as she approached the door and motioned her to the back corner of the auditorium.

"Where are they?" he said. It wasn't the first time he had asked her where she hid the intercepts removed from Shelby's bottom desk drawer. She refused to say. Greyson wasn't accustomed to being stonewalled. Most people in the Mines were too afraid of him to try, but Thelma had a rare and highly irritating brand of courage that set him back on his heels.

"Where are they?" he repeated. The papers must be somewhere in his old office. He was determined to find and destroy them before he left the headquarters compound today.

She shrugged.

Greyson took a pad and pen out of his pocket and shoved it at her so she could write him an answer.

Thelma's eyes remained serene under Greyson's glare. She ignored the paper.

Greyson caught a slight smile on her lips as she turned away, and this pushed him over the edge. He grabbed her arm hard. She looked down at his hand and then back up at his face. She raised her brows in a way that let him know that he was crossing a line and that she believed in consequences for crossing lines.

Greyson dropped his hand. He didn't need another sexual harassment complaint. Then he spotted something else he didn't need—a livid Karen barreling her way through the crowd. She suspected that Greyson wanted to replace her with Thelma, so now she inserted herself between them whenever possible. He had seconds to get his answer. Greyson injected a double shot of menace into his voice as he asked again, "Where? I'm not going to drop this. You know that."

Thelma rolled her eyes, took the paper and pen, and scribbled, "I put them where they belong." As she handed the note to Greyson, Karen came up behind her and bumped her hard, not bothering to make it look like an accident.

"He doesn't need your help," Karen said. "If he needs anything, I'll handle it."

"Good," Thelma said. "You do that." With exaggerated dignity, she turned and walked away.

Greyson glared at Karen. "I don't need anything from you."

Karen retreated with a pout. She would probably stir up trouble somewhere, but he had more immediate worries. Greyson considered what Thelma's words might mean. He reached in his pocket for the mini flashlight he kept there in case of the need to prowl in dark places—a need which arose more often for him than for most. He headed for the underground tunnel that connected the Bubble to the Old Shafts Building. A security officer had been stationed at the top of the stairs to keep people from straying into the damaged building. Another sat by the badge machines in the tunnel itself in case anyone got past the first one. Greyson blew past both with a look that dared them to stop him.

He plunged into the darkness of the tunnel. Vibration had caused such extensive damage to electrical connections that it would be a while before power could be restored to the main headquarters buildings. Greyson's flashlight offered weak counter to the murk. He suddenly felt an unfamiliar fear. He had no way of knowing if someone was behind him. His spine tingled. He wheeled and flashed his light in an arc. In these dark corridors, the eerie ringing in his ears sounded to him like the soundtrack to a horror film. He wouldn't hear it if someone sneaked up on him with a chainsaw. Fighting disorientation, he found his way to a stairwell that took him to the first floor. Light from the plastic-covered windows guided him to the stairway closest to his office. He took a breath and stepped into the blackness again. His broken coccyx throbbed with each step. He tripped over a bit of fallen ceiling tile and almost took a tumble. The throbbing intensified.

When Greyson finally made it to the joint Black Mines/White Mines executive office suite, he was panting hard, as much from heat and mental exhaustion as from climbing seven floors. With no HVAC running and windows covered in plastic, the atmosphere in the building was stale and suffocating. He opened the door to his office and let the light from the windows wash over him. Thanks to that sunlight, it was even hotter in here than it was in the rest of the corridors. The windows here had held. They were webbed with cracks, but only a small corner of the glass had fallen out, offering little in the way of fresh air. He thought for a second that he might pass out. He grabbed a tall brass lamp with a marble base, ripped the shade off, and grasped it near the bulb. Covering his eyes with his arm, he was about to swing the lamp at the window. Then he remembered the last time he had tried to break something. The thought of his coccyx hitting the hardwood floor caused a fresh throb of pain. Then he looked out the window to see a few people still clustered in front of the building, talking. He backed up, dropped the lamp, and grabbed his chest. His heart jolted and skipped at the mistake he had almost made. Someone might have looked up at the sound of breaking glass. They would have sent a security guard to investigate. What had he been thinking? Greyson Earl didn't make mistakes like this.

He wasn't making good decisions. He probably shouldn't have taken that last Percocet. He needed to think clearly, but his tobacco-clouded lungs weren't coughing up enough oxygen to his brain. He had to find those intercepts, but he needed air. Maybe if he opened the door to the corridor, it would somehow suck air in through the hole in the window? It was worth a try. His limbs felt slow and heavy as he made his way back to the suite door, found the rubber door stop, and propped the door open.

Was this wise? Suppose someone came down the corridor? Greyson hesitated a minute, then dismissed the thought. The investigators were finished on this floor. He went back into his office.

Where would Thelma hide the intercepts? She wouldn't have the combination to his safe, so she must have left them unsecured somewhere. Greyson's eyes did a slow sweep of the room and stopped on his desk, which was identical to the one in Shelby's office. He suddenly knew exactly where she hid them. He went to the desk and opened the lower lefthand drawer. He kept personal and not-too-sensitive files there. He had to flip through half of them before he found a folder labeled "Miscellaneous Skeletons" in Thelma's precise handwriting. He cursed her under his breath. Inside of this folder, he found another labeled "LI." He opened it and saw the intercepts and a stack of cryptic notes that would have been even more incriminating than the intercepts.

What to do with it now? Another decision. Greyson's brain hurt, but he had to think carefully. He could staple the papers into a burn bag and throw it down the chute, but that wouldn't do. The bags weren't being collected now. It would lie there for weeks. He would have to burn them himself. He grabbed Shelby's trashcan, then decided that it shouldn't be Shelby's trashcan. It should be Thelma's trashcan. Bitch. He went back to the outer office and picked up the can by her desk. In the Mines, all discarded printed material, whether classified or not, goes into burn bags. It's easier that way. Trashcans are for candy wrappers, takeout containers, and tissues. Most of the tissues in Thelma's trashcan had been used to blot lipstick. Greyson paused to press one of these to his own lips and indulge in a brief Thelma fantasy. Then he tossed it onto the floor, upended the trashcan, and dumped the contents. He tore the plastic can liner out and threw it aside. He flicked his lighter and began to burn the papers, starting with his notes. It was a slow process. He read each note first and tried to commit it to memory before touching the lighter to a corner, watching it flare up, and dropping it into the can when his fingers felt the heat.

Slinky Nardovino tried to escape from the suits crowding the small lobby of the Bubble. Everyone wanted to shake his hand, squeeze his shoulder, and nod their approval. He was a hero. Again. During the Screamer Attack he had stayed in the building, first directing evacuation efforts from his computer, then moving through the complex, checking on the stragglers, leading first responders to the wounded, and helping to put out the small fires that erupted when vibration wreaked havoc on the wiring. Because he stayed so long, he sustained complete and permanent hearing loss. Not even a hollow ringing remained.

Many curious glances fixed on the Boss of Paper Mines. The attack had transformed him in a good way, unlike the other victims, who suffered various degrees of post-traumatic stress disorder. Slinky already had PTSD before the attack—along with the Hosmer hook he wore in place of a left hand; it was a remnant of the first Gulf War. The explosion of an IED had left him with a vexing tinnitus. The PTSD created tics and twitches. It had been painful to watch as his left eyelid jumped, or the right corner of his mouth broke out in micro-spasms. Now the tinnitus was gone. The tics were gone. He had dropped the nervous habit of chewing on pencils. His face had settled into an expression of calm, but pensive preoccupation. People noticed for the first time that he was quite a handsome man. All the ethnicities that once seemed at war in his blood had achieved harmony. The Italian, Irish, and African genes collaborated to produce a uniquely compelling façade that piqued the curiosity.

During the swearing-in, he had mentally run through a list of contractors and calculated costs. He loved the details of his work and, strangely, he loved having the silence necessary to devote his full attention to them. Perhaps the biggest benefit of deafness was that he would never again have to listen to the idiocies spouted by the other horsemen or the inane small talk that accompanied events like this.

Slinky had perfected a swift gesture toward his ear to convey his deafness and regret at being unable to converse. He used it liberally as he pushed through the crowd and finally reached the officer who guarded the stairway to the tunnel. The man got a pat on the back and a genuine smile from his boss.

Slinky clicked on a small flashlight as he descended the stairs. He had arranged generator power for the Bubble for this ceremony, but restoring electricity to the rest of the complex would take weeks if not months. He had electricians lined up, but they must wait for the crime scene investigators and the engineering inspectors to finish before they could begin their work, and no one could tell him when that would be.

In the tunnel, another security guard sat by the Mines tag machines under a battery-powered light. He pulled a sizable Maglite from under his desk and offered it to his boss. Slinky accepted. He would need to order a lot more flashlights and D batteries. Noted.

The Maglite cast its beam down the tunnel. Wires hung from the ceiling. Investigators had removed the screamer lights and carted them off to a warehouse in Maryland for study. They left ceiling tiles stacked along the wall. Slinky made a mental note to get an okay from the chief investigator to destroy them. He calculated replacement costs in his mind. He paused and ran the light along block walls painted with abstract bands of color. He didn't see any cracking in this area. The harmonic vibration had limited effect on the underground tunnel.

The effect on the people escaping through this tunnel had been dire. Sound bouncing off the hard surfaces had magnified panic. His flashlight beam crawled along the floor until he found the chalk outline of a victim who had been trampled to death: Lisa Whitman. He knelt to touch it. Such a small woman. He had attended the funeral and met the victim's doll-like daughters, Kira and Lily. Slinky rubbed away a bit of the outline and then put his finger to his lips to taste the chalk. He closed his eyes and said a quick prayer.

The compound was his responsibility. The deaths here weighed heavy on him, even though he was not responsible for hiring Kreative Industrial Sunlight Solutions to install the lights. Dashiell Aspling had done that over Slinky's strong protest. Lucky for Dashiell that he had died during the Screamer Attack. He would have had uncomfortable questions to answer. Also, Slinky would have punched him at the first opportunity and damn the consequences.

It didn't matter to Slinky that none of the elevators worked. He never used them. He usually took the stairs two at a time to his office, but darkness and clutter slowed him down. The larger debris had been removed, but bits of ceiling tiles and the occasional lost shoe or purse remained.

Slinky planned to retrieve his clipboard from his office and then tour the building. The heat and stale air didn't bother him. He had tolerated worse in the Gulf War. Every day since the attack, he had walked miles through the corridors of the Old and New Shafts buildings. He could have delegated this task, but the darkness and silence of the building drew him like a magnet. Now the place known as the Mines truly resembled a Mine. Islands of battery lights interrupted the darkness here and there. Figures scurried about. Flashes of light indicated that damage was being recorded. As a longtime Tolkien fan, Slinky could imagine dwarves following veins of mithril and beating sparks with hammers.

Despite the damage, the deaths, and the challenges ahead, Slinky was filled with a strange joy. He didn't miss the sound of his footsteps or the sound of anything at all. He had never realized how much the prevailing noise of life had weighed on him, especially since the war. Now he felt light enough to fly. His very existence was a meditation, and this building was his church and his responsibility. He had limitless quiet to work on the unique logistical challenges left in the wake of the attack. When he got home from work, he could happily take the colicky baby from his frazzled wife and go into his study. He could read and dandle the screaming child on his knee while his wife took a soaking bath. Even the horror of the attack and nagging guilt couldn't keep a feeling of peace from descending over him. Deafness. What an odd thing to be thankful for.

When he reached the seventh floor, Slinky found the corridor dark. The investigators were finished here. He shined the flashlight along the walls. Most of the artwork had fallen off the walls and been trampled. Frames were splintered, glass broken, and delicate images torn beyond repair.

Police tape dangled from the door to the BOM's office. An autopsy had revealed that the cause of Dashiell Aspling's death was indeed a heart attack. Slinky thought that Dashiell had been the sort of man you could kill with a fly swatter. He passed the office without going in.

Slinky worked the combination lock leading to his own office suite. Inside, he deposited the trash into a burn bag and pulled a gym bag from his lower drawer. He quickly changed into running shorts and shoes and a T-shirt. He hung his suit on the coat rack and headed out for an inspection tour of the third floor.

Out in the corridor, he clicked on the Maglite and started when it illuminated a small, female figure thirty feet away. She advanced on him quickly, finger to her lips. It took him a moment to recognize

Maddie James. He had seen her in her disguise, but it was still hard to accept this perky blond as the dark and grumpy bomb dissector.

When she reached Slinky, Maddie grabbed his Maglite and cut it off. She clamped her small, cold hand around his wrist. She was remarkably sure-footed in the dark. She led him to the end of the tunnel and turned the corner. She slowed as they approached the door to the joint Black Mines/White Mines executive suit. It was open. A light flickered and smoke hung in the stale air. Maddie let go of his arm and pushed him toward the suite door.

Slinky saw Greyson lighting papers and dropping them into a trashcan. He considered a confrontation. How stupid to set a fire in a building with non-functional water sprinklers. Greyson was undoubtedly burning something self-incriminating. Then Slinky knew what those papers were. He had read the intercepts and even committed them to memory. He stepped back into the darkness. He must approach this problem carefully.

Back out in the corridor, Slinky waited for Maddie to return his Maglite. She didn't. "Maddie?" he called softly. Nothing. Dragging one finger along the wall and stumbling over debris, he slowly made his way to the intersection of the tunnels, calling now and then. What was he supposed to do, grope for her in the darkness? Awkward, and it had EEO complaint written all over it. Like most senior officials of color, Slinky had once headed the Office of Equal Employment Opportunity, so it would be particularly embarrassing if he accidentally grabbed some delicate part of Maddie's anatomy, fake or no. He took one more step and a foot clad in a heavy leather shoe caught his ankle and sent him sprawling to the floor. That wasn't Maddie's foot. "Who's there? Who did that?" Slinky yelled.

✢ ✢ ✢

I was livid. Slinky wasn't going to do a damn thing. He was walking away, leaving Greyson to trash and burn at will. He deserved to lose his Maglite. I stood still and listened to him bumble down the tunnel. I waited until he had turned the corner. I heard him fall. I hoped he didn't have another flashlight squirreled away in his office. He might come back for me.

I crept back to Greyson's office. My dance training served me well. I had developed excellent spatial awareness—you have to, or you collide with other dancers. I also had great night vision. As a child, I used to get up and wander around the house in the wee hours. Since receiving my assignment from Brand, I had been walking the tunnels of the Mines without the benefit of flashlight, sidestepping the investigators. They never saw me. They were blinded by their lights.

I entered the office suite, hugging the wall. I couldn't let Greyson feed anything else to the fire. As he stared into the flame, I leaped into action, performing a perfectly timed échappé sauté to achieve the elevation necessary to bring the Maglite down smartly on his head. The landing sent a pain through my foot that nearly brought me down, but I recovered myself. He dropped like a shot buffalo. The folder fell into the trashcan. I lunged for it and stomped it out. I got some minor burns on my hands, but I ignored them. I checked Greyson's vitals. He would be fine, other than a nasty headache. I gathered up the damaged papers and stuffed them into my clothing. The trashcan still smoldered. I lifted the lid of the large coffee urn on the credenza. It was still three quarters full of coffee dotted by spots of yellow-green mold. I poured it into the trashcan and wiped the Maglite free of fingerprints with the tail of Greyson's suit jacket. I left it by his side. I straightened up and sensed a movement by the door. I crossed the room and looked out into the corridor. My eyes had no time to adjust to the darkness, but I thought I saw something. Not someone, something. It was not on all fours, but neither was it walking upright. I had heard rumors about wildlife getting into the building through broken windows. I lit out in the opposite direction and scurried down the nearest stairwell.

Greyson couldn't decide which hurt worse, his head or his ass. What the hell had happened? The world had gone dark shot through with stars. He had been attacked and he must have re-injured his coccyx. That would account for the pain in his ass. Pain or burning? The feeling was so intense he couldn't tell. He gingerly put his hand to the area. It wasn't on fire, but the smell of smoke was in the air. Sweat rolled down his face. His head throbbed so hard it might come loose from his neck. That might be a good thing.

He had to clear the smoke out of his mind and get control of this situation. He was vulnerable. His assailant might return. Greyson rolled over to sit up, forgetting that he had to be wary of his tailbone. The resulting pain made him turn back over and heave, but he didn't bring anything up. He shifted to one hip and propped himself up with his elbow. Greyson blinked until the number of trashcans in front of him went from four to two. If he remembered correctly, there should only be one. He had been using it to burn papers.

Who hit him? Must have been a big son of a bitch. Greyson looked around and saw the Maglite on the floor. He felt his head. It was wet. He sniffed his finger. Blood. But a damn flashlight? He would have thought from the pain that it was a steel pipe or a baseball bat. He reached for the Maglite but stopped himself. There might be fingerprints. Every Mines employee was fingerprinted on day one. He would catch this brute and send him on a ten-year tour of duty to some mosquito-and-insurgent-infested hellhole.

Greyson tried to remember what he had been burning. Bad secrets. Intercepts. Yes, the intercepts he had Alberta suppress. Why would he be burning intercepts? Someone had been talking to a terrorist who shouldn't have been talking to a terrorist. Greyson pressed his fingers to his forehead. If only the room would stop moving so he could think. Westerly. Harrison Westerly had been talking to a terrorist. Westerly worked downtown. Greyson blinked and tried to concentrate. Holy crap, Westerly was the former chairman of the Mines Oversight Committee. That's why they had suppressed that intercept and decided to surgically plant a bug in Westerly's pet cockatoo to find out what he was up to. Then the bird died, then ... Wait, was all that real?

Greyson didn't know anymore. He knew he had burned some papers. The intercepts? Wasn't that what he was burning when the lights went out? With a feral groan, Greyson leaned forward and grabbed the trashcan, but his hand found only air. Wrong trashcan. He grabbed the other one. It was still warm. He was hot. It must be 100 degrees in this room. He swallowed the vomit that rose in his throat and pulled the trashcan closer so that he could look inside. He saw a file folder soaked in coffee. Coffee? Greyson picked out the dripping folder. It was labeled "LI" in pencil. LI stood for Little Issue. It was the acronym the horsemen had used to refer to the awkward problem of finding a U.S. senator's name on an intercept concerning terrorists. It also covered the subsequent problems created by efforts to bury the original problem.

His head was caught up in a blood-stained throbbing. Greyson tried to think in the space between the throbs. He had to find the intercepts. The folder was burned along its spine. The only thing that held it together was the glue-effect of the coffee. Greyson pulled the two parts of the folder apart. Nothing. He dipped his hand into the slimy coffee and felt around. Nothing but wet and blackened shards. Had the intercepts slipped from the folder and burned or had someone stolen them? Greyson pulled his hand out of the trashcan and contemplated the dark stain on his cuff. Then he upended the trashcan, and a pool of sludgy coffee spread over the patriot blue carpeting.

He felt a light touch on his tailbone. Must be imagining it. Greyson looked back to see Alberta standing over him with her mantis eyes. Terror radiated up his spine from the shattered coccyx. She was standing on one foot. Why? The word "kick" was the last thing that passed through his mind as her pointy toe, moving hard and fast, contacted his tailbone. Pain raced up Greyson's spine and exploded in his head. He vomited and passed out.

Alberta couldn't stop chuckling when she thought of Greyson on his hands and knees, facing away. How could she resist? It was as if a bright red target, pulsing like a heartbeat, hovered in the air over his broken tailbone.

She knew it was broken because she'd heard it happen. That Ossetian had worked for her longer than he worked for Greyson. She heard the pacing, plotting, and fuming, then the sound of wood striking glass. Then the wounded bawl and Birdie's 911 call. She heard the EMTs tell Greyson that it was a probably broken coccyx before they hauled him off to the emergency room. He returned home after a few hours and came into the room muttering, "Where is the mother fucker?" Muttering, muttering, muttering ... "Aha!" The last thing Alberta heard was the sound of the bug being smashed.

So, yes, she knew Greyson had a broken coccyx, and there she was wearing three-hundred-dollar pumps with a sharp, metal cap toe. Retribution in high style. She kicked with all the strength she had, and, thanks to her devotion to the leg press machine in the Mines gym, that was no mean strength. Then she backed out of the door and listened to him vomit, giving in to pure, malicious delight.

The next morning, she was still laughing as she parked in front of an office park in Northern Virginia, one of the many facilities newly leased by the Mines. When she reached the executive suite, Thelma greeted her with the news that she had finished arranging next week's London trip and secured a much-coveted ticket to the West End Theatre production of Oliver! One of the perks of being BOM was that Alberta could take the best trips for herself. The MI6 anniversary celebration promised to be three straight days of high dining and VIP-level entertainments.

"By the way," Thelma said. "Carlos has asked for a meeting. Shall I put him on your schedule for this afternoon?"

Alberta smiled. "Yes, do. I've been too busy to visit with him lately."

Alberta took great pride in Carlos. She had been assigned as his mentor when he was fresh out of career prep, skinny and unsure. She had found it enormously satisfying to watch him grow into himself and gain confidence. At first, she had worried that he was too open and honest to make a good sharper, but he had turned those things into assets. He could get people to trust him because he radiated trustworthiness and good will. He believed in what he was doing and made others believe. He was assiduous with the safety and well-being of his assets and single-minded in rooting out any malfeasance in the units under his management. Alberta felt like the parent whose child has turned out so much better than oneself.

She could tell something was wrong, however, when he walked into her office that afternoon. The disarming dimples disappeared as soon as he sat down. He got to the point.

"Yesterday I paid a visit to the seventh floor after your swearing-in. I wanted to see for myself what the attack did to the building. I heard moaning and found Greyson lying on the floor of his office in pain. His head was bleeding. He had been burning something in a trashcan. I called an ambulance and managed to get him down to the front entrance to meet it. I stayed with him at Fairfax hospital until he was released, but he wouldn't tell me what had happened, and he threatened me with dire consequences if I called the police, even though he had obviously been attacked. He wouldn't tell me what he had been burning. I'm sure he's trying to cover something up. Moreover, he's made a couple of sudden and rather disruptive reassignments in the Counterterrorism Sector, sending Jason Talbot and his deputy overseas on short notice."

Alberta let nothing show on her face, but she felt a little shock because she knew why the men had been reassigned. If Carlos started to dig into the matter, he would unearth her own connection to it. She listened as he outlined his suspicions.

"Let me take care of Greyson," she said. "I know how to get the truth out of him. You're going to be busy. Something has come up and I need you to take over the MI6 anniversary trip next week. The speechwriters are working on the remarks and toasts, but they'll need your input. We need to make a good impression. You'll be checking up on the progress of their investigation in Manchester. Oh, and how do you feel about musicals? You'll have a ticket to Oliver!"

6

A Little Light Payback

Greyson lay on a massage table, peering down through the hole of the headrest. He wasn't getting a massage. The idea of hands anywhere near his throbbing coccyx was unbearable. No, this was simply the only position in which he could bear existence, and this only because he was laced with Percocet.

Greyson was in his study. The table was set up at the far end of the long room, the part with the frosted glass walls. He found the filtered light conducive to creativity. He needed to plan his next move against Alberta. The table had been modified. A chunk cut out of the side allowed him to reach a pad and pen that had been placed on a short table directly below his head. Also on the table were a glass with a straw and a hand bell. So far, the only words Greyson had written on the pad tonight were "vulnerability," "timing," and "weapon." His eyes strayed to a Waterford glass with a film of buttermilk. He no longer drank kefir. He'd done nothing about the bugging situation and the Ossetian. The man had probably disappeared when Birdie told him his services were no longer needed. Greyson should have confronted him himself, but he wasn't up to it.

Greyson needed more buttermilk. Where was that damn maid? His hand reached for the bell. He rang it vigorously until Birdie finally appeared at the door, breathless and huffing.

"Well, I guess Mr. Sore Bottom is out of sour milk," she said. "Don't worry; even though cleaning this vainglorious barn of a house would be a trial for a woman half my age, I have nothing better to do than to drop everything and attend to your slightest whim. I swear, a naked baby does more for itself than you do."

Greyson couldn't make out anything that she was saying. All he heard was the infernal ringing in his ears. Her damn mouth seemed to be moving all the time these days. She never talked like this when he could hear her. He suspected that she was being impertinent.

"This empty glass has been sitting here for half an hour!" Greyson bellowed.

Thanks to a hip injury, Birdie moved with a rolling waddle that made her look even more hen-like than she did when she had acquired her nickname. She kept up her running commentary as she made painful progress down the length of the room. "I can see why you're so upset. Staring at a dirty glass is so much worse than anything else I can think of. Poverty? Hunger? The plagues of Egypt? Those were nothing compared to staring at a dirty glass." She finally reached the table and plucked up the offending item. "You know what I think? I think if your mama had broken your tailbone with a paddle back when you was little, you and I would both be better off today."

"Refill," Greyson bellowed.

"Right away, sir. Sorry I can't get down on these old knees to gen-u-flect. You probably want another one of those perky sits, too. Even though you won't be sitting perky for some time. Ha ha." She made this joke frequently.

"Percocet!" Greyson bellowed. "And this time you'd better bring it to me when I ask for it and not sometime in the distant future or I will kick you to the curb."

Birdie turned and headed back up the length of the study. "As if you could get anyone else to work for you longer than an hour. We've been down that road before. So, I'm as sorry as I can be, but you don't get one until six o'clock. I intend to follow the instructions on the bottle. Even though you're as shoddy a copy of Adam as God ever put on this green Earth, I don't want you to overdose and kill yourself dead. Then I would have to look for a new job. No, you're my cross to bear and I cannot shrug you off much as it might do my heart good to see them cart away your cold, stiff carcass." She slammed the door shut on her way out.

Greyson groaned. His tailbone would drive him to drink if he couldn't get the doctor to up his dosage of Percocet. If she refused, he would strangle her.

No, he shouldn't waste any venom on a stupid doctor. He needed it for Alberta. Greyson considered the second word on his list, timing. A sense of calm came over him. Of course, timing. He had been torturing himself over not moving fast enough to prevent Alberta from becoming BOM and Mr. Boring Normal Pretty Dimples Carlos from becoming her deputy. Now that Alberta and Carlos had taken up their positions, however, Greyson might as well bide his time and wait for the right moment to move against them. In the meantime, he could observe and assess. He would design a weapon that would bring them down and humiliate them. Or maybe he would get someone to kill Alberta. That would take some planning. He could allow himself time for the pain to subside, and his head to clear. It would be crazy to take them on while he was in this condition. He could wait. He relaxed.

When Birdie returned with the buttermilk, she heard the snoring before she even opened the door. Greyson had fallen asleep with his arms hanging over the side of the massage table, his big paws dangling. He could snore louder on his stomach than most men snored on their backs. Frequently he stopped breathing altogether for a few seconds, then started again with a gurgle.

Birdie heaved a sigh. "The apnea. If your mama had fed you with her titties like God intended instead of squirting milk into you from a bottle so you didn't have to work for it, then you wouldn't sound like the first beast of Revelations. I suppose I should take this sour milk back to the kitchen and go fetch your machine before you stop breathing altogether. Lord forgive me, but I'm tempted to skip it, but I could hardly read my verses after leaving you to die. Wouldn't it be funny, though, to watch them carry you out dead and stiff with your arms sticking up in the air." Birdie paused for a chuckle. Greyson stopped breathing. She waited until he started up again before hurrying to get the machine.

When Birdie returned, she removed the notepad from the small table. It was wet with drool. "Like caring for a baby," she muttered. "A big, ugly, hairy, foul-mouthed baby." She set the notebook by a vent to dry and pulled a cloth out of her pocket. She wiped down the table, moved it out of drool range, and set the CPAP machine on it and plugged it in. "Now how am I going to get this mask on you?" Birdie bent to peek at Greyson's face sticking through the headrest. "Well, ain't you even uglier from this angle?" She held the mask to his nose and turned on the machine. She waited as his breathing returned to normal, and then she gently poked the head straps between Greyson's face and the headrest. With difficulty she reached around on top and pulled the straps through the other side and pushed them to the back of his head. Greyson moaned but didn't wake.

"There, you'll live whether you deserve it or not, Mister Sore Bottom."

✛ ✛ ✛

The next morning Birdie hauled herself from her bed early and grabbed a fleece robe that had faded from bright pink to gray. "Merciful Lord, grant me the forbearance not to kill the swine. He makes me tell him it's time to get up, then shoots the messenger every blessed morning. I'm already shot so full of holes it's a wonder my coffee don't leak out before I put the cup down." Because he couldn't hear an alarm clock, the task of waking Mr. Earl for work had been added to her many burdens. Since he had begun to abuse painkillers, the job had grown more difficult, even dangerous. She'd sooner roust a bear from hibernation.

Birdie found Greyson in his study, still face down on the massage table wearing yesterday's clothes and hooked up to his CPAP. She took a deep breath and gently placed her hand on his shoulder. She squeezed. No response. She increased the pressure and added a back-and-forth motion. No response. She upped the intensity of her movements slowly, but to no avail. He awoke suddenly and violently. His body jerked, and he cried out. The CPAP mask warped the sound into something animal. Greyson flailed his arms. The movement aggravated an old back injury and the new coccyx injury, and his bellowing grew angrier.

Birdie patted his shoulder. "Now, now. Don't go and throw yourself off the table again. I ain't in no fit condition to pick you up." But Greyson's head was too fuzzy to take her good advice, even if he could have heard it. He made a move to roll over. "No, not again! Mercy!" Birdie cried. She tried to push him back down, but he struck out at her. She backed off, and Greyson flipped himself over and fell to the floor, tangled in the CPAP hose. Birdie grabbed the mask and pulled it off his face before he strangled himself. He screamed in pain. Birdie took the bottle of Percocet out of her pocket and shook it in front of his face. Greyson reached for it. Birdie pulled it away and doled out one pill. He swallowed it and glanced up at the clock.

"It's an hour too early!"

Birdie scribbled an explanation on the notepad she kept in her pocket, next to the pills. "Special meeting this morning," it said.

Greyson howled.

Thelma was now the senior secretary in the Mines. She should be happy, but working for Alberta was more stressful than working for Shelby had ever been, even when he was at his boozy worst. She'd been with Alberta for a few weeks, helping her prepare for her hearings. It was enough time to learn her routines and name the uppermost cell on Alberta's daily planner Siberia.

Siberia was generally blank and white. Alberta used that time to sip a cup of coffee and eat a bowl of yogurt and fruit from the executive dining room. It was a terrible sign if a name marred that whiteness. Nothing good was in store for the person called in to Alberta's office before 8 a.m. Thelma had no idea what went on in there. She never heard a raised voice. All she knew was that the subject would stumble out thirty minutes later stunned and pale.

When she saw the name scrawled across Siberia that morning, she popped another antacid. Greyson Earl. Thelma was well tuned in to the rumor mill, so she knew the history of Greyson and Alberta, from the extramarital affair to the pre-swearing-in breakup. She was careful to never step between them because of the foul vibrations in the ether. The thought of them alone together in that room made her shudder.

Greyson arrived a minute before the appointed time. His appearance only increased Thelma's unease. His face had the color and gloss of overcooked oatmeal. The word that popped into her head was "undead." If this was what he looked like going in, she might have to call logistics to carry him out.

Thelma touched the intercom and announced Greyson's arrival. Alberta's usual reply was a crisp "Send him in," but today she chuckled and said, "I'm so ready." Thelma gestured toward the door, but Greyson had frozen in place. He looked unsteady and unwell. Thelma got up and gently led him to Alberta's office. She gave him a little push inside and softly closed the door. "Like tossing a bobcat into an alligator pit," she thought. She went back to her desk, but she couldn't concentrate on her work. Her eyes kept returning to the spot where Greyson had disappeared. She would not have been surprised to see blood oozing from under the door.

Alberta had been waiting for this day. The idea had first popped into her mind when she found out that the Screamer Attack had left Greyson deaf. She waited until it was clear that the deafness was permanent and profound, until she was sure that he had no skill in lip reading, until she had observed the effects of the painkillers. She waited until she was installed in this office that Greyson wanted so badly. She waited until he was at his worst. Now everything was perfect.

She was delighted to see how bad he looked this morning. "Sit down, sit down." Alberta smiled and gestured to a chair.

"I won't sit," Greyson said.

Alberta rose from behind her desk and approached him. She stopped a foot away and peered into his face. "I can see the imprint of the CPAP mask on your cheek. That tough hide doesn't snap back like it used to, does it, old man? Do you remember when you could drink yourself senseless and wake up the next morning fresh as a daisy with your memory and your conscience wiped clean?"

"You know I can't hear a word that you're saying. Use the writing tablet," Greyson said.

"No," Alberta said. "I won't use the Doodlebug today. I don't want you to understand. Not that you're capable of understanding."

Greyson pushed past Alberta, grabbed the tablet from her desk, and shoved it into her hands. She tossed it into a chair.

"What are you playing at?" he said.

"Playing is the last thing I'm doing."

"Cut the crap," Greyson said, "What ..."

Alberta reached out and pressed a finger to his lips. "You will be quiet." Her face changed. All polish and pretense melted away, leaving something raw and ugly.

Greyson took a step back.

"Hatred," she said. "What you see in my face is pure hatred. I had to hide it for so long, but now I'm going to let it out for air." Alberta walked to the window and stared out at the generic landscape of office buildings, parked cars, and Bradford pears. "Do you know why I came to work at the Mines?" she asked. "The boys came because they had read some Ian Fleming confection. I came because I had read *The Gulag Archipelago*. Read it the year it came out. I was fifteen and already a senior in high school. I felt something unique and powerful inside myself. I wanted to aim that power at the biggest evil I could find. Solzhenitsyn convinced me that evil was the Soviet Union.

"My parents fought me for my life every step of the way. They put me on this earth to produce grandchildren and care for them in their dotage. I would have none of it. You can't imagine their anger, shock, and bitterness. A daughter who thought she owned her own life? What an abomination! They refused to pay for college and tried to undermine me at every step. I petitioned the court to be emancipated from them and won. I got a scholarship and left. I got out, but it cost dear."

Greyson interrupted. "What is the point of you yammering at me when I can't hear anything?"

Alberta ignored him. "Meanwhile," she continued, "your daddy sent you to the best schools and bailed you out when you got into trouble. He twisted arms and slipped money under tables. He got you into the Mines and groomed you for this chair, which you regard as a birthright." Alberta turned and pointed to the historic desk chair that had been brought here from Langley. "This chair that I occupy."

Greyson sensed that she was rubbing his face in something deeply unpleasant. He tried to speak but couldn't get a word out before she was there again, her face inches from his and terrible.

"You," Alberta said, "raped me."

Greyson took an unsteady step back and almost lost his balance.

"You raped me," Alberta said, "and you blacked out, and you were so sloppy drunk you didn't remember the next day. I'm going to tell you the story now, even though you can't hear what I'm saying. I didn't understand what was happening to me then. It's only fair that you don't understand what's happening to you now. I want you to feel the out-of-body confusion. I want you to feel the ground beneath your feet cave and your heart melt."

"I've had enough of this shit. You're wasting my time." Greyson turned to leave, but Alberta cut him off and blocked the door.

"What galls me," Alberta said, "is that I actually sought you out."

1977

Alberta was the first of her class to arrive at that famous Mines training facility dubbed "the Unmentionable" because its existence was officially classified, even though it had been featured in movies. That was lesson number one for the new class of recruits—even the silliest of pretenses must be maintained. If you scrape off the most superficial layer of secrecy, it might expose some deeper layer below. It's best to learn early on how to shift the conversation.

Alberta had tacked a few extra dollars onto her school debt to get a cheap hotel room near the facility so that she could arrive early and fresh. An instructor had to unlock the dormitory for her. His name was Bob. She would meet so many Bobs!

This Bob was friendly and talkative, perhaps because Alberta was so pretty. He helped carry her bags from the car. As they passed the sign that marked the dorm as "Earl House" he asked her if she knew who Major Earl was.

"Yes," Alberta said. "I do my homework. He was a legend. Boss of Black Mines. I was reading his autobiography when he died in that plane crash last year. I wish I could have met him."

"Well, you'll get to meet his son, Greyson. He's in your class."

"Really?" Alberta had never met anyone famous, so this was close enough to impress her.

"Big son of a bitch," he said, "six foot five and dresses like a pimp. Even when he was a kid, Major let him tag along to places where he shouldn't have been allowed. Now, at least, he has his clearances."

Later that day, Alberta stood at the window of her dorm room and watched as recruits arrived and walked in from the parking lot. No six-foot-five pimps. Greyson was late. She looked for him at dinner and orientation, but he wasn't there either.

He didn't arrive until after 10 p.m. By this time, the rest of the class was in the small, dimly lit bar that served as a space for relaxation as well as a place to practice the art of extracting information while socializing.

The beer and the wine were cheap. Thanks to her accelerated education, Alberta was barely over drinking age. Furthermore, she had strictly avoided any underage indulgence in favor of her studies. She was acutely aware that she was the youngest person in the Career Prep class—and perhaps the youngest ever to enter a Career Prep class. She hated this fact and determined to appear more worldly than she was. She sipped at a beer, but it was nasty.

"Terrible stuff, isn't it?" said a deep voice.

Alberta turned to see a young man who could have come from her own hometown. He had that square, solid, close-cropped look. Cotton plaid shirt. Plain, pleasant face. He reminded her of every boy she'd turned down in high school. Her first instinct was to give him a cold nod and sidle away, but he grinned and held out a bag of pretzels. "These will take the taste away."

She took one and bit into the saltiness.

"I'm Brian Mason," he said, "but everyone calls me Brick, and, yes, that is lame."

Alberta laughed. Brick was easy to talk to. When she found out the Mines had trained him in Russian, they switched the conversation into that language. He was every bit as proficient as she was, and she had been the best in her class. She felt she was stepping into the big leagues, where she belonged. She forgot about legends and their offspring.

"Nobody Does It Better" was playing when Greyson finally appeared. Alberta later wondered if he had waited outside the door through "Margaritaville" and "Brick House" for more appropriate theme music. He was a master of calculated spontaneity.

Her tastes were so dulled by the seventies that his appearance didn't strike her as clownish, despite the glossy orange print shirt, the bell bottoms, and the platform shoes and permed hair that brought his height to nearly seven feet. Alberta herself was tall, just shy of six feet. She wasn't accustomed to being dwarfed. Greyson's nose was too hawkish and his forehead too sloped and bumpy, but it was obvious he considered himself handsome and that he was the kind of man who could talk you into it, too.

Later it would shame her to think how her heart raced when she saw Greyson's eye pause, ever so briefly, on her golden head before continuing to scan the room. *He's pretending not to notice me*, she thought. Greyson wasn't the sort to make a beeline for a woman who intrigued him. No, he circled his target and deliberately avoided eye contact. The word "predatory" would only come to mind later.

Greyson kept a glass of Coke in his large left paw, but she guessed he had brought something stronger to spike it with because his voice grew louder as the night wore on. "After Harvard," he said, "I could have done anything. I could have chased money on Wall Street, or power in Washington, but I chose the Mines. Noblesse oblige. My father hammered that into me." Alberta heard those words float across the room and, bless her foolish young heart, she was impressed.

It was nearly midnight before Greyson finally approached Alberta. He deftly elbowed Brick aside, offered his hand, and said, "Greyson Earl." She shook the hand and replied, "Alberta Bennet."

"Peach," Greyson said with a smile.

"Alberta," she said firmly. People had tried to stick her with that nickname before. "And this is Brian Mason." As she spoke, Greyson kept hold of her hand. She wasn't quite sure what to do about that. It was awkward. Perhaps if she had been more social in school or if she had been less affected by the beer, she could have handled it better. Greyson raised her hand to his lips and gave it a wet kiss. Alberta flushed.

"You're Major Earl's son," Brick said.

"Obviously." Greyson took Alberta's beer, handed it to Brick, and said, "Get rid of this shit." Again, he insinuated his body between Brick and Alberta.

It struck her as funny, but she didn't want to hurt Brick's feelings by laughing. He was a good sort, if less exciting than Greyson. She ought to bring him back into the conversation, but suddenly there was a cup at her lips.

"Here," Greyson said, "this is better than what you've been drinking." He tipped the cup into her mouth.

Caught off guard, Alberta swallowed and coughed. She was too inexperienced to identify the form of alcohol, but it was strong. She didn't like being fed like a toddler from a sippy cup. She took a step back, but Greyson moved with her.

Then Brick was there, pushing Greyson away. "I don't think she wants your germs."

"I can speak for myself," Alberta said, "and I can drink for myself." She took the cup from Greyson and took a big swig. This gave her the feeling that she was back in control of the situation. Besides, a sharper had to learn to hold her alcohol.

But she wasn't in control of the situation, and the men were not in control of their tempers. Brick and Greyson faced off with chests puffed out and fists clenched. The last thing she wanted was to have two men fighting over her on her first night. That was no way to start a career.

"Brick," Alberta said. "Could you get me more pretzels?"

Brick reluctantly broke eye contact with Greyson. He gave Alberta a hurt look and headed for the vending machines. Greyson cawed with triumph, thinking he'd won the round.

"If you'll excuse me," Alberta said to him, "I have to go to the ladies' room."

There was no women's restroom inside the bar at the time. The Mines had built a freestanding cinderblock bathroom for women twenty feet outside the back door, located so that it could serve two buildings. It was a temporary measure while a new, larger recreational facility was under construction. Alberta didn't mind because the night air was delicious. She looked up into the black sky and stumbled on the path. The stars swam like bright little fish. Suddenly the cock sparring between Brick and Greyson seemed funny. Laughter spilled from her throat.

She sat, emptied her bladder, and considered the damp patches on the concrete floor. She imagined she would be traveling to places where this toilet would be a luxury. She laughed again as she stood and turned to flush. Later, Alberta would learn to take closer notice of odors. The smell of sweaty polyester would have alerted her. She was too drunk to take in details that night. She unlatched the door of the stall and there was Greyson, filling up her view, stumbling, falling forward and pushing her back onto the toilet seat. He covered her mouth with his and stuck his tongue so far down her throat she gagged.

Alberta had no experience with men. She'd avoided any entanglements that might divert her path from the Mines to the altar. She didn't know how to effectively use her tall, strong body to fight off a drunk, horny man. She was paralyzed for the first critical moment. He pinned her arms and turned her so that she faced the back wall. When she came to herself and tried to get free, he grabbed her hair and banged her head against the lid of the toilet tank. She lost consciousness briefly. She thought he might kill her.

His voice slurred as he told her how much she wanted him, really wanted him despite all this coy shit she was trying to dish out. He clawed at the fly of her jeans until the metal button popped off and clinked against the bowl of the toilet. He told her she should not be here, trying to be a spy, that it was a man's game, and he would show her the equipment it took to do the job.

The equipment was outsized, blind, and clumsy. It slid off in three directions before he finally used his hand to jam it in. The pain was acute, but it was the humiliation that made it hard to breathe. The consciousness of her own stupidity and vulnerability. The knowledge that she had stumbled into victimhood like legions of women before her on the very night she had been exulting in a new life.

Greyson came quickly, belched, and then emptied the contents of his stomach over her back. He passed out and slid onto the floor. She remained hunched over the toilet and dripping. She had been quiet through the attack, but now she let out a howl.

That's how Brick found them. He had worried when Alberta didn't return and Greyson disappeared. He would castigate himself later for how long he stood outside, hesitating to enter a ladies' room. He didn't know if this was an assignation by agreement or an ambush. Then the rawness of Alberta's howl told the story.

Brick's first instinct was to kick Greyson into pulp, but Alberta pushed him out of the stall. "They'll throw us both out," she said. "That's how this works. That's our first lesson."

Brian trembled as he absorbed this fact. Alberta could see what it cost him to regain control of his impulses. It cost her dearly, too. "Can I piss on him?" he finally asked in a voice that was oddly childish.

"Please." Alberta turned to give Brick privacy while he baptized Greyson in cheap, recycled beer.

"I didn't cry," Alberta said. "Not once. I never thought of giving up and going home. I wasn't even late for breakfast the next morning. You missed breakfast and morning classes. And you remembered nothing. Nothing."

Alberta paused to take in Greyson's appearance from head to toe. "You look like shit," she said, "but I'm not fool enough to think I've defeated you. You're still dangerous. That's the point of today. I get to unburden myself and say everything I've wanted to say for years without telling you anything, because I know that information is ammunition. I won't give you any ammunition. Get the hell out of here." Alberta gestured to the door, and Greyson fled.

When he was gone, Alberta reached into her desk, pulled out playing cards, and dealt them out for what Americans call Klondike solitaire and Brits call Patience. She preferred the name "Patience," because playing the game calmed her whether she was having a good day or a bad one. It reminded her to proceed with care and prudence no matter how things were going. Enjoy your successes, but don't dwell on them too long. Make the bold moves, but don't get carried away. Remember that the success of one bold move does not ensure the success of the next. Keep your eye on all the cards.

7

The Other Brothers

The Brotherhood of the Blood Drop Cross was the latest name for a splinter of a splinter group of Klan-inspired, testosterone-poisoned Hitler fanboys who loved Jesus, flags, guns, cosplay, and beating the shit out of others. What could such a group have in common with the fleeing terrorists, Fahad and Akil? More than you would think. They had the same goal—a final, glorious, global war. They had many of the same tactics for reaching that goal. They differed only in who they thought would win the war and the shape of a reborn world. Fahad and Akil envisioned a caliphate practicing a "pure" and rigidly patriarchal form of Islam. The Brotherhood saw a whites-only utopia practicing a "pure" and rigidly patriarchal form of Christianity.

The name "Brotherhood of the Blood Drop Cross" likely would outlast earlier identities because the group had invested in a sizable quantity of swag with the blood drop cross logo. It glimmered on the face of a gold-plated medal strung onto a thick ribbon and laid in the center of a table draped in white. Blood-scented candles and men in chasubles surrounded the table. They bowed their heads.

An elderly man cleared his throat. Deacon Davenport, Sublime Arch Sovereign of the Brotherhood of the Blood Drop Cross, wore the most elaborate chasuble. The blood drop logo was embroidered on its front with metallic threads. He was a slight man who employed a series of colorful affectations to boost his visual impact. Mutton chops bushed from his jowls. Round, rimless glasses magnified his rheumy eyes. Underneath the day's ceremonial garb, he wore a leather bolo tie and a velvet vest with an antique gold watch in the fob pocket. This outfit gave him the air of an extra in a spaghetti Western. The whole effect was one of a man layered in clichés like an onion in scales.

Davenport lifted the medal from the table and raised it to his lips. He let a moment of silence pass before speaking in solemn tones. "Allow me to read the words engraved here, 'To Gordon Harold Grant, for Exceptional Fealty to Our Cause.'"

Gordy stepped forward glowing with pride, shiny hair product, and a gloss of sweat. He dipped his head modestly under the attention of the brothers. The occasion called for solemnity, but his mouth twitched with a suppressed smile.

Davenport laid an arm around Gordy's shoulders. "Exceptional fealty only hints at what Gordy has done for the Cause, for this Organization, for his country, and for God. He would be the first one to tell us not to put his accomplishments in writing. To hold us to a high standard of operational security. Let other men get all the credit for the Screamer Attack. They'll also take the heat."

Gordy wriggled under the praise.

Davenport continued. "Do you remember how you reacted when he said, 'Maybe we should help the terrorists attack?' You gasped with disapproval because these were evil and not righteous men. But Gordy saw that each attack carried out by Muslim terrorists led to an influx of money and recruits for our cause. I was the only one of you who saw his genius. Saw that aiding the other side would magnify and accelerate the cycle of retribution. They would attack us again. We would blow up a mosque, and on it would go. Anti-American demonstrations over there. Anti-Muslim demonstrations over here. One shock after another until the sinful world as it exists now collapses, and our new and pure state rises.

"I must take a little more credit for myself. I was the one who recruited Gordy into the Brotherhood. His contacts among our enemies—both in the government and in the Muslim world—have borne magnificent, chaotic fruit." Davenport solemnly draped the medal around Gordy's neck.

Gordy felt the weight of honor on his chest. His heart threatened to burst. He didn't feel ten feet tall. He *was* ten feet tall. Maybe twenty. He had not felt anything like this for years. His career had nosedived after his disastrous tenure as counterterrorism liaison to the Mines. The Mines had caught him in various misdeeds from careless handling of classified documents to lewd acts with a summer intern on a conference table. The wanted him fired and his clearances stripped. The Organ merely demoted him to an admin job working with government contractors. If it hadn't been for the Brotherhood, the ignominy would have suffocated Gordy.

Instead, Gordy became the miracle-working broker between a terrorist cell in Manchester struggling to fund a wild idea, deep-pocketed white supremacists in the U.S., and a cognitively impaired but influential senator who could arrange for a small British company to get a juicy contract with the Mines. Gordy had done his job well, providing Fahad's group with money, photographs of the interior of the Mines headquarters, and other information. He dealt the Mines a humiliation so much greater than the one they had dealt him.

But this was only the beginning. Gordy Grant could be the 100-foot-tall man. He could do it again. He had his own operative. "Give me one man for a follow-up attack," he had told Fahad. It took some convincing, but finally Fahad had given him Hamid's address and code name. He had not made the contact yet. It wasn't time, but soon.

A few weeks later, Gordy was in his Gaithersburg condo preparing to nuke a frozen block of mac and cheese when he got word that Davenport had called an ad hoc meeting of the Brotherhood. Gordy smiled with the thought that more praise might be coming his way. He shoved the box back in the freezer, changed his Versace slippers for topsiders, and headed for the Virginia suburbs.

He got caught in a road repair backup and arrived fifteen minutes late. Velma, the wife of the brother who owned this home, opened the door. The smell of something burning hit Gordy, and he wrinkled his nose. "Toast," Velma said as she swept strings of hair from her forehead. "I was making a tuna sandwich, and I burnt it." She snorted. "Speaking of toast, they're waiting for you downstairs." Gordy took a step back, but Velma grabbed his arm and pulled him into the house. "Too late now." She shoved him toward the basement door, still chuckling at her own joke.

As he descended the steps, everyone looked up. Eyes narrowed. Something fluttered in Gordy's chest. His right knee buckled, and he grabbed the railing. He was a hero. Why would they be looking at him like this?

Gordy started to take a seat in the corner, but Davenport said, "No, sit here," and motioned him toward a metal folding chair placed in the center of the room, the very spot the medal table had occupied such a short time ago.

Gordy sat down and avoided eye contact with the men installed in a mismatched assembly of lumpy chairs and couches. No chasubles today. Most were wearing camouflage fatigues. His nostrils quivered with the smell of burned toast. "What did I miss?" he said.

"Not miss, misplace. Wait, no." Davenport adjusted his gaze so that it bore more directly into Gordy's soul. "Steal. Steal is a better word. Steal, the thing thou shalt not do according to the commandments. Or have you forgotten them?"

Gordy struggled to keep his face blank. "I don't understand." But he did understand. In his time serving as the Brotherhood's Grand Vault Master, he had diverted funds to himself with a few strategic accounting errors. Gordy believed in his cause, but he also believed he deserved an occasional treat. It had started small, and then got out of control as he developed a taste for the finer things just as the Brotherhood's hate rock music label scored a string of hits. The money bought him a mouth full of dental veneers, upgrades for his new condo, and a sweet, fully loaded Range Rover he named "Désirée."

Davenport continued. "Thing weren't adding up, so I recruited a forensic accountant. He reckons you've stolen a quarter of a million dollars. Probably more, but that's the figure we have now."

The cold, hard knot in Gordy's heart dropped through his stomach and lodged in his descending colon. "I don't know what you're talking about. The money went for the Screamer Attack." He tried a casual smile but then shut his mouth to cover the dental veneers. He needed time to think, to come up with an explanation, to find a shovel to dig himself out of this deep, deep shit. His eyes wandered to a display of guns on the wall.

"We tracked the movement of money to your own accounts. We do not—cannot—tolerate thieves," Davenport said.

"I can explain," Gordy said.

But he could not.

"I don't want your explanation. I want the money," Davenport said.

A large bead of sweat on Gordy's forehead exceeded critical mass and ran down over his brow and into his eye. He teared up from the salt sting. He thought he might burst out crying. He wanted to ask what they would do to him if he didn't come up with the money. Then he didn't want to ask.

"Do you know the story of Hank Barker?" Davenport said.

Gordy searched his memory. The name was vaguely familiar.

"Barker worked for a former affiliate of ours," Davenport said. "He handled the group's finances much like you handled ours. Very much like you handled ours. He embezzled a large amount. When he was caught, he was so full of remorse that he blasted his own head off with a shotgun." Davenport shrugged. "At least it was ruled a suicide."

"I'll get you the money," Gordy said. "Give me a little time and I'll get you the money."

"You've broken our trust," Davenport said. "We can't afford to let it slide."

Gordy reached deep inside and pulled out his last ounce of bravado. "If you give me some time," he said, "I'll not only get you the money; I'll pull off another attack on the Mines."

Deacon Davenport raised a brow. "And how will you do that?"

"I have an ace in the hole," Gordy said, "another terrorist ready to strike."

"The rest of you out." Davenport waved his hand, and the men hurried up the stairs.

Gordy preferred to maintain an air of mystery, but Davenport scooted his chair forward for an interrogation. He demanded every detail. He wanted to know why this information had been kept from him. He scowled at Gordy's plan for a simple suicide operation.

"That won't cause enough damage," Davenport said. He smoothed a mutton chop with his finger. "There might be a way to enhance the impact."

Gordy opened his mouth, but Davenport held up his hand. "Set it in motion. I'll give you instructions soon. Meanwhile, cough up the money. I can't let thievery go unpunished."

✦ ✦ ✦

At work the next day, Gordy scribbled a list of assets he could cash out. He'd taken out a second mortgage on his condo the year before and already spent the money. His addiction to the high-end catalogues had left his credit rating in the toilet—a costly Japanese toilet with dubious resale value. He couldn't very well hock his dental veneers. He would have to sell Désirée, as much as it broke his heart, but that would barely scrape the surface of his debt. His pencil lead broke as he pressed down too hard.

A shadow fell across the list, and Ken Jasper's piercing voice bit into Gordy's neck. "Good to see you hard at work for a change," he said, "although I doubt you're doing anything connected to the mission of this unit. Come into my office and close the door."

Gordy meekly followed his boss into the tiny room and closed the door.

Jasper was new in the department and a decade younger than Gordy. He was a cold and correct man who was going places and didn't mind steamrolling a few bodies to get there. He spoke rapidly, as if trying to finish before the sound of some buzzer. "The Request for Proposal for that security software should have been on my desk at the beginning of the week. I would say you're on thin ice, but the ice has already broken and you're treading water and approaching hypothermia. I've already composed another letter documenting your failures. If I don't get that request on my desk by close of business, the letter goes into the file, and the termination process begins. I'm tired of wasting my budget on deadwood. This unit has been a dumping ground for screw-ups for too long."

Gordy started to say something, but Jasper cut him off. "I've heard your excuses. Get out."

Gordy left the office, stumbling over his own feet and nearly crashing into a printer. As he headed for his desk, he heard an exclamation of triumph.

"They have a name!" The voice belonged to an old colleague, Bill Hanlon. Like Gordy, Bill had been demoted to this department after a career in counterterrorism. Like Gordy, Bill was on thin ice, because he spent more time following news about his old subject matter than doing the dry work of his current job. Lately, he had been obsessed with the Screamer Attack.

Gordy should have gone straight back to his desk to crank out that Request for Proposal, but he stopped to look over Bill's shoulder. The sight of the face on the screen almost took his legs out from under him.

"Fahad Syed," Bill said.

"They caught him?" Gordy asked.

"Not yet, but the manhunt is on."

Gordy knew this would come, but he had hoped it wouldn't be so soon. The man staring at him from Bill's computer screen was the same one he had met in a London pub, the man to whom he had given money, a layout and interior photographs of Mines Headquarters. He had handed over one more item to persuade Fahad to trust him— sort of collateral, ammunition against Gordy himself in the form of a dirty video recorded in a Mines conference room. Where was it now?

Bill scrolled through exterior photos of Fahad's flat and the home of a conspirator named Akil. Investigators would be crawling all over both places, prying up floorboards, looking into vents, taking them apart piece by piece.

What had Fahad done with that flash drive? Had he uploaded it to his computer? Were the Brits viewing his conference-table antics at this moment?

And what about Ace? Gordy had promised another attack in the hope of buying time, but the news had made Davenport more impatient than ever. Gordy had to get to Ace quickly and set the attack in motion.

✦ ✦ ✦

No one had ever knocked on the door of Hamid's apartment. When the sound came in the middle of the night, it broke into his dreams and brought him to his feet, trembling. He stumbled to his one small window and opened it with every intention of hurling himself to the pavement six floors below. He climbed to a chair, lunged, and found himself on his back on the floor. He'd forgotten that American windows have screens.

The knocking continued. Hamid's brain cleared as he lay on the floor and listened. This was not the sort of pounding that signals a midnight raid. It was subdued but persistent, as if the person on the other side of the door wanted to get his attention without waking the neighbors. The Internal Investigative Organ, he reasoned, would have already forced the door. Perhaps it was a brother? The contact Fahad had promised? Hamid got up, went to the door, and looked through the peephole. The man didn't look like a brother. His dark hair had a synthetic gloss in the dim light of the hallway. He wore khakis and a pink polo shirt. He had a black suit bag slung over his shoulder. The way he was holding that bag showed off the sort of gaudy watch that no brother would wear. Hamid opened the door a crack without disengaging the chain lock. "You have the wrong flat," he said.

"Ace, let me in," the man whispered.

Hamid sucked in a breath at the sound of his assigned code name. He undid the chain lock, pulled the man in, and reengaged the chain. "Who sent you?" he asked.

"Fahad," the man whispered.

"Don't use that name," Hamid said.

"I don't remember his code name, but I'm an ally. I have something for you." The man held up the suit bag.

This strange night visitor, who stank of money, hair product, and hubris was everything Hamid hated about Americans. During training, Hamid had drilled in techniques of silently taking down and killing an opponent. Instinct told him that this would be the most prudent path now, but then the visitor unzipped the bag.

A sigh escaped from Hamid's lips. This was what he had longed for—death. The suicide vest was more sophisticated than the sort he had trained with in the camps, but all the necessary parts were there, explosives, detonator, pocket trigger, shrapnel. This was glory and an end to his suffering, but ...

The visitor zipped the bag back up and offered it to Hamid, but the operative made no move to take it. The visitor lowered the bag and looked around the small apartment. It had only two interior doors. The man went to the near door and opened it to find a closet. He hung the suit bag on the rod. "There. It's ready when you are. Now let's talk about your target. It's a place called Hale Plaza. The top brass of the Mines have moved in there while headquarters is down. Security is thick, but I have a way to get you past the front gate." The visitor reached into his pants pocket and pulled out a card. "Call this man and tell him an old Penn State friend sent you. He will give you a job with Caterico, the company that handles the Mines' food services. I couldn't get you anything inside the building. They're much tougher on security checks for those jobs. I got you a job driving the food delivery truck. That'll get you past the gate, close enough to take a run at the building. I'll leave it to you to plan the approach."

"A vest isn't enough," Hamid said. "I want a lorry full of explosives."

Gordy shook his head. "I can't get you that, and the dogs would sniff it out anyway. Do the deliveries until they get used to you. Until they wave you through. Then wait for me to give you the signal to attack."

Hamid didn't take the card. "The signal must come from Fahad," he said.

The visitor smiled. His teeth were too white and too big to fit his mouth properly. Hamid found the smile repellent. The man spoke slowly, as if explaining something to a child. "Fahad can't send a signal. He's on the run. The authorities have his name. He may be arrested any day."

Hamid knew this. He followed the news closely. The way the visitor spoke offended him. Everything about this man offended him. "I can't believe Fahad would trust you."

"He doesn't trust me, but he's willing to use me. He couldn't have pulled off the Screamer Attack without me. Take the card," the visitor said. "Take the job. This is what Fahad wants."

Hamid took the card. An attack was what he wanted, too, more than anything else, but this man could not be trusted. "I'll take the job. I'll prepare; then I'll wait for the signal from Fahad. Not you."

8

Off the Face of the Earth

Their post-attack high spirits had soured to something closer to postpartum depression. It was a common phenomenon among terrorists after attacks, but one that remains unstudied by psychiatrists. They had expected that the attack would change the world and make them giants, but instead it made them dirty, hungry fugitives. Fahad missed his *Daily Telegraph* crossword puzzle, his clean bathroom, and his Dunhill toiletries. Akil missed his wife and regular meals. They were constantly on the move and on two occasions escaped capture by minutes. The stress exacerbated Akil's rosacea, and he was out of his medication. The inability to bathe properly left Fahad itchy and irritable.

They huddled behind crates of canned mango pulp and sacks of rice in the basement of a halal butcher shop and grocery in a small town on the southern coast of Sicily. The owner of the shop was unaware of their presence and would have turned them over to the authorities if he had known. It was his teenage daughter who had hidden them. She was carrying on a relationship with a young extremist on the sly. The extremist was a friend of a relative of Akil's.

This was the fraying remnant of their support network. For food, the men had a stale round of Moroccan bread, some of the spicy turkey sausage that was a specialty of the shop, and a few packages of blood orange hard candy. The next morning, they would set out from the coast on a trafficking boat making the return trip to Libya. And from there? They didn't know. The elaborate plans they had made before the attack had fallen apart, and they were living hour by hour.

They had grown to hate each other's company as much as each other's stink. They argued constantly over whether to stage one more attack while the Mines was vulnerable.

"I need it," Fahad whispered. "I need to hit them again."

Akil held his thumb and index finger in front of Fahad's face showing a half centimeter gap between the two. "We are this close to spending the rest of our lives in an undisclosed location."

Fahad sat back to put distance between his face and the none-too-clean fingers. "We have nothing to lose. They have our names already. If we are going to go down, we should go down big."

"I would prefer to go later rather than sooner," Akil said. "Have you even got a secure way to communicate with your man?"

"I do," Fahad said.

"Well, are you going to tell me what it is?" Akil said after a pause.

"No, I'm not. You don't need to know," Fahad said, and he thought, *You don't need to know that I'm sending out the signal tomorrow. I'm done arguing.*

Fahad waited until the shop was closed for the evening, the owner had gone home, and all was quiet above. He waited until Akil was snoring. He unzipped his backpack and pulled out a pencil, a graph paper notebook, and a travel book light, which he clipped to the notebook.

Tonight, the image would be a simplified ram's head. It meant "Go." Fahad filled in the squares of the nonogram carefully, checking with the edge of an envelope to make sure that they aligned properly with the numbers. When he was finished, he used a pen knife to slice the page from the journal. He folded it, slipped it into the envelope, and wrote in the address of the magazine under the name of the editor. He wrote "Nigel Smith-Jones" in the upper lefthand corner. The people at GRIDZ were under the impression that Nigel Smith-Jones was a lovely elderly Brit who was not computer savvy enough to send in his submissions electronically. They put up with the snail mail because he was a longtime contributor, an excellent puzzle constructor, and occasionally wrote them charming letters.

At 2:00 a.m. the shop owner's daughter led them to a hooded figure waiting by a rusted Fiat. Akil started to get into the back seat, but the driver pushed him toward the open boot. Akil clambered in, swearing, while Fahad slipped the envelope to the girl with whispered instructions to post it without fail. Then he crammed his body into the tight space next to Akil. The car burned oil. Fahad vomited up bread and sausage before they had traveled half the distance to a deserted stretch of beach. Akil punched him in the arm in protest. Fahad wanted one of the orange candies to take the bitter taste from his mouth, but they were out of reach in the backpack at his feet.

When the motor cut off, wind filled their ears. They were unsteady on their legs when they climbed out of the car. Loose stones, ground smooth by waves, tripped them up as they followed their contact down to the beach. Fahad squinted at dark water boiling with people. How many? He couldn't make out individuals, only a wretched mass of body parts struggling against the waves and wind. Fahad squinted and made out a small boat yawing in the dark waves beyond.

"We have to go through the water?" Akil shouted. "I can't swim."

"You won't have to," said the hooded man. "It won't be over your waist." He shoved them toward the waves.

Fahad could not move. This wasn't water; it was the anonymity of human misery. He had felt outrage on behalf of the refugees. He would have been willing to die—loudly and heroically—for them. He did not want to die like them, to sink nameless into their fate. Akil clung to his arm. The hooded man prodded them from behind with something metal. Fahad willed himself to move. They waded in, and soon the water was up to their shoulders. A swell lifted their feet off the bottom. Akil panicked and almost dragged Fahad under the surface, but he managed to right them both. Fahad spat saltwater and tried to hold his backpack high. It contained nothing of value but everything he had left in life—his notebook, underwear that needed laundering, a photograph of his brother, a sliver of Dunhill soap, a small sum of money, and a few foil packages of orange candy. The water was to their chins by the time they reached the flimsy craft. Rough hands dragged them aboard. Someone shouted, but the wind carried the words away.

The shopkeeper's daughter was careless with the envelope. When Fahad handed it to her, she folded it and slipped it into her jeans. Back in her bedroom, she removed it and stuffed it under her mattress. The next morning, she overslept by half an hour and had to scramble to get to school in time for a math exam. She failed it. She knew it before she turned in the paper. Her teacher was her uncle. He would phone her parents with the news before the end of the school day. They grounded her. She didn't think of the envelope again until four days later when she slipped out of her bedroom window to meet her boyfriend.

He greeted her with the words "They disappeared."

"What?"

"The men that were in your basement. Never got to Libya. Probably at the bottom of the sea."

She had not liked them much. The short one was rude and they both smelled sour. Still, she felt bad that they might be dead. She remembered the envelope. She resolved to post it as soon as she could get out again.

This gentle beach featured white sand, not stones. The five young mothers were Saturday morning regulars. They'd been joking and laughing, but now they were on high alert. Their charges had strayed beyond the invisible boundaries agreed upon earlier in the day.

"What are they doing?"

The children were down near the water, gathered around something the mothers couldn't see.

"Probably an interesting rock?"

Paola shielded her eyes with her hand. "No, it's some sort of trash. I'll go check." She took off at a trot across the sand. "Faro, what have you got?"

The little boy turned and toddled away, clutching the thing to his chest. "It's mine. I found it!"

Paola accelerated and caught her son by the waistband of his swim trunks. "Don't you run from me."

Faro tried to pull away, but his mother dropped to her knees and locked an arm around his middle. Her other hand reached for his hand. "What have you got? Give it to Mama! Now!"

They tussled.

"How many times have I told you not to pick up trash?" Paola said.

"It's not trash. It's orange candy."

You can't eat that. It's been in the water."

"So what?" Faro said. "I've been in the water, too."

This logic did not impress his mother. She pried the bag away. "I'll buy you some clean candy when we get back to town." She kissed Faro's teary face and went to find the nearest waste receptacle to dispose of the sodden bag.

The children were back home in bed by the time the bodies washed ashore.

9

A Fairy Tale

lberta straightened her posture, took a breath, and entered the conference room of Hale Plaza. It had been named after a different Hale, not Nathan, but people were already calling it "Nathan Hale Plaza." She'd called a "principals only" staff meeting. No deputies or acting chiefs. Alberta had sent her own deputy, Carlos, on another trip. As much as she adored him, he was getting on her nerves with his penchant for prodding sleeping dogs. He'd questioned her about a line item in the executive office budget—miscellaneous expenses. That kitty had paid for the veterinarian who implanted a listening device in Senator Harrison Westerly's cockatoo. Now it was paying for a very different sort of expert, one she planned to introduce at this morning's staff meeting. Carlos must never find out about any of this. He was the future of the Mines and must be kept squeaky clean. Meanwhile, if she was to ensure that the Mines had a future, she had to sweep up some left-over dirt.

Arthur, Greyson, and Slinky waited for her. She read their faces. "Alberta the bitch," she saw in their eyes, and it made her smile. They were underestimating her. She was a bitch, but she was so much more.

"Good morning." She said it, and Thelma wrote it on a pink Doodlebug, added an exclamation point, and turned it around.

"Greyson, please sit down." Alberta gestured to a chair.

Greyson hovered by the table with a fearsome scowl on his face. He had the half-crazed look of a dying beast. Alberta guessed it was the result of sleeplessness and painkillers. She smiled and gestured at the seat again.

"I will not sit," Greyson bellowed.

"Suit yourself," Alberta said lightly. "Now, first—"

Arthur interrupted her. "First we have to talk about the geese. I was attacked by a Canada goose this morning coming in from the parking lot. They're everywhere, leaving their slimy poop and going after people. Something needs to be done."

"Slow down," Alberta said. "You'll give Thelma a hand cramp."

Thelma scribbled furiously on the Doodlebug. She turned it around. It said, "Goose attack in lot. Slimy poop. Action item."

Greyson and Slinky nodded in agreement.

"We need to get a guard out to shoot the damn things," Greyson said. "I'm tired of cleaning shit off my shoes. Time to start serving goose McNuggets in the cafeteria."

Thelma frowned and wrote "Shoot geese?" on her Doodlebug.

Slinky shook his head. "Illegal. I've already assigned someone to hose the sidewalks on a continuous basis. We've had two falls already from people slipping in the droppings. The attacks occur when someone nears a nest, so I'm deploying orange cones to mark the sites."

Thelma wrote, "No shoot. Illegal. Full-time goose poop hoser." She slid the purple erase button and wrote, "Marking nests with cones."

"Enough," Alberta said. "I set the agenda, Arthur. First up, I have a surprise." Thelma scribbled the words "Surprise for you!!" on the Doodlebug and turned it around.

From their faces, it appeared that the horsemen did not like surprises. That amused Alberta. She found the Doodlebugs Slinky had ordered hilarious. She felt like the hostess of Wheel of Fortune with her beautiful assistant Thelma turning the letters.

Alberta nodded, and Thelma went to fetch the surprise. The horsemen's eyes narrowed, widened, then squinted with confusion when an odd, morose-looking woman walked into the room. She was fiftyish. Ichabod Crane physique. Harry Potter glasses but in red. Sensible shoes. Ruth Bader Ginsburg hair, but with a streak of periwinkle blue running from the right temple and disappearing into the bun. Big, dark, hooded eyes with sparse lashes. Dressed in blue to match the streak. What was that thing on her wrist? Good god, it was an age-blackened ERA bracelet.

"This," Alberta announced, "is Justine Moreau."

Thelma displayed the Doodlebug with spokesmodel panache and a dazzling smile.

Only Slinky rose to shake Justine's hand. Alberta frowned at the others until they followed suit. Justine stared at the men as if she were examining statues in a museum.

Alberta continued. "Justine is my new hire. Justine, you can return to your office while I explain what you'll be doing." Alberta waited for the door to close; then she began, pausing after each sentence for Thelma to write her words and show them to the horsemen.

Arthur, the only horseman with functional ears, blurted out, "This is excruciating. Can't you just tell me and write a memo for them later? Are meetings really going to be run with these stupid toys? I could have my people develop something much more appropriate."

"It would cost a fortune and do the same thing," Alberta said. "Only it would be gray. Am I right?"

"It would look streamlined, adult, and it would have significantly more functionality. It could be voice activated," Arthur said.

"Which means it would be a potential security risk. It would also mean that people would have to have training to use it, and they would resent the training and never use the fancy functions anyway. Moreover, it would take months for you to even come up with a beta version, by which time, many more people will have recovered their hearing or obtained hearing aids or learned to read lips or sign. Meanwhile, these are available now. Am I right?" Alberta asked.

Arthur started to say something and then leaned back in his chair, defeated.

"Am I right?" Alberta repeated.

"Yes."

"Don't sulk. If you can find something better off the shelf, I'll consider it."

Alberta nodded to Thelma to resume her translation. "Justine is a novelist." A range of unpleasant expressions passed over the faces of the horsemen.

"Cozy mystery?" Arthur asked.

"Psychological horror," Alberta said. "She also writes biographies. I'm going to have her write us a story of—" She paused here to allow Thelma to catch up. "—the man responsible for the Screamer Attack."

Arthur said, "What the fuck?"

Thelma frowned at Arthur, scribbled on the board, and turned it around. "Language!"

Slinky said, "Excuse me?"

After the meeting was over, Alberta appeared at Justine's door. She knocked but didn't wait for permission to enter.

Justine was grinding coffee beans and didn't hear Alberta come in. She had brought in her own elaborate coffee setup.

"Addict?" Alberta asked.

Justine looked up. "I'm a writer, so it goes without saying. Too bad this office isn't closer to the restroom. It would improve my productivity."

Alberta pulled a chair from the corner and sat down. "You have an office on your first day in the Mines. Some miners work fifteen or twenty years for a door they can close. Most never get that door at all. Be happy with what you have."

"I am. I'm thrilled with the benefits." Justine's hand wavered near the brew button, but then she lowered it to her lap.

"Go ahead," Alberta said. "I don't mind as long as you make me one, too. Black."

Alberta sat, and the two women assessed each other. *She's a parody of an unreconstructed feminist*, Alberta thought, *and she knows it and plays it up.*

As she eyed Alberta, Justine's hand hovered over a selection of mugs arrayed across her desk. It came to rest on a red and blue one with a wing on one side and a forked tail on the other. Curiosity and caution warred briefly in her face. Curiosity won, and Justine handed the mug to her boss.

Alberta read the words on the side out loud, "Watch out. I could go either way." She chortled. "So true. Can I borrow this for my next staff meeting?"

"Keep it," Justine said.

When they were settled with their coffee, Alberta said, "I talked them into it."

"Good, I was afraid the idea would sound too crazy."

Alberta savored her first sip, leaned back, and crossed one silk-panted leg over the other. "Crazy is never a problem with the old boys. The crazier the better. What they hate is that the idea comes from a woman."

Justine nodded. "That stubborn old fart problem."

"Makes me want to have the cafeteria serve more saturated fats to clear them out faster."

"How did you get them to come around?"

"Easy. If you don't create a snipe, then one of them might become the snipe. It's in everyone's interest for you to succeed."

"Snipe?" Justine said.

"Snipe is what we call a scapegoat."

"Why don't we say scapegoat?"

"Snipe is a cover term."

"Thin cover," Justine said.

"Even thin cover keeps us on our toes," Alberta said. "I don't want to hear you say 'scapegoat.' It's too loaded a word. It attracts the wrong kind of attention."

Justine wrote 'snipe' in a notebook and underlined it. "So, now that I'm polygraphed, sanitized, and made fit to view the secrets of the inner sanctum," she said, "explain how is this going to work."

"We need a story to satisfy intelligence committee hounds so the Mines can get back to the business of national security. And get back to it quickly. My people have gone through hell. They don't need a MOC show trial."

"What about the truth?" Justine said. "Wouldn't it be faster to lay out the truth? Not hold anything back?"

Alberta snorted. "The committee wouldn't be satisfied with it, because that's not what they're looking for."

"It's not?" Justine said.

"Of course not. Have you ever watched a hearing? They're looking for ways to advance their own agendas. There is a Republican story and a Democratic story and neither one bears any resemblance to the truth. Sure, there are a few high-minded types who would like to know what happened, but they've become rare."

"You're right." Justine fingered her ERA bracelet. "You're exactly right."

Alberta continued. "We need something better than the truth. Something that will satisfy their needs. You need to come up with a confection with nuts for the nut lovers, raisins for the raisin lovers, and a pretty layer of extra-sweet icing on the top to obscure any flavors we don't want them to taste. That's why I hired you. I need someone who can make fiction more plausible than the truth and create an antagonist that everyone will hate and feel good about punishing."

"How does a fictional antagonist help? They need someone real to grill."

"They'll have someone real. His name is Lyle Voth. He was the executive assistant to our late Boss of White Mines, Shelby Wexler. Lyle is a slimy, misanthropic non-entity. Everyone who knows him hates him, and everything he says sounds like a lie. By making him the snipe, morale in the Mines will improve."

"What did he have to do with the attack?"

"Nothing. That's where you come in. You come up with a story and a motive. We manufacture the necessary evidence, documentation, etc. I'll assign someone to help with the technical details. I want you to study past testimony from the intelligence committees. See what types of information the members latch onto. What makes their eyes sparkle. Learn their agendas. You're going to be watching a lot of c-span." Alberta tapped the top of the coffee machine. "Don't run out of fuel."

Justine squinted behind her thick glasses. "Why would Voth take this sitting down? Won't he call you all out as liars?"

"The man has such an unpleasant manner nobody will believe him no matter what he says. He looks guilty."

"What have I gotten myself into?" Justine asked.

"What you've gotten yourself into is a situation where you can enter your dotage with excellent healthcare and good pension benefits. Work a decade here, and you don't have to worry about the future. Can you afford to turn that down?"

"No, I can't. I really can't."

"One more thing." Alberta reached into her jacket pocket and pulled out a small photo of a smiling man in front of a flag. "This is Carlos Hernandez, my deputy. Do not talk to him. He is to have nothing to do with this project until you're finished. Hide in the ladies' room if necessary."

The job took hold of Justine's imagination. She wasn't just after healthcare and benefits, although she desperately needed both. It was the angle of view. What writer could turn down the opportunity to see this piece of history from the inside? She pushed aside her misgivings about the morality of it all.

Justine's cover job was to write a "lessons learned" paper about the Screamer Attack. This gave her a pretext to interview anyone she wanted. The first person on her list was Lyle Voth. It was her job to ruin this man, who had nothing to do with the attack. She thought it only right that she face him as her first order of business.

When Lyle walked through the door, Justine saw why everyone hated him. He had a way of looking down his nose while wrinkling it as if he smelled something bad. That was how he looked at Justine, even as he extended his hand in greeting.

"I'm a busy man," Lyle said. "I don't have time to waste. Why did you call me in here? If you knew what you were doing, you would start with the bomb dissectors who missed this attack. What is your background?"

"And hello to you, too," Justine said and thought, *This man is guilty of something*.

"You didn't answer my question," Lyle said.

"My background is immaterial, Mr. Voth. Let's talk about yours," Justine said evenly.

"You're not Mines," Lyle said. "Nobody from the Mines would say 'Mr. Voth.' We use first names here and we have since day one."

Justine scratched another note in her Moleskine. "I asked you about your background, Lyle. If you want to save your valuable time, answer my questions."

Lyle sniffed. "I was an alchemist not a bomb dissector."

Alberta had told Justine that *alchemist* was Mines speak for *analyst* and *bomb dissector* was Mines speak for counterterrorism analyst. Justine hoped she wasn't showing any ignorance with her next question. "Isn't *bomb dissector* a subset of *alchemist*?"

Lyle harrumphed. "The bomb dissectors like to think that they're real alchemists, but they're not. Tracking people is not alchemy."

"I'm interested in what you do," Justine said.

"My expertise is in Third World economies. My most recent position, as you well know, was executive assistant to the Boss of White Mines."

"Shelby Wexler," Justine said.

"Correct. Again, I must ask you why you've called me in here, because—"

Justine slammed her empty mug down on the desk, and Lyle jumped. "You don't ask the questions. I do. If you have a problem with that, make an appointment with Alberta Bennet-Mason and ask her to change my instructions. Otherwise, answer the questions."

The look Lyle gave Justine was so hostile that any hesitation she had over ruining his life vanished. The man was guilty of something, and he didn't have the wit to hide it.

Justine peppered Lyle with questions. Ten minutes later, she hit on a topic that caused him visible distress.

"Tell me," Justine said. "As executive assistant, didn't a lot of information go through you before it reached Shelby?"

"Well, some. Naturally. Some went through me; some went directly to Shelby."

"How did it go to Shelby without going through you?"

Lyle scoffed. "Haven't you ever worked in a bureaucracy? These are stupid questions. If you knew anything about —"

"Enlighten me."

"Well, he learned things in B ... B ... BOM staff meetings."

This was the first time that Lyle had stuttered during the interview. Justine leaned in. "What sort of information?"

"The usual. Terrorism threats, s ... sensitive things ..."

"Did he share that information with you?"

"Uh, sometimes," Lyle said and then, "No, he didn't sh ... share that information with me. No. Well, maybe sometimes. I don't remember any specific incidences of information sharing."

"He must not have trusted you much," Justine said.

Lyle sputtered.

"Never mind. If he wasn't sharing information with you, then how do you know he was getting terrorism threat information in staff meetings?"

The color in Lyle's face deepened. "Well, everybody knows that. It's the sort of thing they talk about in staff meetings. Common knowledge."

"Did you ever sit in on one of the meetings? Would you sit in if Shelby was out sick, for example?"

"Well, no. They never let me sit in," Lyle said, "but anyone could guess what they talk about in those meetings."

"Did other executive assistants sit in for their bosses?"

Lyle colored. "Yes."

"You were the only assistant not trusted to sit in?"

Justine watched the color in his face shift. He wouldn't meet her gaze. "What other sorts of sensitive things would you guess that they talk about in those staff meetings?"

"Um, well, um, operations, appropriations requests, that sort of thing. As executive assistant to the Boss of White Mines, I'm certainly qualified to make a good, educated guess about what goes on in those meetings, but I don't know for sure. How would I know?"

Lyle grew so pale Justine feared he would faint. She adjusted her heavy, round eyeglasses, sharpened her gaze, and said, "I don't have to ask. I know how you know."

Lyle gasped lightly and looked to the clock. "It's almost eleven. I have another appointment. I had no idea this badgering would take so long. I would really like to know what your qualifications are for this position." His voice rose. "It's obvious to me that you have none. I must leave now." Lyle pointed a threatening finger at Justine. "I'm going to find out where you came from. You're unprofessional and incompetent." He got up, caught his foot on the leg of the chair and had to grab Justine's desk to keep from falling. He gathered what was left of his dignity and fled.

Justine made no effort to stop him. She had some research she wanted to do before she talked to him again. She drummed her fingers on her Moleskine and considered all the ways an executive assistant might illicitly get information from a BOM staff meeting. Did Shelby take notes?

10

Maddie Smashes into a Brick Wall

I pored over the charred papers pulled from Greyson's trashcan. I could make out some hedge words from the audio analyst: "possible," "suspected," and "believed to be." Only two words remained from the actual conversation: "screamers cost."

Screamers. I didn't see that word in the slag before the attack. I was sure of it. I'd been searching for anything that would indicate method of attack. I would have recognized "screamers" as a method.

The first time that word came up in connection with terrorism was several days after the attack. When I finally turned the news on, I saw it scrolling through the captions at the bottom of the screen. The very word used in this undisseminated intercept had been adopted as the label for the attack. I doubted it was coincidence. Someone who had seen this report had also slipped this word to the press, probably by accident.

Then there was the second word—cost. Who was footing the bill for this operation?

The only other thing on the fragments of paper was the handwritten notation "JT in CS/BM/BAGD." That would be Jason Talbot in the Counterterrorism Sector, Black Mines, Base-Affiliated Groups Division. I guessed that Talbot and maybe his deputy were the only recipients of these reports.

I would try out my disguise on Talbot. I arranged for Joseph to pick me up at the Print and Photography Building and drive me to the Counterterrorism Sector offices in a government car. When he arrived, I got in the front seat. "Good morning, Joseph, how are you today?" I said in a voice that was higher, breathier, and slower than normal.

"What is that?" Joseph asked.

"It's my Jennifer voice. Don't laugh. This is serious."

"I'll try not to laugh, but it will be difficult. You sound like ... I don't know what. A porn star maybe."

"Crap, that's not what I was going for. You've driven Hill staffers around; what do they sound like?"

"Like they're trying too hard to let you know that they're educated, connected, and busy doing important things."

I tried again, this time with more precise pronunciation and a smattering of pretense and impatience. "Yes, Joseph, I'm well aware of that."

"There you go. Now drop a name."

"I've already written a white paper on the issue for Senator Snodgrass," I said.

"Bingo."

I fished a bag of snickerdoodles from my briefcase and placed it next to him. "Mom thinks you're too thin," I said.

"Bless her heart," he said. "I am too thin. Since Lucy died, I microwave whatever comes in a box. She was one fine Southern cook. Nothing tastes like she made it." He selected a cookie and bit into it. "Oh, but these taste just like hers."

"Where did Lucy grow up?" I asked.

"Greenville, South Carolina."

"How do you feel about hominy? Lima beans? Fried onion rings fat as doughnuts? Cornmeal-based cooking?" I asked.

Joseph sighed, "Mother's milk."

An idea formed in my head, but I pushed it aside for the moment. I had to concentrate on being Jennifer.

I had applied my prosthetics and makeup with special care that morning. As Jennifer Morris, Senate staffer working for the MOC, I was bound to meet up with some hostility, but my tenure as chief of the Alternative Analysis Unit had thickened my skin.

I have a distinctive, rapid, arm-pumping stride. Anybody who knew me would recognize it. During my excursions through the damaged Headquarters complex, I had practiced my new "Jennifer" walk, which was slower with shorter steps. Instead of my usual flats or kitten heels, I bought a pair of cheap stilettos high enough to throw my posture out of whack. The uncomfortable footwear and my cast would guarantee that I couldn't revert to my usual gait.

The other thing I had to remember was not to brush my fake hair behind my ear. It was a habitual gesture I had to suppress. The last thing I wanted was for someone to notice my new hearing aids. It would be a dead giveaway that I had been at the Mines during the attack. I doused my wig with hairspray and hoped that the stiff feel of it would stop my fingers in time.

My heart thumped as I watched the SCUDO go over my badges and paperwork. I knew him. A raw scar bisected his forehead. He'd worked at the New Headquarters entrance in the atrium alongside the guard who died under falling glass.

He smiled at me and gave me a wink as he handed my papers back. Good sign. Men never winked at Maddie for fear she'd put out their eye. He motioned to a man standing nearby. The man came forward and offered his hand.

"Jennifer Morris? I'm Gene, your escort." He glared at me slantwise, as if he had vision in only one eye. I knew the greeting would have been warmer if I had been one of his Black Mines colleagues, but I was wearing a red V (for Visitor) badge. In the Mines, V, not A, is the scarlet letter.

"Pleasure to meet you," I lied.

Gene glanced at a form in his hand. I watched his lips to make sure I understood what he was saying. "You want to go to the Base-Affiliated Groups Division?" he asked as if there were something perverse about the request. "Why that particular unit?"

"Are you going to question my every request?" I took a breath and reminded myself not to let my voice go sharp. "The attack was conducted by a terrorist group once affiliated with the Base. Why wouldn't I want to talk to—" I stopped myself before I said, "the BAGGIES." It was an in-house nickname, not something a staffer would use. "—to the Base-Affiliated Groups Division?"

"Fine, this way," Gene said. He led me down a long hallway, up an elevator to the fourth floor, and down two more hallways. When I got to the office, I found a new chief had taken over. "Bob just started a two-year tour to a Middle Eastern country," the secretary told me when I asked for Abbot. "Our new chief has agreed to talk to you."

"No one mentioned this when I made my appointment. Was the new chief here during the Screamer Attack?" I asked.

"He was in Europe."

"Then he wouldn't be useful to me, would he? When did Bob leave?"

Her eyes narrowed. "I can't be more specific without explicit permission from above. You can put in a written request if you like." She seemed pleased to impart bad news.

"Look," I said, "I know you can't tell me what country he's in now, but you can tell me when he left. I will document any failure to cooperate. What's your name?"

"Bob left a week ago."

"Interesting name," I said. "Thank you. Could I speak to Miles Harvey?" Miles was Talbot's deputy.

"In an Asian country. Two-year tour." The secretary had the gall to smile.

Everyone who had seen the intercept had likely been sent to some remote location. Finding out where would use up considerable time and political capital. Even if I tracked one down and flew out for a personal interview, they would stonewall. I glanced at Gene. He pointedly looked at his watch.

As long as I was here, I should talk to some bomb dissectors. As this thought entered my head, a sleazy-looking man with a shaved head, black mustache, and aggressive beer gut walked in the door. Vernon Keene.

Vernon had served on my canary crew before the Stadium Attack. For weeks we sat at a conference table across from each other. Surely, he would recognize me. I turned away.

"You look lost," Vernon said in the velvety, extra-deep voice he used for preying on unsuspecting women. "May I help you?"

I steeled myself and turned around. To be as un-Maddie-like as possible, I gave him a sweet, coy smile. Gene stepped forward. "She's not lost. I'm her escort."

I ignored him and offered Vernon my hand. He had no idea who I was; otherwise, he wouldn't be hitting on me. Vernon was someone I wanted to talk to. Whatever his personal flaws, he was an excellent bomb dissector, the sort who thought out of the box, when he wasn't thinking about sex. Granted, that wasn't a huge percentage of his waking hours, but it was enough to make him useful.

"Hello, I'm Jennifer Morris. I'm working on the MOC report on the Screamer Attack. I was here to interview Robert Talbot, but he's out of the country."

Vernon scoffed. "Talbot is a colossal know-nothing."

I was gratified to see the secretary scowl. "Could I have a few moments of your time then?" I asked.

Gene stepped in. "You can't walk in and talk to anyone you please. Who is this? If his name isn't on my list, you can't talk to him today. You'll have to put in a request."

"My name is Vernon Keene," Vernon said. "I'm one of the most experienced bomb dissectors in the Strategic Threats Group. You might remember me as the man who cracked the Stadium Plot."

"After it had happened," I said and immediately regretted my words. I had to play to Vernon's ego.

"Nevertheless, I'm sure it would be worth your while to talk to me," Vernon said.

"I'll put in a request," I said.

Gene escorted me out. Since none of the people on my list were in the country, there was nothing else I could do. Next time I would bring a longer list.

I got into the car with Joseph. We pulled out of the parking lot and into a mid-day traffic snarl. I opened the window and leaned out. Snarl as far as I could see.

Joseph took the next side street and began to wind through places I had never been. With a little urging, he launched into a fascinating commentary on local history. It seems that Lucy, a librarian and researcher, had been working on a book on the region's Jim Crow history before she died.

"I helped her with the research," Joseph said. "A driver has a lot of time to kill waiting for people to come out of meetings. Whenever I had to wait, I would look around for the oldest person I could find. Most people don't notice them, but they're always around sitting in a dive having a bite to eat or walking slow through a neighborhood. It's easy to get them to talk about the old days. Lucy would take my leads and follow up with her research."

"How close was she to finishing the book?" I asked. Until my rides with Joseph, I had thought of this whole area as prefabricated and soulless. I wanted to read something that would give it some history and humanity.

"She finished the first draft," Joseph said. "I'm tying up loose ends, polishing, doing some additional research. I'll get it finished one of these days. You know I'm not just a driver. I have an English degree from Howard."

"Then why are you driving people around?" I asked. "That's not right."

"When I signed up, that was all a black man would be offered. Later they tried to put me in the Employee Development Program and move me into an Admin job. I thought about it. I thought about how my passengers always look like they're sitting on walnut-sized hemorrhoids. I thought about sitting inside pushing paper instead of driving around and talking to people and helping Lucy with her book. I'm out here every day working on the equivalent of a PhD in local history. I'm happy. I would go crazy in a cubicle."

"It's driven me a little crazy," I admitted. "You're a wise man."

11

Slinky Goes Rogue

Slinky was touring headquarters again. He had replaced his Maglite with a head lamp. The smell of decay drew him toward the cafeteria, a place he had largely neglected since the attack. Ample light came in through the arched, two-story windows. They had shattered suddenly and spectacularly during the attack, killing one sixty-eight-year-old contract officer, Billy Rutledge, and injuring dozens. Slinky paused to acknowledge the chalk outline on the floor near the window with a nod.

Abandoned food and broken dishes littered the tables and floor, but the main smell was coming from the serving area. Slinky picked his way over broken glass to take a closer look. This low-ceilinged room was tucked under the upper floor of the cafeteria. Ambient light from the windows lit the cash registers near the front but left the salad bar and steam tables in darkness. Slinky sidestepped lines of trays dropped during the attack. He almost lost his footing when he stepped in a slick of something gelid. He aimed his light toward the darker recesses in the back of the room and startled a murder of crows feasting on rotting sausages and eggs. A momentary trick of light and shadow made it appear that there were dozens and not a mere handful. Slinky ducked as they took wing and flew close over his head. He turned and watched them wheel out through a large gap where the plastic covering the windows had come loose. They circled above the courtyard. He marveled at his ability to observe the raucous creatures in silence. It gave him an odd feeling of invulnerability. Their screams couldn't tear at his nerves.

Slinky's lamp shone on another steam table. A raccoon dropped onto the floor with six kits close behind. They waddled toward the kitchens. How were they getting into the building? When Slinky's beam of light found the glowing, close-set eyes of a skunk, he opted for a slow backwards retreat.

Time to stop asking permission. The investigators wouldn't find anything in the cafeteria. He couldn't let this building rot any longer. He had already vetted a crime scene clean-up company. He would send them an email and get them started this afternoon. He had a list of retirees available for use as security escorts. Damned if he was going to let the physical plant go to the skunks while he awaited authorization from constipated bureaucrats. He could ask forgiveness later.

Nauseated from the cafeteria smells and afraid the skunk would detonate, Slinky fled to the corridor that ran along the north side of the cafeteria.

There he saw Maddie wearing her curly Jennifer wig. She was headed away from him, toward the east end of the building. Slinky elected to avoid contact. He had already had dealings with a skunk today; he didn't need to deal with Maddie. Slinky turned on his heel and headed west, toward the New Shafts Building to check out a worrisome crack engineers had found in the foundation. A couple of them were advocating for tearing the building down and starting over. Imagine trying to get money appropriated for that.

Try as he might to focus on logistical issues, Maddie's image wouldn't leave him. He now believed Senator Brand had made a serious error when she hired the woman to write the MOC report. From everything he'd ever heard about her, he knew that Maddie only followed instructions up to a certain point, and then she struck out on her own and went places you never intended her to go. She'd put Slinky in a tough spot by leading him to Greyson's office. Even now, he wondered whether he had done the right thing by not confronting the man. He didn't need to confront him to know what he was burning. It had to have been those intercepts of Senator Harrison Westerly.

The day after the Screamer Attack, Westerly had resigned "to spend more time with his family." He pulled out this old saw of an excuse even though he was in the middle of a divorce and estranged from his son. The only family Westerly would spend time with was his new pet bare-eyed cockatoo, Orrin Hatch. Orrin had been bought to replace Dirksen, the cockatoo the Mines had accidentally killed when attempting to plant a bug in him. Slinky winced at the memory.

Surely it was guilt and fear of detection that sent Westerly scurrying from Washington. The intercepts proved that he'd been in contact with a second individual, probably an American citizen, who had in turn been in contact with the terrorists responsible for the attack. Now those intercepts had been deleted from the computer systems and burned, although Slinky had his doubts as to whether anything could ever truly be deleted.

Slinky felt sorry for Westerly. The old man had been sliding into dementia for some time. He probably didn't understand what he was doing. Nevertheless, someone should dig into the senator's contacts, particularly whoever he was talking to in those intercepts.

Yet such an investigation would harm the Mines. The last thing the institution needed was the revelation that the former chairman of the MOC had starred in an intercept and that the Mines had subsequently bugged his pet parrot to find out what was going on. Sure, the only reason Westerly's voice had been picked up was that he had been speaking with someone directly associated with a terrorist, but still, it didn't look good. And yes, the Democrats would be delighted that a prominent Republican senator was caught in wrongdoing, but they would yell about overreach at the same time. The Republicans would be out for revenge. The Mines would be dragged into a nasty partisan battle just when it desperately needed funds for rebuilding.

Maybe Alberta was right. They couldn't tell the truth. The best thing to do was to create a palatable story while moving against the terrorists responsible for the attack. But that meant that no one was trying to find out who Senator Westerly had been talking to in those intercepts.

Once he had reached the New Shafts building, Slinky took the first door to a stairwell. He stopped and turned his headlamp off. He stood in the darkness and let his imagination take him back to the day when this staircase was packed with terrified people. Was he doing right by them? They would suffer if the MOC went on an anti-Mines rampage. They and others might suffer more if evidence was ignored. Crap, he was going to have to tell someone. Not Maddie, someone who could track down Westerly's co-conspirator and yet be trusted not to publicly drag the Mines down.

Back in his Hale Plaza office, Slinky sat down to his computer. First, he arranged for the cafeteria cleanup and the necessary escorts. Then he considered the question of whom to trust with the information from the Westerly intercepts. Someone smart and discreet.

Slinky thought about the Stadium Attack. Who was it who had figured out what had really happened? It wasn't Maddie; it was that fellow who always looked suspicious, the one with the mustache and shaved head who wore black. Vincent? No, Vernon. But was Vernon discreet? He'd helped Maddie air the Mines' dirty laundry in public.

But Vernon seemed more predictable than Maddie. Given adequate incentive, he probably could be trusted to stay behind the scenes.

"Five years," Slinky said. It was a tempting offer. He would arrange for Human Resources to add five overseas years to Vernon's service record if he successfully and discreetly completed the assignment. That meant earlier retirement and earlier entry into the lucrative world of contract work.

Vernon licked his upper lip and stroked the end of his mustache with a fingertip. He wrote on his Doodlebug, "But what exactly is the job?"

Slinky shook his head. "I need your promise first."

Vernon scowled, but he held out his hand, and the two men shook on it.

Then Slinky laid out what he wanted Vernon to do. He watched the man's face as he told him about Senator Westerly, the intercepts, and the task of finding out who Westerly had been talking to.

"The guy was a U.S. citizen?" Vernon wrote.

"American accent, at least. To get around the restrictions, I've arranged to have you work on contract for Heartland Defense. You put nothing on a computer. I don't care if you do all your work on a Doodlebug."

"I have an appt. to talk to Jennifer Morris from the MOC," Vernon wrote.

"I'll get you out of it."

"How could it hurt?" Vernon wrote. "She's hot."

"No." Slinky gave Vernon a fierce frown. "Talk to Jennifer Morris and the deal is off."

«12»

Goldfinger

Joseph let me out in front of the print and photography building. I waited in the rain until he had driven off, then sprinted to the far end of the building and peeked around the corner. I called softly as I crept along the rain-streaked brick. Under the inadequate cover of a bush, I found the small tabby I had been feeding and slowly taming. Her silver-gray fur had darkened with moisture. She looked pitifully thin. She was facing away from me, shivering even though it wasn't cold. I called, but she didn't react. I realized then that she was deaf. Was she in the building during the attack? Had she somehow sneaked in past security? How did she manage to escape without getting crushed?

That's when I cried. Somehow this one little victim made the dam burst. I flattened myself against the wall and let rain and tears wash my face and wet my silly wig. I felt again the darkness, the noise, and the crush. I cried because it was only right that I take my turn as victim. It wasn't right that this little animal had to suffer. The kitten looked over her shoulder and saw me. I thought she would bolt, but she was hungry. She gave a plaintive meow. I wiped my tears, reached into my bag, and brought out a small can. I popped it and dumped the contents onto the ground. She tore into it. I petted her as she ate. She was still skittish, but she was so focused on her meal that she tolerated the touch. I quickly gripped the scruff and scooped her into my oversized bag—the one I had been carrying for a week for this very purpose. I closed the flap. She howled.

I went back around the building to the entrance. Fortunately, George, the security guard manning the Mines tag machine, was still in line for hearing aids. He didn't react to the exorcist sounds coming from my bag.

"How'd you get so wet?" he asked in a loud voice.

I pointed skyward and fluttered my fingers to indicate rain. We did a version of this little question and pantomime routine every day. I had been cultivating George with baked treats from my mother so he would turn a blind eye to the contraband I carried into the building. When George's eyes wandered to my bag, I realized he was thinking about food, not cats. I had promised him a loaf of banana bread. That loaf was indeed in my bag with the feral kitten. I set the bag on the floor in front of George's desk where he couldn't see it. With one hand holding down the flap, I slipped my hand in and grabbed the foil-wrapped loaf. The kitten sank her claws into my wrist, but after a small struggle, I managed to remove both the arm and the loaf without letting her out.

George was so happy to get his banana bread that he didn't notice the claw marks on my arm or on the foil. At least he pretended he didn't notice. He probably would have let me take the kitten in the building, but I wanted to give him plausible deniability.

Once inside my office, I opened the bag. The kitten crouched inside, big-eyed and terrified. I popped another can, tuna this time. Planning for her capture, I had stocked a few cans. I dumped the tuna into a dish and set it down on the floor next to the bag. The kitten followed her nose to the food. I petted her as she ate. I felt her muscles relax.

"I dub you Stella, after the first female head of MI5." Stella was too busy eating to react. When the dish was empty, I picked her up and put her in the litter box I had already set up in the corner. She squatted and peed, neatly covering when she was finished. Then I sat with her in my lap. I massaged her ears, scratched her under the chin, and gave her neck a light knuckle rub. Stella purred and closed her eyes. I understood then why Vivi spent so much time rescuing animals. In a world of bombings and beheadings, the ability to exercise simple kindness was a lifesaver.

I opened my bottom left desk drawer. Anticipating the arrival of the kitten, I had lined it with faux wool. I gently set Stella down. She kneaded her bed briefly, then fell asleep.

My wig felt like a wet animal on my head. I took it off and hung it on the back of a chair in front of the air vent to dry.

I couldn't take Stella home, because Abu Bunny hated cats, but I could let her live here for a while. It would ease the strangeness of being the only Mines person working in the building. The other temporary occupants were members of the various investigative teams. George was super vigilant with them, but he hadn't blinked an eye when I had brought in the litter box and other cat accoutrements. I suspect that he had been feeding the kitten, too, because I had seen other empty cans near the building.

George had also overlooked the microwave and mini-fridge I had procured and stocked with snacks and beer. If I was going to have to look at Buddy's beer magnets all day, I figured I might as well indulge. No one ever checked up on me. Slinky seemed to be avoiding me. I took the opportunity to make myself comfortable and happy at work.

I'd brought in my ancient boom box. I put on an old Blondie CD and watched the kitten. She didn't wake up, even when I turned up the volume. Nothing like "Kung Fu Girls" to get yourself pumped.

I scanned my notes. I'd struck out on interviewing insiders. Vernon was suddenly "unavailable." Audio analysts claimed no knowledge of the undisseminated intercept. The bomb dissectors I'd talked to knew nothing of the intercept. They'd uncovered the Manchester-based terrorist cell and were tracking down the perpetrators. God speed to them, that wasn't my job. My task was to figure out who dropped the ball on our side.

I focused on the decision to hire Kreative Industrial Sunlight Solutions to install the lights. According to Slinky, Dashiell Aspling stepped over the rules for competing government contracts. Now that I was working for the MOC and not the Mines, I was free to investigate American citizens. I'd spent a day searching for possible past contacts between Dashiell and KISS. I couldn't find anything, and no one in the Mines had heard of KISS before Dashiell arrived. Maybe it was a family contact?

I spun my Rolodex and stopped on the name Thelma Madison. She was the most connected person I knew. She could get Dashiell's wife's phone number. I sent her an email, and she produced the number promptly.

To my surprise, Shannon Aspling agreed to talk to me that day. I had a suit hung on the back of my door for such eventualities. I put it on, and the long-sleeved jacket covered the scratch marks on my arm. I shook out the wig, plopped it on my head and ran a brush over it. I went to the mirror I'd hung on the wall and checked my prosthetics. I repaired some rain damage. I was presentable.

I called Joseph for a ride. Even sitting in the back of a government car, I felt like I might be arrested at any moment as I approached the enclave of McMansions ten minutes from headquarters. *Enclave.* The word came into my head even before I saw it carved into the stone sign at the entrance: Wellington Enclave. These people were a different species, and I did not belong here.

The Aspling McMansion oozed pretension from its Italianate loggia to its semicircular topiary-lined driveway, to its fountain filled with putti. It looked like a mansion that should be on a hundred-acre estate, but it was squeezed onto an undersized lot. That was the thing about this neighborhood. The proportions were wildly off. Didn't the residents notice?

If Dashiell's house was the epitome of everything I hated about McMansions, then his widow was the epitome of everything I hated about rich women. Shannon Aspling was ridiculously young—thirty at most—but she was already botoxing her lips. As I shook her hand, I tried to imagine what would make a beautiful woman pump a substance weaponized by terrorists into the tender flesh of her face. I must have been staring, because Shannon backed up a step and said, "Excuse me?" There was something childlike in her hesitation.

I shook myself out of my catatonia and smiled at her. I guessed Shannon spent more money maintaining her looks than I did maintaining my house and car combined. She was manicured, pedicured, and probably sugar-cured. I had nothing in common with her, but I felt a sudden connection.

"I'm so sorry for your loss," I said.

"Thank you." Shannon smiled shyly, then launched into a rapid-fire monologue punctuated with fluttery movements of her hands and shallow gasps for air. I stopped her and asked her to speak louder and slower, lying that I had an ear infection. "It's been so incredibly hard," she said loudly. "None of my friends will hang with me because they think Dashiell might have had terrorist connections. The only people who come are men with badges who look at me like I might have explosives in my bra. I mean, I'm a widow. Aren't widows supposed to get sympathy? All I've gotten is suspicion. I mean, it's not so much that I miss Dashiell. He was losing it, getting strange. Now I'm losing it. No one will treat me like a normal person. I refuse to talk to them anymore. But you sounded nice on the phone."

I realized that all I had to do was be kind to her and she would tell me anything. "I don't think you're a terrorist," I said. "I've spent my career studying terrorists and I can't imagine why anyone would mistake you for one."

Shannon swiped a tear. "Come in. I can't believe I'm talking while you stand in the door." She abruptly turned and led me into the house.

I followed, marveling at her waist-length extensions, which reminded me of the wig I had rejected. We left the marble-floored foyer and were about to enter a library when I said, "Wait a second" and slipped off my shoes.

"You don't have to do that," she said.

I pointed to the white carpet.

"People come and clean it," she said. "That at least is something I don't have to worry about."

I didn't put the shoes back on. They had charcoal on the bottoms from walking through the fire-damaged section of headquarters. I was not going to leave my footprints in this room. I sat down gingerly on a pale, silk-upholstered chair and put my shoes upside down in my lap. I feared my period would begin even though it was a week and a half away. To ease my discomfort, I looked around for a conversation starter. "You have some nice books," I said. The shelves were laden with beautifully bound volumes.

"Our decorator curated the collection."

I didn't want to think too deeply about that remark, so I got to the point. "You said Dashiell had gotten strange?" I'd heard rumors that he was losing it in the weeks before the attack.

"God, yes. He was fine when he first took the job, but then he got so ..." Shannon screwed up her face and stared at the ceiling so intently that I couldn't help but glance up myself. More putti. They swooped around in fluffy clouds. Shannon searched for an answer in those clouds. At last, she said, "My kitty used to stare at a spot on the wall or suddenly perk up his ears and get wide-eyed like he had heard something I couldn't hear. Dashiell started doing that. I mean, it's a normal thing for a cat and but when it's your husband it's freaky." Shannon sniffed. "I miss my cat. I lost him a month before Dashiell died. Merkin was the best cat."

"Merkin?"

"An old boyfriend named him that because he liked to nap in my crotch. Cute, isn't it?"

"Adorable. It sounds like Dashiell was acting paranoid."

"God yes. Sometimes I would deliberately drop something to see how high he would jump. That was the only way I could get any sort of reaction out of him. He stopped looking at me, talking to me, listening to me. It didn't matter if I changed my hair color or wore a super sexy dress. He didn't see me. No communication, period. I felt invisible. Sometimes I would look in the mirror to see if I was still there. I'd say something to Dashiell, and he didn't even acknowledge me. Toward the end even his personal hygiene ..." Shannon wrinkled her nose. "I had to beg him to shower. I'm lucky that he had mostly lost interest in sex by then, because I'm not putting anything in my mouth that isn't clean."

"I can see you have high standards," I said. I had to steer this conversation in a better direction before the mental images got too vivid. Was Dashiell's strangeness natural or drug-induced? "Did your husband have a history of depression?" I asked.

"You'd probably have to ask one of his exes. We were only married eighteen months. I never saw him depressed until he became BOM."

"Anyone else in his family?" I asked.

Shannon shrugged. "I don't know. They're all cold fish. The only way I could deal with them at Christmas was to get drunk as quickly as possible. I barfed eggnog all over his mother's escritoire." She frowned up at the putti, and a tear rolled down her cheek. She turned back to me. "I hadn't thought of it. Suppose his strangeness is hereditary? I'm four months pregnant. That was the last time we had sex. Suppose I have a strange, ugly, cold fish baby? Dashiell was so ugly.

God, I hope I don't have a girl. When I imagine that face on a girl ..."
Shannon started to cry in earnest.

"I bet she'll be as pretty and sweet as you are." I reached over and
squeezed Shannon's hand. She gave me a grateful smile.

"Thank you. I don't know anything about genes. I should learn,
so I know what to expect." Shannon's hand went to her belly.

"Well, I've heard strangeness is a recessive trait," I said. This was
total nonsense, but it seemed to ease Shannon's mind. She smiled.
Then her face clouded.

"I haven't offered you coffee or anything to drink. I can't even
remember to do the simplest things. Is it too early for a cocktail?
Would you like a beer?"

I hesitated. I shouldn't drink, but if Shannon brought up her sex
life again, I might need it. "Thank you, a beer would be lovely."

"Pilsner, IPA, something darker?" Shannon asked.

"Pilsner."

Shannon touched a button and relayed my request through the
house intercom system. She asked for milk for herself. A maid
appeared shortly with our orders.

I took a sip. "Wow, I've got to get me one of those buttons."

Shannon frowned at her own glass. "I don't like milk, and I don't
like taking pills, and I don't really like religion. But I'm going to drink
milk and take my vitamins and pray every night that this baby doesn't
turn out like his father." She took a big gulp from her glass.

"Did the strange behavior start slowly?" I asked.

Shannon dabbed at her mouth with a cocktail napkin and
checked with the putti before answering. "The first time I noticed it
was a few months after he started his job. He came home from work
and said, 'Welcome wagon,' and then went upstairs and crawled into
bed. I went to check on him, and he was crying. He kept saying, "It's
all classified. It's all secret. Unless it all comes out."

"Welcome wagon" was a Mines term. The full term was "welcome wagon briefing." This was when the horsemen briefed a new BOM on the "toxic turds" or nasty secrets that might bite him in the ass in the coming months.

"You say this was a few months after he became BOM?" The horsemen had waited an unusually long time for the briefing. The toxic turds must have been extra smelly. "Was his behavior all downhill after that?"

"Once or twice, he got a little better, but it didn't last. Then he really went downhill. I didn't tell him about the baby. I wanted to be out of here before it was born. I got a divorce lawyer, Ted. He's been amazing support."

"I bet he has," I said. I had heard that Shannon had brought Ted to Dashiell's funeral and spent the whole time hanging on his arm. I hoped he wouldn't take advantage of her too badly.

"You said you hate to take pills. What about Dashiell?" I asked.

"He never took anything. He ran a drug company once—that was before the insurance company—and afterwards he wouldn't take a pill of any type."

I was pretty sure someone had given Dashiell something. Was it the terrorists? I made a note to get in touch with a drug expert. "Did Dashiell ever mention a company called Kreative Industrial Sunlight Solutions?" I asked.

"Other people asked me that, but no. I never heard the name until after the attack."

"Did Dashiell have any close friends or associates who might have given him the name of the company."

Shannon thought about this. "I don't think he had what you could call friends because he didn't like people. They always disappointed him. I disappointed him."

"What about associates?" I hoped I could steer her back to the subject before she started crying again.

"He belonged to the Congressional Country Club. He didn't really like golf either, but he wanted to be well-connected so he could get the BOM job. That's the whole reason he fired a few hundred people and moved the corporate offices of Circumspectual from New York down here. He said it was a cost-saving measure, but that was an excuse. He wanted to be here to cultivate the people who could make him BOM."

"Why did he want the job so badly?" I asked. "He had no background in intelligence."

"Oh, but he read every spy novel ever written. They're all in his private library upstairs if you want to look."

"You know that's no qualification for the job, right?"

"Really? Well, it doesn't matter now. I'm sorry, I'm feeling a little green. I was throwing up all morning and it tired me out."

"You should take a nap. You don't mind if I look through his library?" I said.

"Not at all. In fact, I would like that. I didn't tell anyone else about it because, well, you'll see. I want you to understand, though."

"Understand what?"

"What I went through. You'll see." Shannon rang for the maid. "Sheila will take you upstairs. Stay as long as you like."

Dashiell Aspling's personal library was on the highest floor of his mansion. Sheila took me up there in an elevator lined with gold-veined mirrors. I stood and warily eyed the curvy, perky-nosed, strawberry blond woman who wasn't me. She was still holding her shoes as she stared back at me from all directions.

The attractive young maid had a funny look on her face as she pointed to the door to Dashiell's library. "If you need anything—or get freaked out—there's a buzzer on his desk. I'll come get you right away. Remember, none of it is real."

She left me to explore. I hesitated before the closed door, wondering what the warnings meant. Dashiell had redecorated the BOM's office in glass and chrome. His house was pure Italianate pretension. What would his personal office look like?

I stifled a scream as I opened the door to a tuxedoed man leveling a gun at my head. I clamped my hand over my mouth and counted to ten as I stared at a wax Sean Connery as Bond, James Bond. Wax figures had skeeved me out since my parents dragged me through a wax museum when I was seven. They shushed me as my comments became more insistent. "Mommy, this is sick. Why would people do this?" They insisted that we go through the entire museum because we had paid for the tickets. I wet my pants. I still have deep-seated issues with waxosapiens.

I was taking a moment to allow my heart rate to return to normal when I became aware of a creepy mechanical wheezing. If there was anything I hated more than waxosapiens, it was waxosapiens with chests that moved slowly up and down accompanied by this noise. Bond's chest wasn't moving. The sound was coming from behind the door. There was nothing to do except to step into the room, close the door, and face whatever monstrosity waited behind it.

Dr. No. His chest heaved to the mechanical whir. He was dressed in white with black gloves and cigarette holder. His cold eyes fixed on me.

I pointed my finger at him. "I am not going to let you and your kind stop me from looking through this room." He continued to wheeze. I stepped around him, found his cord, and unplugged him.

I steeled myself and turned my back on Bond and No. It took me a few moments to take it all in. Dashiell's enormous personal library was a cross between a wax museum, a spy museum, and a teenager's bedroom. Spy novels lay haphazardly on shelves and chairs. Unlike the pristine leather-bound volumes in the library downstairs, these bore the marks of hard use. Scattered among the bookshelves were glass cases full of spy memorabilia. Upon closer inspection, this wasn't the type of thing we had in the Mines spy museum. These were movie props. Each piece was labeled with the film it had appeared in and the actor who had used it. Dashiell must have paid a fortune for this junk. He had two of Roger Moore's cigarette lighters, several Bond pistols and sunglasses, a Maxwell Smart shoe phone, and numerous other artifacts.

I circled a freestanding bookcase and almost tripped over Nick Nack as played by Hervé Villechaize. I couldn't stifle a yelp. I needed to sit and allow the panic to subside. I spotted a large sofa on the other side of the room facing an oriel window. I stumbled toward it, clutched the tufted velvet back, and looked down to see a dead woman, face down, arm dangling, and painted gold. I grabbed a pillow and screamed into it.

I had what we at the Mines call a WAGFUD moment. It stands for "We're all gonna fuckin' die." It's that instant when you're briefing a Very Important Person, and you suddenly realize that he or she doesn't have a clue. Like riding in a car with a driver who suddenly says, "Now which pedal is the brake?" WAGFUD. In this case, the senior official was already dead, and others had died because of him. Somehow the delusional man who created this bizarro theme park had been put at the helm of the nation's premier intelligence agency. I had to pull myself together and find out how this had happened.

I pawed through Dashiell's books to see if he had anything that might have helped him run the Mines, but he did not. No Agency histories, memoirs of former directors, or scholarly works on intelligence. It was all spy fantasy—glamorous, exciting, and nothing like the generally tedious business of gathering intelligence.

Satisfied that the late BOM was an ignoramus, I approached his desk. I sat in an elaborate leather chair that was probably from the set of some movie. I straightened a paperclip and picked the lock on the top center desk drawer. Inside, I found scattered sticky notes in rainbow colors, individually wrapped root beer barrels, and headless Lego mini figures. The notes were apparently written by Dashiell in code. I'd work it out later. I gathered the papers, including the ones stuck to the underside of the desk drawer, and stuffed them into the satchel I'd used to catch Stella. I picked the second lock. This drawer held yellow legal-size pages covered in numbers, probably another code. It also contained more root beer candies and Lego heads without bodies. What kind of person stores Lego heads and bodies in separate drawers? The third drawer held heavy gray stationery with the Aspling monogram in silver script. Tiny, coded writing covered each page. I found more candies and Lego weapons of various types from medieval axes to laser guns.

The contents of the remaining drawers reminded me of things a little boy might keep in a box under his bed: a dry snakeskin, some smooth rocks, and action figures. There was a plastic decoder ring of the type that might come in a box of cereal. I slipped this into my bag. This wasn't Dashiell's library. It was Dashiell's inner child's library.

After I had collected every piece of paper I could find with writing on it, I had to pee. I guessed that the door to the right of the desk was the bathroom. I opened it and flipped on the light to find Ursula Andress emerging from a bathtub wearing a white bikini with a holstered knife. "You have got to be fucking kidding me," I told her. "I am not peeing with you looking at me." I took a monogrammed towel from the rack and threw it over her head. I caught the distinct smell of semen. I peed as fast as I possibly could and tried not to think about how Dashiell spent his time in this room.

When I got back to the Print and Photography Building, I could hear Stella crying all the way down the hall. She ran up the leg of my pantsuit when I opened the door. I sat down and petted her until she calmed down. If this was how she reacted to an hour's absence, what would she be like when I left her overnight? As attached as I was to the idea of furry companionship at work, it wouldn't be fair to her. I gazed into her wide, golden eyes. "How would you like to live in a big, tacky mansion?"

"Meow."

"She'll give you a stupid name, but there are worse fates." I slipped the kitten in my bag and called Joseph to drive me back to Shannon's place. If she didn't want Stella, I had no plan B.

I needn't have worried. As soon as I pulled the sorry critter out of the bag and said, "I found this kitten and thought you might ..." Shannon snatched her up and hugged her.

"Come in out of the rain."

I followed Shannon into the foyer. She sat down on a brocade sofa to take a closer look at Stella. "He looks just like Merkin! My psychiatrist said I needed a mourning period, but this is fate!"

Should I tell her that Stella was female? Would that make a difference? I pulled three small cans out of my bag. "In case you don't have any cat food in the house."

A look of horror came over Shannon's face. "We don't feed commercial foods in this house. You haven't given him any of that junk, have you?"

"Certainly not."

Shannon's face softened as she spoke to Stella. "I'll have the cook fix you Merkin's favorite meal. You're going to be a big, healthy boy."

"She's female." I held my breath in case this caused rejection.

"Even better." Shannon ran her hand down Stella's back. The cat's butt rose in the air and twitched as Shannon scratched it. "Look at that booty move. I have the perfect name for her: Twerkin'."

I hesitated again, afraid to ruin the deal, but committed to the truth. "She's deaf."

"Oh, poor baby!" Shannon said and held the cat closer.

I had one more piece of news regarding the lumps I had felt in Twerkin's belly. "She's pregnant."

Shannon burst into tears and buried her face in the cat's fur. "You and me both! We'll go through it together." She looked up at me. "Thank you so much! We're cat relatives now."

I breathed a sigh of relief. Twerkin' had a forever home, one much nicer than my own.

«13»

Vernon Runs into a Brick Wall

S linky isolated Vernon in the break room of the headquarters' motor pool. The drivers were now working out of a building near Hale Plaza, so it was available. He upgraded the windowless room with a vault door and security system.

It was the best office Vernon had ever had. It was the only office he had ever had, but it was way cooler and larger than any entry-level Mines manager's lair. It had a stained concrete floor, two vending machines, and a full-sized fridge. It smelled like oil. A nice-sized Formica lunch table served as a desk. Three cases of Gatorade were stacked in one corner of the room. A metal cabinet in the opposite corner held a well-curated collection of porn magazines. Slinky would have consigned them to the incinerator if he had found them.

Slinky had set up a special computer that allowed Vernon to access Auger, the terrorism database, and other resources, but blocked him from doing anything other than searches. For word processing, Vernon had a stack of legal pads and a jar full of pencils. Slinky had thoughtfully included an electric pencil sharpener. Vernon liked the sound it made and had to restrain himself from sharpening his pencils to nubs.

After a week, Vernon developed painful hand cramps from the unaccustomed manual writing. A Mines doctor prescribed a regimen of exercise—squeezing stress balls and massage with warm oil. Because it was a work-related injury, the Mines provided the balls, oil, and an electric oil warmer with a convenient pump top. When you're a guy and you spend hours every day alone in a room with porn and a dispenser of warm, rosemary-scented oil, one type of massage leads to another. Still, Vernon was getting some work done, too.

Slinky recited Vernon the contents of the Westerly intercepts from memory. If he could have provided the original recorded conversation, the job would be done. Vernon would have recognized the growly whine of Gordon, "Gordy" Grant. The bomb dissectors called him "Loop," short for "Fruit Loop." Vernon had gotten along with him better than most.

Because that recording had been deleted, Vernon had to take the long path to identifying Senator Westerly's interlocutor. He focused on Manchester. The bomb dissectors, working with British counterparts, had identified the homes of the planners and the factory where they had manufactured the lighting/amplification equipment. Vernon surmised that the interlocutor had been in Manchester when that conversation with Westerly was recorded. He was now composing a travel request. He thought a week in Manchester would do it. Now he had to think up a justification for spending a few days in London afterward. He loved going to the Tower.

Vernon finished the request shortly before his scheduled ten o'clock with Slinky. The knock came as the "Sound of Mustang" clock above the door played a clip of the 2000 svt Cobra. Vernon grabbed his Doodlebug and buzzed Slinky in.

Slinky sniffed. "Why does it smell like Williams Sonoma in here?"

Vernon deflected the question. "You hang out at ws?" he wrote on the Doodlebug.

"That's where I buy gifts for my wife. It's an idea I had early in our marriage when she complained about a calculator—a nice one—I got her for her birthday. I told her to find a store she liked and register there. Now my calendar alerts me on all gift-giving occasions. I call Williams Sonoma and ask them to wrap the most expensive item on her list. I pick it up on the way home. Problem solved elegantly. If people put half the energy they expend complaining into coming up with solutions, the world would be a better place." Slinky sniffed again. "So why does it smell like Williams Sonoma here? Rosemary, that's the scent."

"Something I microwaved," Vernon scribbled on his board. Then he handed his boss the travel request.

Slinky read it. "Maybe Manchester, not London. And only Manchester if you have your ducks in a row. Prepare your questions and let me review them. If they look good, I'll approve it. I don't want you to embarrass us by going off half-cocked to meet with the Brits. Meanwhile, how are your efforts going here?"

Vernon gave the thumbs up and wrote, "I have a domestic strategy."

A "so so" hand waggle might have been more apropos than the confident raised thumb. Vernon had indeed devised a domestic strategy. He planned to confront Harrison Westerly and pry the information from his arthritic fingers. Vernon had been trained to brief and write papers, not to interrogate or do interviews, but he had watched enough police procedurals to be an expert in his own mind. The problem was that he didn't know where Westerly was. The man owned properties all over, and no one would say at which one, if any, he was currently residing. Old phone numbers were no longer in service. He could be living in a high-end care facility or an elite resort.

Unlike Maddie, Vernon had never learned to cultivate the people who keep track of schedules and contact information. Vernon's approach was to try to barrel through the gate keepers and go straight to the top. Unfortunately, that was a strategy that only works for people who are already on the top.

Vernon wasn't helped by the "look" he had cultivated. He thought his shaved head, thick mustache, and black shirts said, "man of intrigue." Unfortunately, many people, and most especially women, interpreted this look as "douchebag" or "possible serial killer." Adele Westerly, the senator's estranged wife, had slammed the door in his face. One of Westerly's former aides threatened a restraining order. Even the senator's mild-mannered former chief of staff, Roger, stiff-armed him.

Vernon was left combing through open sources—press articles, interviews, speeches and the like—to get a hint of who the senator really was and where he might be now.

Who was Senator Westerly?

His supporters described him as an old-school Southern gentleman, distinguished public servant, and faithful Christian. His detractors used terms like "neo-Confederate nut job," "obstructionist fossil" and "sanctimonious shyster." Other reporting revealed him to be a one-time segregationist, a Sunday-school teacher, an avid bear hunter, a believer in visits from alien life forms, a serial divorcé, an heir to a boatload of Louisiana oil money, which he had managed badly, and an expert on bare-eyed cockatoos. Taken together, these things amounted to absolutely nothing that could help Vernon locate the old man.

«14»

Justine's Suspicions

Justine brewed a strong pot of coffee, grabbed a legal pad, and scribbled her prompt at the top of the page. "What scares a bureaucrat?" She wrote until the page was full and the cup was empty.

What scares a bureaucrat? Space. The 'crat is only comfortable in the box, no matter how many times he may parrot the term "out of the box." 'Crat equals box. Cubicle. Den. Lair. A warm, comfy, vaguely smelly nest. Anything that might flush the 'crat from the box provokes existential dread. If he's low-level, it might be reorganization. At the upper echelons, there is nothing a 'crat likes better than to reorganize those below him, flushing them from their boxes. He would like them out of their boxes, but not out of his. That's where the line is. What really scares a 'crat? Accountability, which could roust him from the box altogether. The biggest fear? Destruction of the box.

Justine saw the evidence everywhere. The Screamer Attack had almost destroyed the physical box, the headquarters complex. Now it might destroy the institutional box. The Esteemed Legislative Body might "reform" the Mines into oblivion and farm its functions out to different boxes. The idea had surfaced in editorials from both sides of the political spectrum. The bureaucrats couldn't wrap their minds around this cavalier discussion of their fate. She could see it in their eyes and hear it in their voices. This wasn't Post Traumatic Stress Disorder from the attack, but Anticipatory Loss of Box Anxiety. ALBA wasn't in the medical books, but it was real. At the worker bee level, the fear was not as severe. After some confusion and pain, the troops would land in a new box because the work they were doing had to be done by someone. The top managers, however, would be asked to pack their institutional baggage and leave. That fear explained why Alberta had hired her to do this assignment, which was either pure genius or pure folly, depending on the outcome.

Unfortunately, Justine's fate was tied to Alberta Bennet-Mason. So maybe she wouldn't be able to count on this job and its benefits after all. She supposed she could go back to living as she had been before. She hadn't invested much in this place yet. Still, maybe if she wrote her story well enough, she could save herself and the Mines.

Justine jumped at the knock. She hadn't scheduled any interviews.

"Come in," she called.

When Thelma appeared, Justine assumed she was there to relay some message from her boss. "What does Alberta want now?"

Thelma shut the door. "It's not what Alberta wants. It's what I want. I know what Alberta has you doing."

"Do you have a problem with it?" Justine asked.

"Not as long as you leave Shelby out of it."

Justine sensed that Thelma would make an invaluable ally or a dangerous enemy. She'd best tread carefully. "You were Shelby's secretary before you worked for Alberta?"

"I was his secretary for my whole career. I know he had faults, lots of them, but he was a good man. I don't want his name dragged through the mud when he can't defend himself. You know how they make everything sound so bad on the news. Shelby did a lot of good for the Mines and for the country before he lost it."

"You don't think he had any responsibility for the Screamer Attack?"

Thelma looked down at her elaborately manicured nails. "He did, but so did a lot of other people. After an attack, everybody goes looking for one big villain they can pin everything on so everyone else can go about their business. I don't want people to make fun of him like he was stupid or something. I don't want that to be the only thing that people remember about him." Thelma looked Justine in the eye. "Tell me the truth; is Shelby going to be the snipe?"

Justine was glad she didn't have to lie to Thelma. She wasn't sure one could lie to this woman. "No, he's not the snipe."

Thelma let out a breath. "Thank you. It's been keeping me up at night. Well, that's all I came to say." She made a move to get up.

"Wait. Could I ask you a couple of questions?"

"About what?"

"Lyle Voth. I have some suspicions."

Thelma sank back into her chair. "You and me both. Now there's a dirty sneak. I've always thought he was up to something."

"What made you think so?"

"I caught him going through Shelby's burn bag one evening like a raccoon in the garbage."

"Do you know what he was after?" Justine asked.

"I made him empty his pockets. He had the notes from the morning executive meetings with the BOM."

"Did you read any of those notes?"

"I wouldn't do that." Thelma looked offended. "They were scraps. Shelby always tore the pages of his notebook into quarters before putting them in the burn bag."

"Would you like some coffee?" Justine asked.

"It smells delicious."

Justine pushed a basket of sugar packets and artificial sweeteners toward Thelma. She selected a mug that said "Strong and Unfiltered" and poured a cup. "Why do you think that Lyle was going through Shelby's trash?"

"Well for one, he was mad because they never let him go to the meetings. When the other principals were out, they would send their executive assistants. The only time Lyle tried to go, they kicked him out."

"Why?"

"Nobody trusts Lyle." Thelma tipped her head. "I wonder if his own mother even liked him. Maybe he was raised by weasels."

"Is there any other reason he would be stealing those notes?"

"That's what I wonder about. After I caught Lyle, I started dumping Shelby's burn bag down the chute whenever I left the office."

"Did you tell Shelby about it or report it to anyone?"

"No."

Justine thought she detected guilt in Thelma's face. "Why not?"

"Well, that's not important."

Justine didn't press.

The thought of Lyle put Thelma into a foul mood. As she drove to work the next day, she tried to shake it off. It felt wrong. She had a sunny personality. Thelma parked her van in front of Hale Plaza and stared into the rearview mirror, bucking herself up with affirmations.

She mentally ordered her facial muscles to rise, relax, and assume a pleasant expression. Then she spotted Karen getting out of her car. Instantly, her efforts were undone. She did not want to have to make conversation on the way into the building. Thelma scrunched down behind the wheel as the gnome hustled past, carrying a Santa-sized sack slung across her shoulder.

Now what? Thelma waited half a minute and then got out, closing her door softly. She stepped up her pace as Karen opened the doors and approached the security desk. Thelma paused inside the door, turned partly away, and pretended to rummage in her purse for her Mines Tag.

The two guards behind the desk stood. They knew Karen, but a large sack could not be ignored.

"What have you got there?"

"Just gifties for Secretary's Day," Karen sang as she handed the thing over. She gave them her most charming smile. "Stuffed toys. Feel free to run them through the X-ray machine."

I know what you're up to, Thelma thought. You've pulled this one before.

"I didn't know it was Secretary's Day," a security guard said.

"It's not regular Secretary's Day," Karen said. "It's Black Mines Secretary's Day. It's special, because we do so much more than a regular secretary."

Thelma spilled her bag to allow more time for observation as the guards emptied the bag out on a table and pawed through dozens of pastel stuffed bears with plastic wings and halos and the words "Angel Secretary" on the chest. They poked them, prodded them, and ran them through the X-ray machine. A canine officer appeared with his handler.

The German shepherd gave the bears a once over. He paused over the last one, eyed his handler, and whined.

"Something suspicious?" a SCUDO said.

"No," said the handler. "He's asking me if he can have it. He likes nothing better than to shake the stuffing out of a toy."

Karen grabbed the bear. "Sorry, dog, I need all of these."

The shepherd watched in disappointment as Karen gathered up the rest of the bears, thanked the security guards, and continued down the corridor.

Thelma waited for her to disappear around a corner before slipping her Mines tag into the machine. She grumbled under her breath all the way up to the BOM's office. "She's done it again," she said to Carlos's secretary.

"Who has done what?"

"Karen has declared it Black Mines Secretary's Day to get everybody mad at everybody else."

"What did she bring this time?"

"Stupid stuffed bears. She's done this every year since they collocated the Black and White Mines front offices. She'll stroll into every joint office without so much as a nod to the White Mines secretary. Then she'll smirk while she hugs the Black Mines secretary and gives her a gift. This is no way her job. She makes me look stingy because I'm not going to waste money I need for my family to buy a bunch of useless junk and pass it out. Karen made it her mission to undo everything they were trying to do when they collocated the offices in the first place. It was supposed to make people work together better, but it's tenser now than ever. And a big part of that is her doing. She never met a pot she didn't stir."

Thelma had a long and aggravating day filled with emails from friends complaining about Karen's stunt. A crisis in the Middle East kept Alberta at her desk until late, writing cables that Thelma had to format and send. By the time she finally secured the office, it was dark. As she trod the ground-floor corridor, she realized that she had adopted the same hunched pose and put-upon scowl as Karen. She stopped, took a deep breath, straightened her posture, and repeated her favorite affirmation: The good you give out will be reflected back on you. She ordered her facial muscles to be high and smooth. When she passed the security desk, she gave the officer a lovely smile and a pleasant "Good night." She sailed out the door, thinking that a simple smile could lift one's mood and put everything in perspective.

She would have maintained this attitude for the rest of the evening had she not glanced back toward the building. Her high, smooth muscles went slack when she saw ghostly wings and halos hovering in dozens of windows. "The witch," she said out loud. "The stupid bears glow in the dark. I bet she made sure they put them in windows. This is so wrong for a government building."

«15»

Maddie Runs into Vernon

I take my dreams seriously. I figure my conscious mind can access only so much of the data that floods across my screen. My subconscious takes it all in, chews on it, comes to certain epiphanies, and spits them out in dreams. Dreams are chewed up epiphanies. They have meaning but finding that meaning is like sifting through a pile of cat barf to figure out what the cat was thinking when it ate that mouse.

I had the first marionette dream shortly after I visited Shannon Aspling.

I head to the Starbucks for a desperately needed double shot latte. I don't have much time before my next meeting. I pick up speed, race walking down the corridor. Abruptly, my right leg goes out from under me. I don't fall; instead something jerks my leg up towards the ceiling until I hang upside down with my skirt covering my face. Humiliating. Then an invisible string attached at the top of my head pulls me upright. My limbs involuntarily jerk. I try to

*regain control of them, but my feet won't stop moving.
People stop to stare. I recognize the movement as a
clumsy version of the Charleston. I am dancing the
Charleston in one of the main corridors of the Mines
without benefit of coffee.*

Over the next few days, I had new and disturbing versions of the
marionette dream. I moonwalked on conference tables during
interagency briefings. I wobbled in line at the credit union. I tap
danced onstage in the Bubble. I woke up clawing at my hands to
remove the strings.

It wasn't hard to interpret these dreams. Something or someone
else was controlling me in alarming ways.

Why had Senator Brand hired me? She didn't just want me to
write a report. She wanted a certain type of report, one that would
implicate the horsemen. I gave my stupid forehead a slap because I
realized then that Brand didn't care about the horsemen. She only
mentioned them to get me to take the job. All she cared about was
implicating the intelligence community. Get everyone to focus on the
intelligence failure to keep them from focusing on policy or legislative
failures or ...

Or what? Legislative failures were the least of the ills emanating
from the Hill. Why had she insisted that I work out of the Mines?
Why had she quarantined me like I had the plague? Normally,
someone doing my job would be working on the Hill. Was there
something there she didn't want me to find?

It annoyed me that none of these commission reports ever
implicated Congress, as if it had nothing to do with what the Mines
had become. As if selective budget cuts had no impact. As if their
micromanaging produced anything but busywork that distracted
from actual work. As if politicization of intelligence reform could
produce anything but a monster with three left feet and no head.

Brand was trying to hide something.

✦ ✦ ✦

The next morning, I waited until I heard Joseph's knock, then opened the door and thrust a platter of my mother's homemade ham biscuits into his hands.

His brows arched. "What's this?"

"Farewell. I'm driving myself to work and I'm ditching the disguise. There's no need for it. It's overkill. It's a silly senator's chance to play spy games, and I refuse to play anymore."

Joseph put on a stern face. "I have direct orders from Slinky to drive you in every day."

"I'll handle Slinky. I'll deal with him as soon as I get to work."

"But—"

"But nothing," I whispered back. "I'll miss you, Joseph, but I have to drive myself. I need some independence." I pointed to a patch of red on my chin. "I'm developing a reaction to the prosthetics. I'm telling you: I will not do this spy fantasy shit anymore."

"But—"

I returned to my normal voice. "Don't argue with me or I'll take the biscuits back."

"You won't take them back." It was Mom. She stood in the door wearing a pink peignoir I had never seen before. "Good morning, Joseph. I hope you'll like the breakfast. Maddie tells me you love Southern cooking. I'm so sorry to hear you lost your wife. You need looking after. You're thin as a rail."

Joseph gave my mother a radiant smile beautifully framed by his mustache. He could have been a movie star with his deep voice and good looks. I noticed then that mom was wearing an immoderate amount of war paint for this hour of the day. I had been too caught up in my own drama to pick up on the signals. Well, this was one situation I was going to exploit to the hilt.

"Maddie tells me she doesn't need me anymore," Joseph said.

My mother dropped her jaw in an exaggerated look of shock. "You need Joseph. Suppose you pass out while you're driving to therapy?"

"The doctor gave me the green light," I said. "As long as I feel fine in the morning, I can drive myself. Tell you what. Joseph, you can stop by here mornings and do a quick check. If I'm not feeling 100 percent, you can drive me. Otherwise, you can have breakfast with Mom and then drive other people around for the rest of the day."

"I couldn't impose," Joseph said.

"No imposition at all," Mom said. "I would love to see someone eat the food I make instead of shoving it around the plate." She gave me the side-eye and took Joseph by the arm. "Come on, while the coffee's fresh." As she pulled him into her lair, I made my escape.

I felt no guilt about pimping out my mother. Joseph would be the best thing that had happened to her in years. It felt great driving my own car again, at least for two blocks. Then I remembered that my pass to get into the compound sported Jennifer's picture. Crap. I drove to the building where I donned my disguise every morning. I put it on, vowing that I would confront Slinky and make him end this nonsense. My chin itched, and red bumps had blossomed on my nose. I took the prosthetics off as soon as I got back into my office and rubbed lotion into my skin. I hadn't seen any of the senior officials I needed to avoid in weeks, and I had to air my face.

I made a plan. One: confront Slinky and make him give me credentials in true face. Two: stop following Brand's other orders. Three: find out why she had issued those orders in the first place.

Nothing got my brain moving like a brisk walk around the compound. I liked to start out with a question in my mind. Today it was "What is Brand hiding?"

The sidewalks of the Mines compound were an obstacle course. The investigators had collected their evidence and left, and workmen had moved in to renovate. Dumpsters of broken glass and ceiling tiles waited to be emptied. Trucks unloaded pallets of new glass and tiles. Back-up beepers sounded all around as forklifts moved through the labyrinth. I took to the grass to avoid the mess. My intent was to head out the front gate and take a turn on the jogging path that ran through the woods outside the fence. My plans changed when I saw Slinky with his Doodlebug talking to a workman. I was about to intercept him when I spied Greyson Earl. Crap, what was he doing here? Just my luck he would return the day I ditch my disguise. I ducked behind a dumpster.

I looked around for an escape route and spotted a familiar bald bullet head. It was Vernon Keene in running gear—running gear?—hiding behind another dumpster. We saw each other at the same instant. Vernon mouthed the words "What are you doing here?" I mouthed the same question back.

He peeked around his dumpster. Greyson was getting into a car. Slinky disappeared into the building. Vernon took the opportunity to sprint over to me. He whispered something too low for me to hear. I pointed to my hearing aid. He shouted, "What the hell are you doing here?"

"Don't shout; you'll blow out my ears. Let's go someplace without background noise."

"This way," Vernon said. He led me to the motor pool of all places. Vernon worked the combination on a door labeled "Break Room."

Inside, my eyes fell on a stack of porn magazines. Vernon scooped them up and stuffed them into a metal cabinet. I sniffed. The room smelled like motor oil and some strong herb.

"You're going to tell me it smells like Williams Sonoma," Vernon said.

"Do you seriously think I've ever been in a Williams Sonoma?"

"Good point."

"Looks like you've been nesting here for a while." I saw that the trash can was running over with frozen food boxes and beer bottles. "Why?" I asked. "And why are you avoiding Slinky?"

"I'm here because he put me here, and I'm avoiding him because he forbade me to wander around the compound—or to talk to you, for that matter."

"Really? He put me in the print and photography building. No one is supposed to know I'm here. Why would Slinky randomly stash bomb dissectors around the compound?" I asked. "At least he didn't make you wear a disguise. Until today I was running around in a blond wig and fake nose."

"And fake boobs?" Vernon asked.

"Yes. I talked to you at the counterterrorism building, and you didn't suspect a thing."

Vernon pulled a tragic face. "That was you? Crap. I saw you again here about a week ago. That's why I was out jogging. I was trying to run into the hot strawberry blond. And it turns out to be you."

"And I'm not hot unless I'm in disguise?"

"You are, but in a scary, chilly way. The blond was hot in a hot way, and, as far as I knew, she wasn't a potty-mouthed, over-seasoned bomb dissector."

"Fuck you and the horse you rode in on." I smiled and batted my eyelashes. "But to get to the point: why did Slinky put you here?"

"He has me doing a special assignment. I can't tell you about it."

"He has me doing a special assignment, too."

"What?"

"I can't tell you about it."

"Well, shit." Vernon went to the fridge, pulled out a beer, and held it up. It wasn't even lunch time, but I nodded. He popped the top, handed it to me, and pulled out another for himself. We sat down at the table, clinked bottles, and took a swig in silence. "So, neither one of us can talk," Vernon said. "Where does that leave us?"

I studied the scarred tabletop. "It leaves us following orders we don't understand and that leaves me with a bad feeling in the pit of my stomach. My hidden agenda radar is quivering."

"Mine, too."

"Do you know why Slinky isolated you?" I asked.

Vernon scooted his chair back, put his feet on the table, and folded his arms in front of his chest in a habitual thinking posture. As always, it was accompanied by a vicious scowl. "Yes," he said slowly, "I know why."

"Can you tell me?"

"I promised not to."

"How good is your word?" I asked.

Vernon gave me an evil smile accompanied by a finger twirl of the mustache. "Oh, I'm a sneaky double-dealing bastard, so my word isn't worth shit."

"Exactly, so tell me why Slinky put you here."

Vernon hesitated a beat but only for appearances sake. "Before the attack there were some intercepts that were never disseminated."

I sat up straight. "You have them?"

Vernon held up his hand. "I'll get to that. They weren't disseminated because one of the speakers was a U.S. senator. Senator Harrison Westerly, former head of the Mines Oversight Committee, to be exact. The other was a U.S. citizen, not further identified. They were talking about the Screamer Attack. Slinky gave me the task of finding the identity of the second speaker."

"Harrison Westerly? Holy crap. I caught Greyson Earl burning those intercepts after the attack. I knocked him out with a Maglite and salvaged fragments, but there wasn't much left. Do you have the actual reports?"

"You knocked him out?" Vernon's eyes lit with delight. "He'll have you killed."

"He has no idea who did it. I sneaked up on him from behind. And I wiped my prints from the Maglite."

Vernon whistled. "And you with a broken arm. If I had done that, I'd have it carved on my tombstone as my life's greatest achievement. Remind me to stay on your good side."

"I don't have one. You didn't answer my question. Do you have the intercepts?"

"Not the physical intercepts," Vernon said. "Slinky told me what was in them and made me memorize it. He had memorized them earlier, so who knows how accurate his recall is. Although there wasn't much there to remember. A few lines in each." Here Vernon recited the intercept on the cost of the screamers and the one on moving the date of the attack.

"Screamer," Maddie said. "Nowhere did I see that word before the attack. How could they have withheld this information? I could have done something with that word. I knew there was a threat coming from the U.K. If I had the word *screamer* maybe I would have investigated audio engineers. Maybe I would have found an odd little electronics company called Kreative Industrial Sunlight Solutions that hired more audio engineers than lighting experts."

"Or maybe you wouldn't, but you're right. We should have seen it, but if they had shown it to us, someone might have leaked it. It was too explosive not to leak. Then the MOC and the media would have killed us. Either way, it was an existential threat to the Mines."

"I think I would prefer being 'killed' in quotation marks by the MOC to being killed with no quotation marks by terrorists."

"I have to agree with you there." Vernon took a swig of beer and wiped his mouth thoughtfully. "Punctuation is everything."

"Senator Harrison Westerly. A U.S. senator talking about screamers. Maybe that explains my assignment."

"Which is?"

"Constance Brand has me drafting a committee report."

"Who in their right mind would pick you for that job?"

I explained the odd setup and Slinky's involvement.

Vernon tapped the mouth of his beer bottle while he mused. "I still think it's crazy. Why wouldn't Brand choose a MOC staffer to write a custom report? Does she know about Westerly? They're on opposite sides of the aisle. Why would she protect him?"

"I think she's protecting herself and hoping that I find something over here that will divert attention from her sins," I said. "Her name was on some notes I took from Dashiell Aspling's home office, otherwise known as the Museum of Weird Shit. I came out with stacks of coded notes and a mild case of PTSD."

"How did you get in? Shannon Aspling threatened to call the cops on me."

"I gave her a kitten, so now she considers me a relative."

Vernon frowns. "A kitten? I never thought of buying access with a kitten. What did you find out?"

"That our late BOM was an adult child living in a fantasy world."

"So, what else is new?" Vernon said. "We're all gonna fuckin' die."

"Dashiell used three separate code systems. They weren't sophisticated, but he kept messing up his coding, which is slowing me down. The first code turned out to be the names of people with influence—the people he had to cultivate to get confirmed as BOM," I said. "The second listed meetings: golf outings, lunches at pricey steak houses, and dinners at his own home. I'm still working on cracking the third code."

"I'll help," Vernon said. "Where are the notes?"

"In my office."

We made the trek over to the Print and Photography Building. Vernon sat down and spied my Jennifer wig draped over the chair. He patted it wistfully.

"That is just too weird," I said. I grabbed the wig and stuffed it into a file drawer.

"Can I play with the fake boobs?"

"No, no, and fuck no."

We worked for an hour with no luck. Then I remembered the decoder ring. I fished around in the bottom of my bag, found it, and held it up.

"You are fucking kidding me," Vernon said. "Are we about to find out that this is all about Ovaltine?"

The ring worked, but it was tedious twisting the fragile dial. The information was getting ever more interesting and varied. It included some insider tips on stocks that were about to rise or fall sharply; account numbers from foreign banks; a list of initials and phone numbers for "useful contacts"; and the names of companies, including Kreative Industrial Sunlight Solutions.

"Bribes," I said, "that's how an unqualified twaddle head ends up as the nation's chief intelligence officer. We're still missing the linkages. Who got what out of which meetings? There must be something that ties them all together."

"There's a better approach," Vernon said. "Some financial sleuthing to tie those insider trading tips to stock purchases by various Congresspersons. I know a guy."

"Of course you do." I stretched my back and looked up at the clock. "Crap! I didn't realize how late it was. Slinky is probably gone by now."

"What's the problem?" Vernon asked.

I explained why I needed new credentials.

"No," he said. "You need to keep up the disguise, it could come in handy."

"No. I'm done."

«16»

A Cold, Cold Affair

"It worked, Brick." Alberta addressed a photo of herself and her late husband taken on a raw, rainy day in Brussels in 1984. They were in a tacky little tourist trap. Young Alberta and Brick grinned in front of a display of corkscrews in the shape of the *Manneken Pis*—the city's famous statue of a little boy peeing into a fountain. The screw was in place of his penis. They bought a couple of dozen to give as gifts to their upright, abstinent, and humorless midwestern relatives.

Brick and Alberta were in high spirits. They were in Brussels to speak to a NATO experts meeting on the state of the Soviet Union's clandestine war with the West. The assignment was a sign that their careers were flourishing. After the meeting, they planned to take a few days leave and see how many Belgian waffles they could eat.

They had the strangest of marriages. Unromantic in the traditional sense, yet strong. Brick and Alberta loved and hated all the same things. They loved the Mines, a sense of mission, spicy food, travel, in-jokes, intrigue, and unusually large, furry cats. They hated the Mines, sentiment, weakness, affectation, the behavior of

American tourists abroad, paperwork, and, most of all, Greyson Earl. They hated what he had done to Alberta. They hated his arrogance, privilege, misogyny, and amorality. They hated the way he spoke and the way he moved.

Early on they had tried to get Greyson fired by arranging for reports of his alcoholism to reach the right ears, but he had too many protectors in the old boy network. In the end, he rallied, joined AA, and got sober. On the strength of his pedigree and ruthlessness, his career soared.

Brick and Alberta had to work twice as hard for their success and make fewer mistakes. They had to watch their backs at every turn. He knew who had turned him in for drinking and he sought payback at every opportunity.

His latest dirty trick was waiting for them when they lugged their bags of Manneken Pis corkscrews back to their hotel. A message greeted Brick at the front desk. He was to take the first flight out of Belgium the next morning and return to D.C.

"What the hell is this about?" Brick said. "I have a presentation to give tomorrow."

"That's not a problem," said a familiar voice. Brick and Alberta wheeled around to see Greyson standing behind them trailing his luggage. "I'm here to take your place."

Alberta was afraid Brick would throw a punch. She put a restraining hand on his shoulder. Greyson gave an infuriating smile, turned, and headed for the elevator.

Later that night, Brick fumed as he packed for the return trip. He had stopped in at the U.S. embassy and found out that he had been called home because he was in trouble and that trouble was the result of another one of Greyson's dirty tricks.

"He's gone too far this time. I'd kill the bastard if it wouldn't land me in jail," Brick said.

Alberta sat cross-legged on the bed and considered their options. "He has all the cards. He has the contacts. He knows where the bodies are buried because his daddy wielded the shovel. We need what's in his head."

"And how do we get it?" Brick asked.

The idea that came into Alberta's head was outrageous and repellent. She dismissed it, but it returned again and again because ... it would work. She knew it would work.

Brick watched the emotions play across her face. Finally, he said, "Spit it out."

Without altering the gravity of her expression, Alberta slipped her hand under the white cloth of a conference table and squeezed Greyson's penis. Each seat was equipped with a microphone and a headphone for simultaneous translation. The surprised sound Greyson made was untranslatable, however, even though it was transmitted to the entire room because he had forgotten to flip his microphone off. "Oooomf." The sound was girlish, growly, and breathy. All eyes looked up with surprise and curiosity. Greyson adopted the same expression as cover. The meeting resumed, Greyson flipped his microphone off, and Alberta returned her hand to her own lap.

She wore a red suit with a skirt so short it restricted her range of motion. She would have never worn a mini at Mines Headquarters—although other women did. She disdained "pink suit women" who didn't know to guard against the appearance of frivolity and fragility at all costs while inside the Mines. If she could have worn chain mail, she would have. In Europe, Alberta felt less restrained. She was not the only female in the room showing some leg, but no one else had so much leg to show. Sheathed in silky, smoke-colored stockings, Alberta's long legs drove Greyson mad. She had calculated the effect in advance.

When Alberta grabbed Greyson's penis, she did it with the full knowledge and approval of her husband. Not that Brick was thrilled with the idea, but as soon as Alberta had brought it up, he, too, knew it would work.

And it did.

That squeeze was the turning point, the beginning of a long, globe-trotting, almost glamorous affair that gave off the scent of bitter almonds, not roses. Alberta knew how to stroke Greyson's ego so that he didn't guess until too late that he was the object of espionage rather than desire. It was the beginning of a gradual shift in power that eventually led to Brick's swearing in as Boss of Mines and then, later, her own. They reached the pinnacle while Greyson watched from below.

How upset Greyson's daddy would have been. When it became clear that Major Earl would never achieve his ambition of becoming BOM, he had groomed his son for the post, teaching him all the secrets to achieving pull in the Mines. These secrets Alberta had extracted delicately, like a surgeon removing parasitic worms from the brain.

Alberta looked at the photo again. "Well, Brick, it worked, but I never thought I would be here alone."

«17»

Justine Oversteps

Justine had a 6:00 p.m. with Alberta. That was an hour after her normal departure time, but that's how things worked. If you weren't a senior official, your only hope for a meeting with the BOM was at the butt end of the day. For a 6:00 p.m. you would likely have to sit and wait in the semi-darkened outer office until seven. You could doodle in your notebook, do muscle clenches to keep your butt from going numb, or make funny faces at yourself in the curved brass surface of the lamp base. Sometimes Thelma would come out and gently tell you to go home, the BOM was done for the day.

Justine was too excited to sit. She had something important to tell Alberta and she'd find a way to tell her even if she had to break into her office. She eyed the door. At 6:45, Thelma came out and said, "You can go in."

At the sight of her hired pen, Alberta removed her reading glasses, pushed back a stack of papers, and smiled. "You asked for this meeting, so I assume there's progress?"

"A breakthrough," Justine said.

"You have your story line?" Alberta leaned back and folded her hands in her lap.

"Not a story line. I found out the truth." Justine was on the verge of a grin until she saw Alberta stiffen.

"What truth?" Something flashed across Alberta's face, a twitch, a ripple, a movement reptilian in its speed. Then it was gone under a wash of self-possession.

"Lyle is guilty of something," Justine said. "I'm not sure how it ties in to the attack yet, but he stole Shelby's staff meeting notes and shared them with someone. Maybe terrorists. I found evidence of covert meetings in his appointment book."

"You looked in his appointment book?" Alberta said.

"I thought it was part of my job," Justine said.

"Fine," Alberta said, "go on."

Something in Alberta's face rattled Justine, but she continued. "Usually, Lyle was meticulous about recording whom he met and what was discussed, but some entries just had the notation 'G2' and a time. And there were lots of crossed-out numbers, like G2 was using different phones."

"Did I ask for the truth?" Alberta said. "When you're sent on a snipe hunt, you're not supposed to find the damn snipe." She sat up straight, snatched a pen from the desk, and began to roll it between her palms. "Why would I hire a novelist for the truth? I've got alchemists to do that. Do you think they haven't figured this out already? Do you think I didn't already know everything you just told me? No, I hired you to come up with a story to satisfy the public and the committees. And you play spy girl. I thought my instructions were clear."

A stupid question almost slipped from Justine's tongue. Isn't the truth better than fiction? But she saw the fear in Alberta's eyes. She was lying. She hadn't known any of this or else she would never have pointed Justine toward Lyle in the first place.

Alberta finally spoke. "Bring me all the information you've collected. Get it now and don't keep anything or copy anything. I'm going to send Thelma with you to make sure you follow instructions this time."

Back in her office, Justine shook as she collected notes she took from her conversations and other information she had found in Lyle's desk.

"This isn't right," she said to Thelma. "Do you think this is right? I have evidence against Lyle, and she wants to bury it. People died. Does this seem right to you?"

"No," Thelma said. "I'm a good secretary, but I'm a good person first, and this does not seem right."

"Help me xerox it," Justine said.

Thelma hesitated a minute, then got busy. She was in a panic of guilt. She could have turned Lyle in when she caught him raiding Shelby's burn bag, but she didn't. Not because she was trying to be nice to Lyle or give him the benefit of the doubt, but because she took it as an opportunity to blackmail him into buying several hundred dollars' worth of the products her sons were selling for the Boy Scouts and the band. At the time, she had thought Lyle was just being nosy and she might as well take advantage of it. Now it seems that Lyle might have had something to do with this attack—this attack that killed her dear Shelby, and several other, more innocent people.

"What do we do with the xeroxes?" Justine asked.

"I'll take them out," Thelma said. "Security knows me. I take boxes of coffee grounds out for my compost pile. They don't even look anymore. All we have to do is put this stuff in a plastic bag, tape it up, put it in the bottom of the box, and cover it with grounds. I'll take it home and then you can come to my place to pick it up."

After Thelma left, Justine sat shaking. She was not the sort of person who broke laws; she was the sort of person who studied the psychology of law breakers. Justine Moreau, who hadn't collected so much as a parking ticket in her whole quiet life, was doing something that could land her in jail.

18

Things Close in on Gordy

Alberta guessed that Lyle Voth was the molothrus Greyson had told her about. The one who was passing Mines dirt to the Internal Investigative Organ. Lyle had found out about its most damaging secrets simply by reading Shelby's notes. Why had they let Shelby write those notes? Because he was one of the horsemen, and rules were not for horsemen.

Alberta knew Lyle was, at best, a marginal player. Who was running him? What did G2 mean? It had to be Lyle's Organ contact. Alberta pulled out her cards and began to shuffle, snapping them loudly against the blotter. Her mind ranged over the long list of her own contacts at the Organ. After a time, her mind, her breathing, and her heart stumbled over the answer—Gordy Grant. Alberta had been the Mines Inspector General when Gordy was banned from the Mines for his sins. She had interviewed him and been struck by his utter contempt for his colleagues in the Mines and the Organ.

Who was Gordy spying for? He hated the Organ as much as he hated the Mines. Maybe Hunter Johnson didn't know the Mines' worst secrets. But who did? Who else could Gordy be working with?

Who would he know who would want information on the Mines? Alberta pushed the cards to the side, turned on her computer, and accessed the files she had kept as Inspector General. She found Gordy's file and began to read. And to remember. And to sweat. The more she read, the more she wondered at the Organ for merely demoting the man and not firing him. He had worked terrorism long before his rotation to the Mines and had run informants in the terrorist world.

Justine had come too damn close to the intercepts Alberta had suppressed. She'd discovered things Alberta didn't know. Lyle couldn't be the snipe now, because he would lead the wrong people to the right trail.

The whole thing could come down around her ears thanks to a novelist. A damned novelist who couldn't stick to fiction.

She wouldn't let that happen. The first order of business was to take care of Gordy and Lyle Voth.

When Alberta Bennet-Mason invites you to lunch, you clear your schedule, whether you want to lunch with her or not. When she suggests a restaurant, you agree, even if you don't like foreign food. Gordy Grant could think of many things he would rather do today than break bread with Alberta: have a colonoscopy without drugs, go to the ballet, listen to his third-grade nephew play "Free Bird" on a plastic recorder.

But he had to go.

Gordy grew more uneasy when he discovered that Alberta had arranged for a small private room at an Ethiopian restaurant. The staff of the restaurant obviously knew her and her preferences. They were on a first-name basis. He caught one winking at her. What he didn't know was that the owner was a former asset she had resettled in the

U.S. She compensated him generously for allowing her to bring a team to sweep this room for bugs so she could use it for meetings she did not want to conduct in the Mines.

For a power lunch, Gordy liked a well-done steak with ketchup at The Monument. It was a time-honored tradition. You ate your steak and potato, and you left your goddamn salad on the plate. That's what movers and shakers did. What was this shit? He could not focus on the menu. Alberta sat across from him still but hyper alert and focused.

When the waiter came, Gordy tried to order the wat or stew, but Alberta laughed. "The Organ has to have its meat cooked to a pulp as if you had no teeth over there. At the Mines, we eat it raw. You should try the kitfo. It will put hair on your chest."

Gordy wanted to rip open his shirt and say, "I have hair on my chest, lady." But that was not the sort of thing any man in his right mind would say to Alberta. He gave the waiter a sullen look and said, "I'll have the kitfo and a dry martini."

"No, no, no. A martini isn't the thing to have with kitfo. You must try the tej," Alberta said.

"Is it alcoholic?"

"Oh yes."

"Fine, what she said." Gordy shoved the menu back at the waiter, who again winked at Alberta. The exchange put a sick chill in Gordy's gut. He glanced toward the exit.

"That exit might as well be in another country." Alberta leaned close and whispered, "By the time you reach it, you'll be even less of a man than you are now."

Gordy's heart felt compressed. He itched all over. The only thing he could think of was to counter with bluster. "What are you talking about? Out with it. I hate riddles."

"I find them delightful," Alberta said with a musical laugh. "Here's one. Why do you think I invited you to lunch? I'm the BOM. My Organ counterpart is your boss, Hunter Johnson. Why would I bother with Gordy Grant, a man we kicked out of the Mines because he was untrustworthy, perverted, and less useful than a buggy whip in a Ferrari?"

"I'm not a mind reader," Gordy growled.

"Neither am I. I don't need to read minds because I have intercepts. So many incriminating words plucked out of the ether. Our net is so wide we catch a lot of unintended fish. Like a doddering senator. We didn't want that one. Too big and toxic. Can you imagine what oversight committees would do if they knew we had recorded him? But you, Gordy, are a helpless little fish. Almost too small to bother with. Nevertheless, I intend to bone you, filet you, and grill you with a sprig of rosemary stuck up your ass."

Gordy shifted in his seat.

The waiter arrived with small glasses of tej. Alberta offered a toast. "To just desserts." She raised the glass and let her lips touch the alcohol, but she only pretended to drink.

Gordy, meanwhile, had never needed alcohol so much. He took a swig and then spat it back into his glass. "Christ. What is this?"

"Fermented honey. Drink up. It's soothing for the throat. It will help you sing, because you are going to sing."

"I'm not going to tell you anything," Gordy said. "You have more to lose than I do."

"You gained access to notes taken at senior staff meetings. What did you do with that information? Who did you pass it to? You're going to tell me all about it."

"I don't have to tell you anything," Gordy said.

The kitfo arrived on a big platter atop injera, a thin circle of sour, spongy bread.

"One platter?" Gordy said.

"Sharing a platter is a mark of friendship and trust in Ethiopian culture."

Gordy grunted and thought, I trust you as far as I can throw you, lady. "Where are the tools?" he asked.

"You eat it with your fingers," Alberta said. "Like this." She pulled off a bit of injera and expertly scooped up the raw meat marinated in hot chilis. She had the ability, rare for an American, to eat Ethiopian food neatly, while watching her dining companions besmear themselves like toddlers.

Gordy tore off a bit of bread and fingered it. "Feels like sheet foam. Real bread has a crust." He tried to scoop up some meat and winced at the way the juices soaked into the injera. He tossed the scrap back on the plate and wiped his fingers on a napkin. "I don't have to eat this crap and I don't have to tell you anything."

Alberta summoned the waiter. "Ebo, could you bring me a knife, please? A sharp one?"

"Right away." Ebo smiled in a way that Gordy found too conspiratorial. The waiter returned with a dagger. It flashed in the light as he gave it a quick swipe with a napkin and handed it to Alberta.

With the point, Alberta inscribed a line bisecting the injera. She fixed her mantis gaze on Gordy. "You will eat everything on your side of this line while you tell me what I need to know. If you don't, I'll tell Hunter Johnson that you were a crow early in your career when you were still busting down doors. A crow who collected shiny things that should have been turned in. You fenced them through a man named Benny Watson. Benny gave me this. Alberta lifted her substantial purse into her lap and extracted a plastic bag holding a watch and a videotape. She held it up so Gordy could see. "Benny called it his insurance policy. He planned to use it if you ever turned on him."

Gordy squinted at the bag. "I have no idea—"

"Cartier watch. Gold and steel with your fingerprints on it. You slipped it into your pocket on the night of February 7, 1994, during a raid on a money launderer, whose name is engraved on the back. The tape is from Benny's security camera. Clear shot of you handing the watch to him and taking the money. Benny keeps excellent records—he recorded every transaction ever made with you. I have other evidence, too." Alberta waited for a response from Gordy, but his mouth was slack. She gestured at the injera. "Eat up." When he did nothing, her voice grew harsh. "I said eat it." She drew a cellphone from her purse. "Eat it now or I'll call Hunter." After a pause, she began to punch the number into her cell.

Gordy came back to himself with a start. "I'll eat it." His fingers shook as he scooped up a drippy mess of injera and kitfo. He stuffed it into his mouth, chewed and swallowed with difficulty. He brought a napkin to his mouth to suppress a gag reflex.

"Even if you could manage to weasel your way out of felony theft charges, there is the matter of your predilection for underage girls."

Gordy fumbled for the tej. It was awful, but it was alcohol.

"Eat," Alberta said. "Come on."

Gordy stuffed more kitfo into his mouth and did his best to chew and swallow.

"You liked to play the pirate from Peter Pan. Oh, the nasty things you did with Wendy. Of course Wendy isn't her real name. Her real name is Kaitlin Shaw. Poor girl has been in therapy for years."

"Shut up," Gordy said.

"Eat your kitfo." Alberta waited while he took an excruciating bite of raw meat and humiliation. "If you don't want to end up in a prison where the other inmates know that you're an ex-agent of the Organ who molests children, then I suggest that you talk. I want every contact you have." Alberta took a small recorder out of her purse, turned it on, and placed it in front of Gordy. "Eat. Talk. You don't leave until you've told me everything and cleaned your side of the platter."

By the time they left, Alberta had a stomach full of bloody, peppery meat and a head full of toxic information. Some of it was obviously fake, but it was clear that the plot was more wide-reaching than she thought, full of unlikely allies, strange connections, and treason. She would have to move swiftly and carefully.

I need to get out of here, Gordy thought. Need fresh air, or I'll be sick. He wasnt thinking straight, or he would have remembered that there is no fresh air in D.C. in summer. He stumbled from the air-conditioned chill of the Ethiopian restaurant into concrete-amplified heat and almost collapsed on the sidewalk. He grabbed a parking meter and held on as his stomach twisted. Fearing that Alberta could come out of the restaurant at any minute, he stumbled down the street. He had no memory of where he had parked his car, but it didn't matter. He was in no shape to drive.

He had told Alberta some truth and some lies, and both could get him into deep trouble. He hadn't the time or presence of mind to fabricate a strong web of lies. Now, at every step, he saw another weak point that could cause the whole sticky thing to collapse. He was barely conscious of his surroundings. He ran into an elderly woman and almost knocked her over. He didn't apologize. He crossed a street against the light and didn't hear the car horns. He stepped in fresh dog shit and didn't notice.

Gordy didn't see the van that slowed and pulled to the curb a few feet in front of him. Its side door opened as he came even with it. His brain moved slowly, while the hands that yanked him into the vehicle moved swiftly.

So many swords of Damocles. As Gordy sat in the metal folding chair in the familiar basement, they flashed above his head like danglies on a nursery mobile. He was helpless as a baby under the uncanny gaze of

Deacon Davenport. When the light caught the man's thick glasses a certain way, his eyes briefly disappeared in the glare only to reappear a second later larger than before. Then they doubled into four and hovered. Gordy repressed an urge to swat them out of the air.

"What did you tell her? Don't leave anything out," Davenport said, "because I will know."

Gordy didn't doubt this. Lately he had begun to suspect that Davenport had superpowers. How had he known about the meeting with Alberta? Was he tracking his movements? Gordy felt violated and sick. He'd already emptied his stomach, vomiting out the door of the SUV while one of the stickmen held onto his shirt. Now his voice shook. "I didn't tell her everything," he finally said. "I told her about Westerly, but she already had most of that story. I told her about Lyle. I didn't tell her about the Brotherhood. I made up a fictitious group called the Knights in—" Gordy broke off.

"Knights in what?" Davenport prompted.

Gordy blushed. "Knights in White Satin. It was the only name I could think of."

"Idiot," Davenport said. "It doesn't matter that you didn't give her our real name; you told her what to look for. How long until she finds it? There is only one solution. Get your Ace moving. And make sure he gets within forty yards of the building. Forty yards. Don't forget. What are you waiting for?"

Hamid recognized the knock and didn't panic or leap from his bed. It was that man again, the one whose name he didn't know. Hamid's instincts told him to push the heaviest piece of furniture in front of the door, but he couldn't go against Fahad's plan. Hamid rose slowly, shut the blinds, turned on a small desk lamp, and peered through the peep hole.

The hair was different. Last time, it had been glossy and monolithic. Now it had separated into greasy strands that revealed a bald spot. The eyes had grown rabbity and wild. Hamid stepped back as they fixed on the peephole. He undid the chain lock.

"Are you ready to go?" the visitor whispered as he pushed into the room.

"What?"

"I know you took the job. I know you're making deliveries to Hale Plaza. It's time to move. To attack."

"I'll move when I get the signal from Fahad."

"Fahad is in no position to give you a signal. I told you that last time. I'm in charge of this operation now."

Hamid took another step back. He remembered a lecture Fahad had given him on how the impatience of Americans was their downfall. Everything about the visitor spoke of impatience, haste, vanity, and a dangerous foolishness. Fahad had told him to accept help from an unlikely source, but he had also told him to wait for the signal.

"No," Hamid said. "If you control the timing, you can set a trap. You don't tell me when. I'm not ready yet."

At this, the visitor launched into an unmanly torrent of assurances, pleas, and, finally, threats. He swore and shook his fist, but he had no real power over Hamid. At last, the visitor wore himself out. He stood panting. Hamid could smell his sweat. He opened the door and said, "Get out." With a few last whispered obscenities, the visitor left.

Gordy reasoned that paying back some of the money could buy more time from Davenport. Where to find money? Look up. The most expensive real estate is in the higher elevations. Gordy called in sick and drove south and west and into the hills.

An old man and a large, white bird shared a stainless-steel cage atop a mountain. Mist swirled in the gaps and hollers; the sun crawled over blue ridges; and wind raced through leaves with a sound like ocean waves. Former Senator Harrison Westerly reclined on an Eames chair, wrapped like a burrito in a gaudy fleece throw printed with the Southern cross. The bird, a bare-eyed cockatoo named Orrin, sat on the old man's arm. Orrin dipped his head to snag a slice of banana from the bowl of Cheerios nestled on the man's lap. He shifted to one leg and delicately transferred the banana from beak to talon. Milk dripped from the fruit onto the sleeve of the old man's robe and sodden Cheerios stuck to his chest and his forehead.

The cage was a cross between an aviary and a folly. It was large and elaborate and had been designed by a famous architect. It took up most of the deck that overhung a steep and rocky slope overgrown with laurel and flame azalea. You could walk from the former senator's wood-paneled living room directly into the aviary. Westerly had always retired to this house during the heat of the summer, away from the scrabble of Washington and the babble of his Louisiana constituents. With his career a thing of the past, he had made this his full-time home. He had no desire to return to Louisiana.

The property had been in the family for generations. As a boy, Harrison had hiked to every local waterfall and outcropping of rock. He sat at his father's feet and listened to stories of the good old days. He heard the man rail against all the people who had ruined a once great nation. Then he took up the railing himself.

Harrison didn't rail against anyone or anything anymore. On his lucid days, he knew he was lucky to be in this cage and not another, less attractive cage in the flatlands, but Hell worried him more than prison. During his years in power, he had never worried about that infernal pit, but now he didn't see how he could escape it. Details were fuzzy, but he thought he had killed some people and wrecked the

Mines, although he remembered calling the whole thing off. Harrison had been deathly quiet since the screamers hit the Mines. He didn't mean it to happen. How could he have planned to kill people? He didn't believe in that. He remembered being angry, but now the hot, carbonated feel of anger in his belly had faded. Even the causes of that anger had gone as limp and illegible as the pages of a book after a flood—all stuck together, moldy, and impossible to separate one from the other.

After the attack, Harrison shrank in stature overnight, even before the press conference announcing his resignation from his Senate seat. His ramrod-straight posture folded. He hunched his shoulders and avoided looking anyone in the eye. His former chief of staff, Roger—the only human being on Earth who really cared about Westerly—hired a strong-bodied, level-headed, no-nonsense local nurse named Nancy to care for the old man. She lived on the south side of the house and came into the aviary every hour or so to make sure he was still breathing and to see if he needed anything. Harrison rarely spoke to her, but he didn't resent her. She never made him come inside when the wind was blowing, like most nurses would do. She understood that at the far end of life, feeling the wind on your face is worth more than longevity.

Other than that mountain wind, the only thing that still brought joy to Westerly was Orrin. Westerly now called the bird "Dirksen," which was the name of his old cockatoo, the one who died when the Mines tried to implant a listening device under its skin. It was a long story too complicated to remember. The senator had merged the two birds into one and forgotten the horror of Dirksen's death, which was the thing that had made him so angry.

Orrin's crest rose at the sound of voices. The words "Well you can try to talk to him" drifted out to the aviary, but only the bird heard them. The senator rarely wore his hearing aids anymore. He started when the devil appeared before him. No, not the devil, it was J. Edgar Hoover. No, Hoover was dead; this was the devil, overdressed and oily haired like you would expect him to be. He wore his fancy clothes badly.

"Gordy," the devil shouted at the cowering old man. "It's Gordy. Don't you recognize me?"

The senator's rheumy eyes twitched. He recognized Gordy as his own petty devil, the man who had persuaded him to sell his soul. The man responsible for consigning him to Hell after a life lived in full expectation of Heaven's rewards. The senator pulled the fleece blanket over his head, sending the bowl of Cheerios crashing to the floor. Orrin, sensing a threat to his beloved daddy, flew at the lacquered head.

Gordy threw his arms up and hit the deck, knocking over a small table. A fine example of North Carolina pottery rolled across the floor. "Money," Gordy yelled. "I need more money for the Cause!"

"Go away," the senator said. "You're evil."

Orrin swooped down on Gordy again and flew up with talons full of dark, gelled hair. Gordy screamed, and Nancy came running. She suffered no fools. She saw the senator trembling underneath the Southern cross. "I told you not to upset him," she said to Gordy. "You get out now. Right now."

"I have business with the senator," Gordy said. He crouched behind a chair with his jacket pulled over his head. "We're old friends. Can you get rid of the bird so we can talk?"

Orrin was fluffed up and doing a cock strut along a perch on the far side of the aviary. His pupils alternately dilated and constricted in a weird, rapid pulsing.

The nurse pointed at Orrin. "The bird belongs here, and you don't. You see what he's doing with his eyes? It's called pinning. It means he's about to take a chunk out of your ass and pin it to his trophy wall. You'd best scoot."

Orrin gathered himself for another attack, and Gordy fled.

Nancy took the senator's vitals. She cleaned up the cereal, righted the table, replaced the pottery, and slipped a fresh robe and blanket over the old man, handling him as easily as if he were a doll. Orrin flew back to the senator's arm. Nancy gave the senator a tranquilizer and the bird a hunk of pine. She left them alone except for the hourly checks. By evening Westerly was covered in bits of shredded pine and bird droppings. Orrin napped on his shoulder with his fluffy head tucked under a wing.

19

Alberta Takes Care of Lyle

Lyle was a marginal player, but one who knew too much. He must be dealt with. Alberta devised an elegant way to do it. On the face of it, it was a promotion, the type that came rarely in the Mines. Only a handful of White Mines officers had ever been put in charge of a Black Mines station. They were influential high-level men who had lobbied heavily for plum posts in Tokyo or Paris. This generated endless resentment in Black Mines. Those who had worked their way up in the field, starting in the most undesirable locations, seethed at seeing a good post taken by a clueless wonk. Such a promotion always came as a surprise, but this one was an entirely new category of surprise. It wasn't the result of heavy lobbying. In fact, the recipient was taken completely unawares.

Thelma called Lyle Voth at 8:30 in the morning and told him to be in the BOM's office at 6:15 that evening. She wouldn't say what the meeting was about. "I have no idea," she told Lyle. "Alberta told me to call you early so you could spend the day thinking about it. So, think. Think hard."

Think, Lyle did. He thought about the questions Justine had asked him. He thought about the notes he had stolen from Shelby Wexler—the notes that he had hidden in his own gym bag. The notes that had later disappeared, along with his Rolodex. He thought about Gordy Grant, who would no longer talk to him. He thought about suicide. He could drive to a bridge over the Beltway and jump into traffic, but he grew queasy at the thought. He put in a call to his doctor's office to ask for a prescription of sleeping pills, but no one got back to him. In the end, he reported to the BOM's office at six o'clock.

It was nearly seven when Thelma finally came out to get him. Lyle was the picture of humiliation as he lowered himself into a chair. Perhaps it would have been better to be an insensate stain on the Beltway than to be sitting here waiting for whatever punishment Alberta was about to mete out.

"I have been reviewing your work, Lyle, and I'm impressed. I think your unique talents are not being fully utilized," Alberta said.

Any sane man would have taken this with a grain of salt, would have been suspicious at the sudden change in attitude. But Lyle was not quite sane. He'd spent much of his life in a fantasy world where his genius was recognized. Alberta's words made no sense in the context of reality, but they came as something long-awaited, even expected in the context of Lyle's fantasy world. He sat up straighter in his seat. A timid smile played across his lips.

"We need men like you to bridge the divide between the Black Mines and the White Mines. The Black Mines needs a more analytical approach. We need to marry street smarts to expertise. You, Lyle, have the brain and the expertise. You have a unique ability to see the big picture. You—" She went on in this vein for some minutes.

It was over-the-top. Unbelievable. Absurd. But Lyle so thirsted for flattery that he was oblivious to subtext. He grew larger as the praise washed over him, like one of those magic dinosaur eggs that expand and crack open when you soak them in water.

Alberta offered Lyle the position of boss of station. A boss of station was like a little king or despot. It was what Lyle had aspired to in his first six months in the Mines, before he'd washed out of the career prep course. Oh, how he would like to call up those smug instructors and tell them how wrong they had been. So what if he froze up and wouldn't do the parachute jump? How many times do you have to jump out of a plane in the real world? They were the ones who had failed to see a future boss of station in Lyle Voth.

Leaving Alberta's office, Lyle said to Thelma, "You thought I was in trouble, didn't you? Quite the opposite. I've been promoted to boss of station. I guess people like secretaries won't look down their noses at me now."

Thelma slammed her day planner shut and marched into Alberta's office. "Why did you promote that man?"

Alberta did a slow blink. "I would not call that a 'promotion.' I would call it 'enough rope.'"

Lyle barely registered the name of the country where he would serve. It was a tiny, fractious state on the verge of failure. It was a haven for criminal gangs and entomologists specializing in the study of aggressive insects. The embassy compound boasted asbestos, leaky pipes, black mold, and exotic rodents. Its staff was a feuding mix of disgruntled rejects who had pissed off a muckety-muck at some point in their careers.

Lyle lasted less than three weeks in his new position. It took less than three minutes for his subordinates to despise him and begin to plot. They didn't intend to do him serious harm. They only meant to scare him back to headquarters.

Lyle made the mistake of dismissing his new secretary's advice with the words "The first thing you'll learn about me is that I dislike talkative clericals." They might as well have booked the dead body transport service then and there.

Bella had thirty years in the field. She'd knifed an insurgent who tried to break into her bedroom, given birth to her first child in a rickshaw, and held a station together while her alcoholic boss dozed on the couch. She didn't take shit from little shits like Lyle.

She listened to the ideas her colleagues offered on how to bring Lyle down, contributed a few of her own, then promptly began to implement them all at once. She sent his ridiculous cables to headquarters unedited. She collaborated with Lyle's translator to turn his efforts to communicate with local leaders into a raft of insults and idiocies. She found him housing in a neighborhood subject to army ant attacks and had the house staff remove the ant barriers. She filled his water bottle from the toilet bowl in the ladies' room. When Lyle came down with dysentery, she arranged a catastrophic failure of his plumbing. When his staff dug a temporary privy in the garden, Bella added half a sack full of snakes—non-poisonous, of course. She wasn't a monster.

It all came together on a hot Thursday night. Lyle was sitting on the privy when a snake slithered up through his legs. He stumbled out with his pants around his ankles and fell into a writhing river of ants. He ran screaming and slapping himself to the swimming pool and jumped in. Unfortunately, he chose the deep end. Lyle couldn't swim and was going down for the third time when his cook dragged him out and resuscitated him. He ended up in a local hospital swollen up like a tick. He contracted blood poisoning. Bella was at her desk arranging a medical evacuation when the hospital called to say that Lyle had succumbed to organ failure.

Those responsible for Lyle's death could not work up much in the way of remorse. If there is one cardinal rule in the Black Mines, it is "Don't cross the station secretary." If you don't follow that rule, if you're too ignorant to even be aware of it, then you deserve whatever you get.

✛ ✛ ✛

Back at headquarters, Thelma read the cable with the news and brought her fingers to her lips. She delivered it to Alberta. "Lyle's dead," she said in a hushed voice.

Alberta put on her glasses and read the tale of woe. "Good god," she said, "snakes, ants, and dysentery." She removed her glasses and brushed her fingers over her eyes. "Thelma, would you give me some time alone?" When the door closed, Alberta repeated, "Snakes, ants, and dysentery. Oh my." She laughed softly. "Yes, that was enough rope."

20

The Wandering Deputy

Carlos tore open a packet of mini pretzels as an old, wistful song played in his mind. "Leaving on a Jet Plane." He mouthed the words "don't know when I'll be back again." He really didn't know. He'd been scheduled to return a week ago, but before he could board the flight to Dulles, Alberta had assigned him yet another liaison visit to yet another intelligence service in yet another country on yet another continent. So now he was on an ancient 747 flying in the wrong direction. Not only did he not know when he would be back again; for a moment he forgot where he was going. Namibia? No, he had already been there.

Carlos was a seasoned traveler, but he was unaccustomed to this pace. He preferred to stay in a place at least a couple of years and immerse in the culture, see the sights, and talk to the people. This station hopping exhausted him. He wasn't experiencing countries; he was experiencing airports, jet lag, and acute homesickness.

Meanwhile, he was letting his family down. He'd told them this new job would mean more time for them, time to make up for all the packing and moves and school changes he had put them through.

Instead, he had missed an important piano recital, a school play, and numerous soccer games. He dreamed about coming home to find his seven-year-old daughter married. He would be lucky if he didn't find his wife remarried.

Lately, communications with Tessa had degenerated into a list of crises she had handled alone. To smooth things over, he bought her a box of her favorite Mozartkugeln at the duty-free shop at the Vienna airport and had it shipped home. He later called from a hotel in Helsinki to see if the chocolates had arrived and, more importantly, if they had improved her mood. What resulted was the worst phone call of his life.

Her hello was flat and vaguely hostile.

He countered by filling his with love. "Hello, babe, you don't know how good it is to hear your voice." Silence. "Did you get the package I sent?"

"Oh, I got it all right." This time there was no mistaking the hostility.

"Did it not arrive in good shape?" Carlos asked.

"I don't know. Your mother's dog got to it first."

"My mother?" Carlos said.

"Short, excitable woman, speaks no English, comes for long, unannounced visits bringing her incontinent bulldog, Dulce. Makes extremely dense tamales. Gets pissed when the kids won't eat them. Never uses my name. That mother."

"Oh." Carlos winced. "When did she arrive?"

"About three years ago, or at least that's what it feels like."

"Oh," Carlos said. He struggled to come up with something else to say, but nothing came.

"Oh," Tessa said.

"If Dulce ruined the package, I'll send you more," Carlos said.

"I never want to see another Mozartkugel in my life." The voice was so strained it didn't sound like Tessa.

"Tell me what happened," Carlos said, although he didn't really want to hear what had happened.

"You know it's a record tree pollen season, don't you?" Tessa said. This seemed like a non-sequitur, but Carlos knew better than to point that out. He knew it was a record tree pollen season. Tessa was an allergist.

"I'm booked solid," she said, "and working late every day. I come home Monday to find that your mother, Dulce, and the package all arrived some time that morning. The nanny and the kids were crying. The cat had climbed the curtains and pulled down the valance. Your mother was screaming. The dog was convulsing. The smell of shit was so strong, I almost vomited."

"Chocolate is toxic to dogs," Carlos said.

"Oh, really?" Tessa said. "You don't say."

Carlos vowed not to interrupt her again. "Go on."

"There was bloody diarrhea and vomit all over the living room carpet. You know, the one we got in Turkey? The one we paid a small fortune to have shipped to Manassas? That carpet. Imagine it covered with dark chocolate, marzipan, and pistachio freshly processed through a twelve-year-old bulldog. Oh, and little bits of foil. He ate the foil, too."

"I'm so sorry," Carlos said.

"Your mother demanded that I take Dulce to the vet. She was speaking Spanish but it was clear what she wanted. So, I wrestled the shitty, convulsing dog into the back of the van and drove to the emergency vet in Vienna where I sat for four hours authorizing increasingly expensive medical procedures and all the while secretly hoping the mongrel would croak."

Carlos knew better than to ask if Dulce had pulled through.

"Damn dog lived," Tessa said. "I paid $2,700 to save his miserable life. I would have paid twice that to get rid of him, but I'm too nice a person. Do you want to know what your mother was doing while I was at the vet? Go on, take a guess."

Carlos didn't want to guess. He knew that a younger, pre-divorce version of his mother would have been cleaning up the chaos but that the current, more eccentric and embittered version would be doing something completely irrational and more than a little passive aggressive.

"She made tamales," Tessa said. "She left the shit to seep deeper into the carpet and made tamales, which the kids didn't like because they've never liked tamales and besides, the house smelled so bad they lost their appetites. It was completely understandable that they wouldn't eat, but your mother got mad and started yelling. She stomped out of the room and our precocious three-year-old took her tamale and flushed it down the front hall toilet. Then she threw in one of Dulce's squeaky toys for good measure."

"It backed up?" Carlos said weakly.

"Of course it did. I went at it with the plunger, but all I got was the strangest sound ever to come out of a toilet. I gave up and started moving furniture off the carpet so I could roll it up and drag it outside. I didn't get to bed until 3:00 a.m. I still had to go to work the next day. You know why?"

"Why?" Carlos said because he had to say something.

"Because I'm a responsible, sane adult. The only responsible, sane adult in this madhouse. I went to work, called the plumber, and arranged for him to come the next day. Then I called the trash service and arranged for pickup of the carpet. Then I briefly felt better because I had taken care of things."

"You are the most competent person I know," Carlos said.

"Put a sock in it," Tessa said. "I came home to find that the plumber had backed his truck over our mailbox. Some anal-retentive busybody from the homeowners' association had already taped a note to our door demanding that I replace the mailbox immediately or pay a fine. Also, they would like us to repaint the door. It was the last straw."

"I'll be home as soon as I can," Carlos said.

"Don't rush. I haven't decided yet whether I'm going to change the locks when I get the door repainted."

"I love you." Carlos tried to put his whole heart into those words.

"Whatever," Tessa replied and hung up.

Carlos was afraid he knew what it would take for these trips to end. He would have to stop asking awkward questions. Or at least he would have to stop asking Alberta those questions. She was an old friend, but one who couldn't be entirely trusted. He knew her well enough to know that something was bothering her. Something serious. Somewhere in the Mines, a support timber was about to give way. He got the feeling that the roof could collapse at any moment. Carlos resolved to pursue his suspicions out of Alberta's sight. First he had to get back to headquarters. When he got to the station, he would send a message to Alberta and plead family emergency.

Carlos shook the last of the mini pretzels out of the bag. His stomach growled. John Denver sang mournfully into his ear. "Don't know when I'll be back again ...."

«21»

Justine Seeks Allies

Justine had no idea what to do now. Lyle Voth was not only off limits but also dead. That spooked her. Alberta hadn't chosen a new snipe and apparently no longer wanted a report. Justine appealed to Thelma. "Ask her what I'm supposed to do." The answer that came back—"Absolutely nothing."

Justine sat in her office drinking coffee, watching C-SPAN, and growing ever more morose. She couldn't take leave because she hadn't earned any yet. She gave up the idea that she would retire with a government pension and healthcare. She marked on the calendar when she would have four hours of sick leave, then scheduled a medical appointment. One wouldn't be enough. Her gallbladder had begun to trouble her, and she should have it out before the attacks became acute. A gallbladder alone could put her in the poor house without insurance, and Alberta could fire her any day now. If she was lucky, firing would be the worst of it. If she was unlucky, someone would find out about the documents hidden in her apartment, and she would land in jail. At least they would take some minimal care of her medical needs there or so she supposed. What kind of dentists did they have in prison? She had a right molar that was possibly going dead.

Justine could not stop thinking about the trouble door in her bathroom, the one that allowed access to the shower plumbing. She had rolled the documents tight, rubber banded them, wrapped them in pink insulation, and shoved them up between the pipes. It was an obvious hiding place, but she could find nothing better. She couldn't leave this evidence to burn a hole in her wall. She had a moral obligation to do something with it. What? She had no idea. This wasn't the type of moral dilemma one encountered as a novelist. Novelist morality involved questions of honesty and truth. Intelligence world morality was more along the lines of "if I get this wrong, really bad shit will happen." The idea of real-world consequences terrified her. She needed to talk to someone with an intelligence background who knew what to do with evidence. Someone she could trust. The natives had networks and allies and experience. That's what she needed.

Justine couldn't keep her head above water in this bureaucracy. She'd lived a solitary life, which suited her. She went to cafes to observe people and take notes, but she wouldn't take any of those people into her life any more than she would go to the zoo and adopt an elephant. She was a sane cat lady, thank you. Now she had to find some human to trust with her life, freedom, and some critical national security information.

Old c-span footage played in the background as she sorted her thoughts. Then something on the screen caught her attention. A roll of the eyes. The camera had panned from the sententious ranting of committee chairman Harrison Westerly to a sharp and skeptical female face in the audience. Then the eye roll. The woman elbowed the man to her right, who mouthed a likely obscenity. The woman to her left lowered her eyes and shook her head.

Justine spent the rest of the afternoon with her attention riveted on the Stadium Attack hearings. The sharp-faced woman was Maddie

James. When she was called to testify, she contradicted everything said earlier and set up an angry whispering and shuffling of papers in the room. Justine watched the faces of Maddie's colleagues. These were not operatives who knew how to hide their feelings; they were wonkish, opinionated alchemists. Of all the subspecies of bureaucrats in the Mines, they were the ones Justine could best relate to.

Those are the people I need, Justine thought. They've been through this before.

Where were they now? What did they know about the Screamer Attack? She turned to Thelma.

"I've never seen this on a file before," Thelma said. "'Long-term medical leave: DO NOT CONTACT.' Somebody marked through her contact information with a Sharpie, which is silly because you can get it anywhere." Thelma handed Justine a sticky note. "Here's her number. I didn't realize she was hurt so bad that she'd still be out. When you call, tell her I asked after her."

Justine was afraid her work phone might be monitored, so she made the call from the receptionist's desk at the veterinarian's office where she had an evening appointment for Susie, her cat.

An older woman picked up. "You'll have to wait while Maddie puts her hearing aids in. I don't know why she takes them out at home. Honestly, I think she wants to tune out her mother. How's that for gratitude?" Justine was surprised to learn that Maddie lived with her mother. She didn't seem the type. The conversation with Maddie was awkward because Justine was unsure what a Mines employee could say on an open line. She had to speak loud enough for Maddie to hear, which meant that the whole waiting room heard. Fortunately, a couple of terriers lit into a barking match. Justine quickly spat out her message. "Hi, you don't know me, but we work at the same place.

I work for Alberta. I need your advice. I need to talk to you. Can I come to your house?"

"Where are you? The pound?"

"Please! It's a matter of national security."

"Well, all right."

It was nearly nine by the time Justine took Susie home and made it to Maddie's place. The woman who opened the door looked both older and younger than the one Justine had seen on TV. The circles under her eyes lent her age, but the bunny print pajamas, small stature, and intense stare gave her a child-like quality. Most children quickly learn that it's rude to stare like that, but Maddie evidently never did. Her eyes took in Justine head to toe and then fixed on the age-darkened ERA bracelet. "Cool," she said, and stood aside to allow her to enter.

"Ignore the bunny crap," Maddie said. "Mom has been decorating. She moved in to help after the attack. I'm working on moving her out. Let's go to the basement where it's private. You want something to drink? Beer? Soda?"

"No thanks." Justine followed Maddie down to a semi-finished basement strewn with derelict bean bag chairs, books, and 80s rock band kitsch. One wall was dedicated to posters with favorite quotes: "I do not wish women to have power over men; but over themselves."—Mary Wollstonecraft. "Sharp like a razor's edge is the path." — the Katha Upanishad. "Never Get Involved in a Land War in Asia."—Vizzini.

"This is my happy space," Maddie said. "Stuff from my first apartment. A whiff of my youth. Have a seat."

Justine was about to do so when Maddie yelled, "Don't sit on my rabbit!" Justine caught herself as a pillow of black fur sprang from the beanbag. Maddie scooped up the creature and gave him a quick hug. "This is Abu Bunny."

"I'm a cat person." Maddie plopped down with the rabbit in her lap while Justine awkwardly lowered herself into crunchy vinyl.

"Who are you and why are you here?"

"My name is Justine Moreau. I work for—worked for—Alberta." Justine explained how she was hired to write the story of the Mines official responsible for the intelligence failure leading to the Screamer Attack.

"It's never just one person," Maddie said. "That's too simple."

"Alberta said the Beltway likes simple."

"Sadly true," Maddie said.

Justine told her about Lyle. By the time she was finished, Maddie was rigid in her seat. Abu Bunny had retreated to a corner.

"Well, that's all I can think of right now."

"What's your address?" Maddie asked.

"What? Arlington. Fifty-two Martha Place. Why?"

Maddie stood up. "Because I'm going to pick up a colleague and come over there to look over your documents. Come upstairs. I'll throw on some clothes."

Justine wasn't accustomed to entertaining. Her apartment had one comfy chair, a lot of cat furniture, a huge collection of coffee mugs, and more books than Maddie's basement. In addition to fiction, she had an eclectic mix of nonfiction useful to a novelist: *An Illustrated Guide to Bloodstain Pattern Analysis*, *Castration Rituals Around the World*, and *The International Cannibal Cookbook*—that sort of thing.

Vernon stared at the titles with growing concern as Justine rummaged through her kitchen looking for something to offer her guests. "This is creepy," he whispered to Maddie.

"Said the man with a bayonet collection," she whispered back.

When Justine returned with a pitcher of iced coffee—she had added cubes to what was left in the pot—Vernon made the gesture of the cross. "No way. Who are you?"

"I'm a novelist. Don't mind the books. I'm nonviolent."

Maddie also waved away the coffee. "Show us what you've got."

In preparation for their visit, Justine had retrieved the papers from their hidey hole, removed the rubber band, and flattened them under a thick volume entitled *Instruments of Torture Illustrated*. She moved the book and offered the papers to Maddie.

Maddie split the stack and gave half to Vernon. They sat on the floor with the papers spread out around them and muttered expletives as they read.

"Holy shit, you xeroxed his personnel file and sneaked it out of the building?" Maddie said.

"Thoroughly illegal and totally badass," Vernon said.

Maddie whooped. "Lyle was kicked out of the Unmentionable for chickening out of the parachute jump. He had to be hauled out of the orienteering exercise on a travois after he stepped in a groundhog hole and broke his ankle. He cried and blurted out everything he knew during the fake interrogation. You know, I think we will need some coffee. Fresh and hot. We may be up half the night."

Justine retired to the kitchen.

"You think it's safe to drink anything here?" Vernon asked.

"Stop whining," Maddie said.

Justine returned with a tray holding three mugs, a carton of milk, and a handful of sugar packets. She handed Maddie a mug that said, "I am smiling, asshole."

"I love this," Maddie said.

"And here you go," Justine said to Vernon.

He read the mug and laughed. It said, "Ask me about penis size. Go ahead, ask." He said, "Well, go ahead, ask."

"Do you always have the perfect mug for everyone?" Maddie asked.

"I do," Justine said. "Whenever I write a character, I have a new one made. I drink from the appropriate mug while I'm writing. I've written a lot of books."

"What's on your mug now?" Maddie asked.

Justine turned it so Maddie could read the inscription "Toxic mediocrity."

"That's Lyle Voth all right," Maddie said. "Alberta chose well. Your notes are amazing. This character sketch of Lyle is brilliant. Alberta gave you his name?"

"Yes, she assumed he was innocent and wanted me to frame him as the scapegoat, although I'm supposed to use the word *snipe* instead of *scapegoat*. When Alberta found out Lyle wasn't innocent, she panicked."

"I can't imagine Alberta panicking," Maddie said.

"I wouldn't have thought so either. The look was only on her face for a second; then she got control of herself. After that, she shut me down. I'm not supposed to have any of this material. I was supposed to give everything back to her. I'm surprised she hasn't fired me."

"I'm not," Maddie said. "She wouldn't want to make an enemy of you. I wouldn't be surprised if she didn't offer you some plum position."

"Like the one she offered Lyle?" Justine brought her hand to her throat. "The one that got him killed?" Her eyes widened behind the round red rims of her bifocals.

"Oh, yeah," Maddie said. "Don't accept any post that involves travel overseas. I don't think she would cause you physical harm as long as you're in this country. Overseas is where she's comfortable operating. Don't worry."

Justine worried. Her imagination veered off into a new direction.

"Lyle Fucking Voth," Maddie said. "We shall refer to him from now on as LFV. Might as well honor the Mines tradition of cover terms. We don't want to let something slip and get Justine killed."

Justine gasped.

"That was a joke," Maddie said. "Really, you'll be fine."

"Maybe we should let this go," Justine said.

"Hell, no!" Maddie and Vernon said in unison.

"I have so many questions," Maddie said.

"There's another thing," Justine said. "I was saving it until I trusted you because, well, you'll see." She fetched a stool and climbed up to reach the highest bookshelf. She selected a large volume entitled *The Human Body After Death*. Inside, nestled between grotesque illustrations, were pages torn from a small notebook. "He had these hidden in an inner pocket of his gym bag." Justine spread the papers out on the floor. They had been torn in quarters before disposal then painstakingly reassembled with Scotch tape. "They're Shelby's meeting notes. Lyle fished them out of his burn bag and reassembled them."

"And you stole them?" Vernon said.

"Thelma stood lookout," Justine said. "I've written about so many searches; it was fun to conduct one myself—and to think about how Lyle would sweat when he found them missing."

As Maddie and Vernon pored over the tiny handwriting on the notes, Justine summarized the contents. "After the Westerly conversation was intercepted, the Mines decided that it would be too dangerous to confront him or turn the information over to law enforcement, but they needed to know what he was involved in. So, while Westerly was out of the country, they tried to plant a bug in his parrot. Although I can't imagine how you would come up with the idea of bugging an animal."

"Accustikitty," Maddie and Vernon said in unison.

Justine squinted. "What?"

"The Mines tried bugging a cat during the Cold War," Maddie said. "It was a disaster. You don't want to know."

"Well, it didn't turn out especially well this time, either," Justine said. "The bird died while they were trying to implant the device. They put it back in the cage, but Westerly had a necropsy performed. The vet found a tiny piece of the device they didn't remove. Westerly rightly blamed the Mines."

"Who was the other voice on the intercepts?" Maddie said. "The one who was talking to Westerly."

"Are you sure it wasn't Voth?" Vernon said.

"I am," Maddie said. "He was way too much of a coward to communicate directly with terrorists."

"I think it was someone he called G2. I have Lyle's Rolodex cards," Justine said. "Hold on a second." She crossed the room and stopped before a three-story kitty condo. "I'm sorry, Susie; I need to get in there." She reached into the middle level of the condo and extracted a small, highly disgruntled calico cat. "She just came back from the vet, poor thing." Justine put the cat down. Susie paused to hiss at Vernon and Maddie, then shot out of the room. Justine reached back into the condo and pulled out a faux-sheepskin cushion. She unzipped it and began to extract the cards. "Can you believe that Lyle would be stupid enough to put his contact in his Rolodex?"

"Yes," Maddie and Vernon said in unison.

"Justine handed over the relevant card. "Here it is—G2 followed by a series of scratched-out numbers."

They spent the next half hour speculating on the identity of G2. The name Gordy Grant did not come to them immediately. Their brains were too tired. If they had known the name was someone from the Organ, they might have guessed, but only Alberta had that information.

"I take it you're a lesbian," Vernon said to Justine, apropos of nothing.

Maddie kicked him.

"Completely asexual," Justine said, "not that it's any of your business."

"Is that possible?" Vernon asked.

"Of course," Justine said. "I'm surprised you haven't run into any number of women who at least claim to be asexual."

Maddie cackled.

"I don't think we're going to have any revelations tonight," Vernon said. "We might as well go home."

"Can we meet here again tomorrow evening?" Maddie asked.

"Can't," Vernon said. "I'm flying out of Dulles tomorrow afternoon. Headed to Manchester. I'm meeting with the investigators looking into Fahad. I want to see if they've uncovered any unusual connections. See if I can catch a whiff of Harrison Westerly's phone pal. Slinky arranged for me to meet with some high-level folks. Should be interesting."

Vernon had viewed a lot of porn in his time. Indeed, he styled himself a connoisseur. He'd never seen anything like this, however. It was enough to render a man permanently impotent.

Michael, an official of the British security service, broke the silence. "The production values are not good, are they?"

Vernon shook his head to clear out the images. "Nothing. Nothing is good. It's all very bad."

Michael's voice was tentative and sympathetic yet condescending. He seemed reluctant but determined to wade through this field of cow dung. "You can see how this presents us with a dilemma. The persons in this video appear to be American citizens. At least that is

211 • SUSAN HASLER

what I surmise from the flag in the corner of the room—correct me if I'm wrong, but isn't that the Mines seal hanging on the wall?"

"Yes," Vernon said. His face colored. He hated it when his agency embarrassed itself in front of these superior-acting Brits, but he had to admit the obvious. "It's a Mines seal. I recognize the photographs on the wall. That's the main conference room of the counterterrorism sector, or at least it was until the sector moved off compound."

"We were afraid of that," Michael said. "It's in no one's interest to have this go public. That is why we haven't passed this along to our counterparts at the Internal Investigative Organ, where it might end up as evidence in a courtroom or ammunition in one of your distasteful interdepartmental squabbles."

"No, that can't happen." Vernon wrinkled his nose. "I used to put my coffee and donut down on that very table."

Michael gave him a sympathetic look. "Let's hope that donut was sitting on a proper plate. But back to the subject at hand. As I said, we found this only last week. It was hidden in the ceiling of Fahad's flat. I haven't shown it to my Mines counterpart here, because he's caught up in an unrelated peccadillo and is somewhat distracted. At any rate, when we heard you were coming at the behest of a senior Mines official, we thought we would show it to you first and let you bear the bad news. Do you recognize the individuals in the video?"

"Two of them," Vernon said. "The man is Gordy Grant, an employee of the Organ who was doing a rotational assignment at the Mines. The dark-haired girl is Melanie Gardner, the daughter of my former boss. She was a summer intern that year. I don't know who the other girl is."

"How did they get the goat inside the building?"

"Lord only knows," Vernon said. "Maybe they put a Mines tag on it."

Michael shook his head slowly and tut-tutted. "What a tangled mess. An employee of the Internal Investigative Organ you say?"

"Yes. He was thrown out of the Mines for this. Not this incident, but another when he was caught with just Melanie. No other girl. No goat. I didn't know there were more videos."

"How embarrassing for the Mines and the 110, and, indeed for the whole United States," Michael said.

"Melanie looks a bit like Christine Keeler, doesn't she?" Vernon said. He wanted to remind his British counterpart that bizarre sex scandals occurred on both sides of the pond.

"I don't see a resemblance," Michael said coldly.

"Was Profumo the guy who was found dead of autoerotic asphyxiation, or was that a different scandal?"

"Different scandal. I get your point. Don't belabor it." He continued. "In addition to this revolting video, we found a drive full of interior and exterior videos of the Mines complex. They must have proven very useful to Fahad as he planned his attack."

Vernon buried his face in his hands. "G2, damn it."

"I beg your pardon?"

"Nothing. I should have known it was Gordy Grant. There was always something off about him."

"After hearing this, I'm more convinced than ever that this is something our government does not want to be involved in. I'm turning this evidence over to you to handle as you see fit, but you must not reveal where you obtained it. If it becomes public, we'll deny any knowledge. Understood?"

Vernon uttered a sulky "yes," and the meeting ended. He had planned to take a couple of days of leave and do some serious pub crawling, but he rescheduled his flight for that night.

22

Go

Hamid had disciplined himself to be slow and neat as he blacked in the squares of the monthly nonogram. Even when the image disappointed him, he made himself finish the puzzle without putting a mark amiss. He loved the sound of the electric pencil sharpener. It wasn't like him to splurge on such things, but the bright blue item had caught his eye. Now he used it obsessively to keep a keen point on his number two pencils. He pressed hard, so that each image was a glossy black. On the day the squares finally resolved into a ram's head, Hamid slid to the floor and gave thanks to Allah.

Go.

He had Fahad's permission to move forward. Ever since Gordy had delivered the suicide vest, Hamid had spent hours staring at the closet door. Once each evening, he allowed himself to take the vest out, put it on, and imagine racing toward his glory.

During the day, Hamid drove a refrigerated truck that delivered ice cream, milk, butter, cheese, and a bewilderingly large number and variety of fruit yogurt cups to the various Mines facilities scattered about the D.C. metropolitan area. Hale Plaza, his target, was a generic, glass-encased, four-story brick structure ringed by Bradford pear trees stuck like lollipops in round hills of mulch.

There was a spot on that road where the view from the guard station was obscured by an island of shrubbery in the parking lot. He would stop there, get out, and run through the lot towards the building. If he was fast, he could get close enough to collapse a wall and create an image of shattered glass that would echo the Screamer Attack. This would deal another blow to the Mines and further ignite anti-Islamic feeling in the country—another step towards the great global war that would purify the world.

Hamid's fondest wish was to kill the unnatural devil woman who headed the mines. He knew her office was at the center front of the building on the top floor right above the main entrance. The main entrance was, unfortunately, the most heavily guarded spot of the building. Moreover, the building was U-shaped, with the entrance tucked in the hollow of the U. He had been thinking about this problem for some time. He had been training at a local track to improve his speed. He timed himself, knew how many seconds it took to run ninety yards. He would have to add seconds to account for the weight of the vest. It was heavier and more lethal than any he had seen before.

Still, the cameras that were everywhere on the complex would pick him up as soon as he got out of the truck. How far could he get?

How to pick the day and time? Hamid would have liked instructions on that point, but Fahad had told him to act independently. Hamid did not like independence, but he must do as instructed. At first, he thought that he would pick a holy date on the Hijri calendar, but Fahad had told him to do the thing that they would least expect. They would be checking that calendar, too, and be more vigilant on the holy dates. It would be better to focus on inflicting the most damage. Then Hamid knew exactly how he would choose the day—the food delivery schedule. If they were going to hold a conference, or a big award event, they would order more food delivered the day before. More and better food. Once a month, he delivered steaks, salmon filets, and sea scallops for a meeting of senior officials, heads of agencies, that sort of thing. He would have to find out more about it. Ask some careful questions.

Hamid knew where the executive dining room was, at the top of the south leg of the U-shaped building. It had glass on three sides and was much closer to the place where he would stop the truck. The plan began to shape itself.

23

Raid

T he message had three words—You are unwelcome. Gordy knew what it meant. The Supreme Lofty Synod of the Brotherhood of Blood was shutting him out of a synod for the first time. He had promised Davenport that everything was ready to go with the operation, that the operative was just waiting for the right day. He handed over small amounts of money earned from selling his treasures on eBay, but it wasn't nearly enough. Davenport was out of patience. Were they meeting tonight to decide his fate?

Gordy's ears burned. It was not a figure of speech; he felt the sensation of burning and itching as he watched the clock. Synods started at 9:00 p.m. with a lengthy prayer spoken by Deacon Davenport. The theme was always the same: lift up our brothers and smite our enemies. Was Davenport praying for God to smite Gordy? He rubbed his earlobe. The tenderness increased. He went to his medicine cabinet and pulled out tubes and jars, reading labels and tossing things on the floor. He finally settled on a vetiver-scented eye cream. He rubbed a generous dab on both ears. It didn't help.

Gordy turned on the television and selected a British who-done-it, but the accents reminded him of Fahad. Gordy thought of Hank Barker, the man who had committed suicide—or so they said—after he was caught embezzling funds. Gordy had at first thought that Davenport had made up the story to scare him; then he found the man in the Organ's database. Barker was real, and he did die by shotgun blast. The files included a photograph that might have as easily been an explosion of hamburger—or a platter full of kitfo—as a human head. Gordy had read the coroner's report carefully. It was inconclusive on the matter of suicide.

Gordy felt a shift in his intestines followed by pain. He hurried back to the bathroom. The stress was giving him diarrhea. He had a delicate gut, which was why he had sprung for a luxury Japanese crapper. He punched a button, and it played Vivaldi to cover his bodily sounds. The seat was warmed to the ideal temperature, as was the gently oscillating spray of water that cleaned him when he was finished, and the waft of air that dried him. He stood, and the flush came automatically. He watched the play of color-changing LED lights in the toilet bowl and felt his blood pressure return to normal. He felt renewed, fresh. This thing was worth every penny he had paid for it. He had even given her a name—Bianca.

Then Gordy remembered where those pennies had come from. He had embezzled them from the Brotherhood. Wait, no. It was a bribe he had taken from an Organ contractor. But that wasn't right either. That money had paid for his zero-gravity gaming chair, the one he had named Lenore. He bought the toilet with the big tax return he got from claiming several large, fictitious business losses. The pain in his gut returned. Gordy settled back down on Bianca's heated seat, but he was thinking about the cold steel of a prison toilet.

It was late when Gordy finally went to bed and pulled the covers over his head. His exhausted brain played images of kitfo, shotguns, and iron bars on a loop. He had barely closed his eyes when he heard a pounding on the door. He looked to the window. He should jump, but he hesitated. The door splintered, and they were in the room. He knew the men. They were Brotherhood stickmen. Everything about them was huge—their arms, their thighs, their necks. Gordy lay frozen in his bed.

"You have been called to the Synod," one of the stickmen said.

"It's still going on?" Gordy asked.

"Shut up and get dressed. Hand over your phone."

Gordy mopped his face with a handkerchief. His heart felt thick and quivery. "Give me another week."

Davenport looked to the ceiling and made a sound in his throat that Gordy could not interpret. "In lieu of money, a Muslim atrocity would do. Say they murder an agent of the Internal Investigative Organ. No, not simply murder, but behead. Imagine the outcry if a video of that landed on the Internet."

Gordy swallowed the beating heart that had risen into his throat and tried to argue. "Experts would know it wasn't Islamic extremists. Those videos go through certain channels and have distinct markers. They would know."

"The experts aren't my audience," Davenport said. "My audience doesn't believe experts."

Gordy knew that was true. He abandoned all dignity and prostrated himself before the Sublime Arch-Sovereign. Tears flowed as he begged for his life, for one more chance to come up with the money and pull off an attack.

Davenport kept a ferocious furrow in his brow, but his lips twitched at the corner. He let Gordy humiliate and exhaust himself. He waited until the man was little more than a heaving mass of human degradation. Then he said, "Another three days."

✦ ✦ ✦

Slinky could have pushed past Thelma if he really had wanted to. He could have made his way into Alberta's office to tell her that the Organ was about to raid Gordy Grant's condo. He could have, but he didn't. Instead, he took the opportunity to get his ducks in a row, to find a non-suicidal way to tell Alberta that critical threat information had gotten from the Mines to the Organ without going through her. To explain how that information had landed on the desk of the Boss of Paper Mines, who should confine himself to issues of logistics and security. And how said BOPM had become entangled with people he should have steered well clear of. He began to sketch Venn diagrams on his Doodlebug, labeling them with the initials of people he desperately wanted to avoid mentioning: VK, MJ, and CB.

Vernon Keene. Slinky wracked his brain, but he could not think of a way to avoid telling Alberta that he had assigned Vernon to the task of discovering the identity of the other man on the phone with Harrison Westerly. He would also have to tell her about sending Vernon to Manchester, where the Brits had passed along the tape that connected Gordy Grant to Fahad. He had no answer to the question he knew she would ask—what made you think this was your job?

Maddie James. The Vernon and Maddie circles should never have intersected. Slinky had specifically told Vernon to stay away from Maddie. When Vernon had given Slinky the news about Gordy, Slinky had said, "I'll have to inform Alberta and the Organ," and Vernon wrote on his Doodlebug, "Maddie already took care of the Organ." Under Slinky's glare, he had continued to scribble. "I told her we had to ... go through chain of command ... She said, 'rusty chain, screw it' ... She called Jill Lippman at the Organ." Slinky made Vernon tell him how Maddie had come to be involved. Vernon wrote until his hand cramped. For all the vows he had made at the onset of his assignment, Vernon was terrible at keeping secrets.

Constance Brand. Slinky did not want to tell Alberta about his arrangement with the senator and Maddie. He had sworn to Brand that he would keep it secret. At the time, it hadn't seemed like such a bad secret, but it would look like gross betrayal to Alberta. Brand, if she found out he had told Alberta, would also feel betrayed. Getting on the bad side of either woman was bad. Maybe he could avoid mentioning Brand.

But Alberta would ask hard questions. Slinky could think of no way to corral his answers inside one segment of the diagram without having them spill into other segments. Was there no way to compartmentalize this?

Thelma tapped on his shoulder. Slinky started and dropped the Doodlebug. She picked it up and wrote, "You might as well go home."

"I have to talk to her tonight," Slinky said.

"Bad time," Thelma wrote. "Hunter Johnson called. She's upset!!"

A look of acute pain crossed Slinky's face. He was too late. He let Alberta be blindsided. What now? All he could do was go home, come back first thing in the morning, and throw himself on Alberta's mercy.

The stickmen drove back to Gordy's condo complex. Their suv stopped in front of the building, and one of them ordered Gordy out. He didn't move. He was staring up at his windows. All the lights in his place were on, and figures were moving about inside. He saw men he recognized milling about in front of the building.

"Get out!" one of the stickmen said.

Gordy stayed put.

The man leaned over him and opened the door. "I said get out!"

"They're in my condo," Gordy said. "They're searching the place. You've got to get me out of here." He tried to close the door of the SUV, but the stickman shoved him out of the vehicle.

"You're on your own, asshole." The SUV sped away.

Gordy's Range Rover, his beloved Désirée, was in the parking garage. He knew that his colleagues would already be searching her. Désirée was gone. Bianca was gone. Lenore was gone. Everything he owned was gone, beyond reach, permanently lost to him. Everything except his freedom. He still had his freedom.

Then one of the agents spotted him and shouted. Gordy turned and ran into the darkness, without plan or destination.

Gordy had never been chased before. He had been the chaser, but that brought him no useful insights on how not to get caught, so he just ran. He ran down bike paths, through parking lots and backyards and alleys. He ran until a pain in his side brought him up short and he doubled over and vomited. When his stomach was empty, he looked up in time to see a search beam slicing through the darkness twenty yards away. He took off again on rubber legs. He tripped over something odd-shaped and plastic, probably a child's toy. He fell hard as another beam of light sliced the air above him. He lay flat and still. The beam moved on. After a time, Gordy stumbled to his feet and tried to run again, but his legs would not cooperate, and his lungs felt ready to burst. His feet hurt. His new topsiders were proving too short in the toe. It started to rain, and the wind picked up. Gordy shivered. He needed to find some place to lie down and shelter long enough to recover himself. As the rain became a downpour, he pushed through a hedge and saw a dark shape that might be a tool shed on the far side of the lawn. He made his way there, only to discover that it was a two-story child's playhouse with a ladder on one side and a slide on the other. The floor of the bottom level was already wet. The top level was more protected by the roof overhang. Gordy crawled onto an ornate balcony. He squeezed himself through the small door. The space was too cramped for him to stretch out, but it was mostly dry. He curled up and let exhaustion take him away.

Davenport was furious when the stickmen reported back to him. "You left him there?" he yelled. "If they arrest him, do you think he has the moral fortitude not to spill his guts? He'll expose the whole organization five minutes into the interrogation. Go back and find him."

"Then what?"

"What do you think? He's a liability. We don't need him. The operative will move when he's ready. Gordy obviously has no influence over him."

The stickmen retreated, and Davenport was left to brood over the paucity of common sense in the modern world.

Alberta sent Thelma home and waited for news. Johnson had told her that the Organ had solid intelligence that Gordy Grant was involved in the Screamer Attack. Agents were preparing to raid his condo. She had argued that they should be patient and surveil him for a while, but Johnson was in no mood to wait. Gordy was his own man and his own problem, a problem he should have dealt with years ago. No more procrastination. He wasn't going to risk having someone tip off the bastard.

Alberta would have tipped off the bastard herself, but she was too late. She sat at her desk and played game after game of Patience. The phone rang. She reached for it, but her arm hit a bottle of Perrier, knocking it over. The cap popped off and fizzing water shot over the cards, her keyboard, and into her lap. Alberta stood and brushed down her dripping skirt as she listened to Hunter Johnson's account of the raid on Gordy's condo. Gordy had fled, but likely would be apprehended soon. Alberta dried off the top of her desk with an old sweater. Maybe she still had time to deal with the situation. She would go home, change her clothes, make some arrangements, and come straight back. It would be no use even to attempt sleep.

When Alberta got back to her office, both Thelma and Slinky were already there. She ignored their efforts to get her attention, strode into her office, and shut the door.

Overcome by exhaustion, Gordy slept too long. He awoke to the pain of cramped muscles and the yapping of a small dog. He opened his eyes to find himself in a glowing pink box lit by sun pouring in through a heart-shaped window. He experienced the sensation of floating down a rabbit hole; then he remembered taking shelter in a child's playhouse. The events of the night before flooded his mind: the threats from the Brotherhood, the men searching his apartment, his lungs bursting as he ran through the darkness. He had to get moving. He twisted around to face the door and gasped to find a small, fiercely frowning girl sitting there. He wasn't good with children's ages, but she was maybe four.

"This is my house," she said. "You got mud on the floor. I'm telling Mommy."

"Don't bother her," he said. "I'm leaving."

"No, you have to clean up your mess first." She pointed to a muddy footprint.

Gordy considered pushing past her, but she might scream. He took out his handkerchief and wiped at the footprints with shaking hands.

"You're making a bigger mess," the little girl said.

Gordy forced his voice to be light. "Are you the princess of this castle? You're a pretty princess. What's your name?"

"I'm Queen Lily. You must obey."

"I am your humble servant. May I please leave?" Gordy said.

"Bow," Lily said, "and say 'please.'"

Gordy lowered his head. He felt faint. The dog was still barking, and an adult could come out at any second. "Please, may I go now? I'll go get a mop so I can do a better job of cleaning your floor. I promise."

Lily considered. "Okay," she finally said. She moved out of the doorway and down the ladder, where she was joined by a frenzied terrier.

Gordy crawled out of the doorway and onto the balcony. The dog leaped at him. "Could you hold your dog?" he asked.

"He's my dragon," Lily said.

Gordy only hesitated a second before jumping down and running for the back fence with the dog at his heels. It latched onto his foot as he climbed the boards. He managed to shake it off before he scrambled over the top and fell to the other side. He got to his feet and ran as best he could with a bleeding leg and a missing shoe. He heard Lily yelling, "Mommy!"

After she questioned her daughter, Lily's mother sent an urgent message to her email list of neighborhood parents. It said, "Pedo wearing khakis, blue shirt, and one boat shoe loose in neighborhood." Then she called 911.

Parents pulled their children indoors and grabbed baseball bats, hockey sticks, shovels, whatever they could find. A couple of people ran to unlock their gun cabinets. Then they went out to find the bastard.

A retired real estate agent saw him first. She was armed with the pitchfork she used to spread mulch. She spotted Gordy crawling under a clump of azaleas. She sneaked up behind him and jabbed the tines of the pitchfork into the back of his neck. "Don't move or I'll skewer you," she said. Gordy flinched, and she jabbed him harder. "I said 'don't move.'" She yelled to alert the other neighbors, and soon Gordy was surrounded.

A black SUV pulled up and two men got out. They flashed badges. "110. We'll take it from here."

Gordy screamed "No!" as they cuffed him and shoved him into the back of the SUV. Five minutes later, a Fairfax County police car pulled up.

"The 110 took him away," Margaret told the officers.

"You called them?" an officer asked.

"I called 911," Lily's mommy said.

"And 911 called us. I don't know why the 110 would show up." He turned to his partner, "Give them a call." He addressed the assembled neighbors. "Did they show ID?"

"They showed something," Margaret said, "but I didn't really look that closely."

A man spoke up. "They didn't hold them up long enough for us to see. Could have been their Costco cards."

"Now that I think about it, they weren't really dressed like 110 agents," someone said, "at least not the ones I see on TV."

The partner returned to the group. "That wasn't the Organ. They're looking for a suspect in the area, but they didn't pick anyone up."

Lily's mother handed him the boat shoe she picked up. "Here's the man's shoe. Does that help?"

✦ ✦ ✦

Alberta took two Ibuprofen and hit the intercom button. "Thelma," she said, "cancel the morning staff meeting. I need to talk to the Organ liaison in the Counterterrorism Sector now."

"Yes, ma'am, but Slinky is still here. He has something urgent to discuss with you."

"Later," Alberta said.

Thelma started to say something, but Alberta cut her off. "I said later!"

Alberta retreated to the small private bathroom off her office and put a cool, wet cloth on her head. She needed to calm herself and stop her heart from racing. Now was not the time to do something stupid. Unfortunately, she had backed herself into a corner in such a way that no smart options presented themselves.

Alberta went back to her desk and took a new deck of cards from her top drawer. A game of Patience would help her think. She slit the cellophane and discarded it. As she shuffled the deck, her fingers slipped, and cards flew up and scattered over the desk and floor. She considered calling Thelma in to pick them up. Bending over aggravated the pressure in her head, but this jumble of cards was such a perfect mirror of the disorder in her mind that it embarrassed her and made her feel exposed. She lowered herself to her knees and picked up the cards herself. She fought back a wave of nausea.

By the time the liaison arrived from a nearby building, Alberta had collected the cards and her nerves. Her posture was straight, and her face calm, but her breathing was shallow.

Thelma's voice came over the intercom. "Neil Porter is here."

"Thank you, show him in."

Neil occupied the position that had once been held by Gordy Grant. His job was to facilitate cooperation between the Organ and the Mines and serve as a conduit of information. Unlike Gordy, Porter was competent, ethical, and dedicated to his mission. He carried no chip on his shoulder.

Alberta stood to greet Neil, but she skipped the pleasantries. "Tell me about the intelligence on Gordy Grant. Where did it come from?"

"From the Mines," Neil said. "You didn't know?"

Alberta blinked and sank into her chair.

"Are you all right?" he asked.

"Fine," she said roughly. "Who gave the Organ that information?"

"It came from someone low level; then Slinky Nardovino called over to confirm it. I thought he would have ..." His voice trailed off.

Alberta felt something collapse inside, but she let nothing show on her face. "That will be all," she said. She hit the intercom button. "Thelma, get Slinky in here, now."

Slinky opened the BOM's door to find Alberta holding up a Doodlebug with the word "EXPLAIN" writ large across it. He swallowed hard but looked her in the eye. "It's complicated." Under pressure, he forgot his preparation. The Venn circles merged into one like drops on a windshield. Then they ran. He looked away from her gaze, focused his eyes on the Hosmer hook in his lap and told her everything in a rush, clearing his conscience of the accumulated weight of secrets and dumping everything on Alberta in an ugly, jumbled mess. Once he started talking, he couldn't stop. He even told her about finding Greyson burning intercepts.

"I should have informed you then, I know I should have, but you know Greyson. Of course you know Greyson." His face flushed with the thought that Alberta had known Greyson in the biblical sense. The more he talked, the sloppier and more confessional his narrative became. "I should have stayed in my lane. Secrets are not my bailiwick. I don't understand alchemists. Sharpers scare me, and people who manage them scare me more. And I should stay far, far away from Congresspersons."

Slinky knew he was straying into dangerous territory, but his mouth moved independently of his brain. He told Alberta things about the Westerly affair that Greyson had never shared with her. "After they killed the cockatoo, their first thought was to replace it with an identical cockatoo. I told them that Westerly would never fall for that, but they assigned me the task anyway. Then, when they decided to put the dead bird back in its cage and make it look like an accident, they didn't bother to tell me to stand down. I did the impossible. I found a bird flipper on the dark web, drove to Bethesda, bought a bare-eyed cockatoo for a small fortune. That's when they tell me, never mind, they don't need it. Do you know how hard it is to responsibly rehome a parrot? While I was trying to do it, my kids got attached, and now we have a cockatoo. He has eaten half our furniture, and my wife hates me."

He paused. For the first time since the Screamer Attack, Slinky was not happy to be deaf. The quiet was unbearable. He couldn't look at Alberta. He didn't know what to do next, so he told her something he didn't need to tell her, something she was in no shape to hear.

"Something else is bothering me. About Brick's death ... I'm sure you guessed the canoe story was crap. Greyson and Arthur called me in the middle of the night and told me to meet them in Brick's office. Said it was an emergency. When I got there, they were standing over a desk covered with blood and some cranial matter. They said Brick was dead and assured me that they hadn't murdered him, but I have my doubts. I asked where the body was, and they pointed to the burn chute. There was a trail of blood. I went down to the basement, assuming that his body had fallen into the collection dumpster, but, no, there was just blood. Quite a bit." Here, Slinky got caught up in the logistical details. "The body had lodged upside-down in the burn chute, below the third floor. He probably bled out slowly. I had to poke him with a broom until he fell. To this day, I'm not entirely sure whether someone shot him and dumped his body down there, or whether he shot himself and somehow stumbled across the room and into the chute. I said we should call the authorities. Only a coroner could determine whether it was suicide or not, but Greyson wouldn't let me. You know how he is about allowing non-Mines people into the building. He insisted we destroy the body. I want you to know that I protested vigorously. I was overruled, like always. I covered Brick with burn bags and rolled the bin over to the incinerator." Slinky remembered then that he was talking to Brick's widow, and maybe he had been less sensitive than he should have been. He changed his tone to one of regret. "I'm not proud that you didn't have a body to bury. I sincerely apologize."

As he spoke, Slinky leaned forward with his elbows on his knees and fixed his eyes on the floor. He should look up in case Alberta was writing on the Doodlebug. He tried to summon the courage that had helped him pull a wounded comrade out of a burning Humvee, the courage that had kept him in the building during the Screamer Attack. But that was a different brand of courage than what would be required to look Alberta in the face now.

Then something fell to the floor and rolled against Slinky's toe. He reached down and picked up Alberta's mug, the one that said, "Watch out. I could go either way." Had it fallen off her desk or had she thrown it at him? He looked up. Alberta was trying to stand. She had planted her palms on the desk blotter, pushing it forward and knocking the mug to the floor. Her eyes fixed on him in the most disturbing way. The pupils shrank to dots. Slinky thought she was about to lunge and attack him. He raised an arm to shield his face. Alberta opened her mouth, disgorged a clot of foamy blood, and collapsed forward onto her desk.

After struggling so long with ethical dilemmas, Slinky was suddenly back in the familiar realm of logistics. He called Medical on the emergency line, told them to come wearing protective gear. He performed chest compressions, demurring on rescue breaths given the possibility of poisoning or communicative disease. After the doctor pronounced her dead, he carefully washed his hands and turned the crime scene over to authorities. He notified all necessary parties, including the Mines Oversight Committee. Because Greyson was at an offsite and not available to interfere, Slinky was able to do everything promptly, legally, and in the right order. He was himself again. Once Alberta was bagged and on the gurney, he saluted her and said "Goodbye," and "I'm sorry for everything" before they took her away.

Something was going on at Hale Plaza. Emergency vehicles and police cars had pulled up to the main entrance. Red lights flashed. Rubbernecking snarled traffic in all directions. Mrs. Cabot grumbled under her breath. She was stuck two miles away from the small park she had reserved for the Girl Scout picnic. It was still early—she always gave herself plenty of time to set up—but if the snarl didn't break up soon, it would be a problem.

After fifteen minutes of idling, the traffic finally got moving. Mrs. Cabot breathed a sigh of relief as she reached her destination. She parked as near as she could get to the pavilion and gathered bags of marshmallows, graham crackers, and Hershey's Bars from the passenger seat of her van. She had signed up for s'mores duty. As she approached, she was surprised to see someone already seated at a picnic table even though there were no other cars in the lot. She slowed her step. At first, she thought the man must be asleep with his head on the table, but as she got closer, she realized that there was no head, only gore. Then she saw the shotgun at his feet. He was wearing only one shoe.

Mrs. Cabot didn't scream or drop her bags. She was a nurse; she had a strong stomach and she prided herself on her level head. By the time the police arrived, she had booked an alternate site for the picnic and initiated a phone tree to inform all the participants of the change in plans.

A solicitous officer told her that trauma counseling was available.

"Oh, please." Mrs. Cabot waved him away. "I've dealt with every bodily grossness, along with snakes, bears, and hordes of preteen girls. A corpse is nothing."

24

Unseemly Celebrations

J ustine looked ten years younger when she met us at the door. Her eyes were bright and happy behind the round red frames of her glasses. She was grinning, something I'd never seen her do.

"Come in!" she said. "I bought beer and chips and a couple of comfortable chairs."

"Is this a party?" Vernon asked.

"Yes. I'm celebrating an increase in my life expectancy. At work, I have to look sad for Thelma's benefit. Here, I let loose. I'm going to live!"

"I really don't think Alberta was planning to kill you," I said.

"We'll never know now, but I feel reborn. I thought she would at least fire me, and I would lose my benefits. Now I can get my lousy gallbladder removed and quit living on applesauce! I spent the day looking at job vacancies. I'm going to apply for an editorial position in publications. I'm more than qualified."

We settled into new Poang chairs, and Justine brought our glasses. I took a sip and gagged. It was like hop-flavored cough syrup. "What kind of beer is this?"

"Cherry. It's from Belgium. The guy at the store said it was special."

Vernon put down his glass. "The word 'special' can have many meanings."

I popped a couple of chips in my mouth to take away the taste. They were jalapeño flavor, an interesting choice with cherry beer. Justine still had to work on her hosting skills.

"Aren't you relieved?" she asked.

"No," I said. "I feel the same way I felt when Shah Massoud was killed. Exactly the same."

"Shit," Vernon said, "I hadn't thought of that angle."

"Who was Shah Ma—whatever?" Justine asked.

"He was the leader of the Northern Alliance in Afghanistan. He was killed on September 9, 2001, by terrorists disguised as journalists. The bomb was in the camera. I didn't hear about it until the next morning, because I was driving home from a trip. I walked in on Monday, and somebody said, 'Massoud got whacked by al Qaida; what do you think it means?' and I swear I heard a string snap. It was the prelude to 9/11. Bin Ladin's gift to the Taliban because he knew striking the U.S. would rain hell on Afghanistan. He took out the leader of their opposition to help them with the battle to come."

"You think Alberta was murdered?" Justine said. "They haven't given a cause of death."

"Yeah, that's why I think she was assassinated," I said.

"Me, too," Vernon said. "The rumor mill is running wild, and the poison guys are working late."

"You think the terrorists got to her?" Justine said.

"If so," I said, "the threat has reached a new level. She was assassinated. In her office. In the Mines. Behind redundant layers of security. With the sort of sophisticated poison the Russians use. And now we wait for the other shoe to drop."

Justine's eyes grew wide. "That's terrible. They wouldn't attack the Mines again, would they?"

Vernon and I exchanged looks.

Birdie sputtered as she moved along the length of Greyson's home office sweeping crushed potato chips into a pile. "What kind of heathen has himself a party to celebrate a woman's death? A woman he used to fornicate with! Then he has the nerve to—" Birdie couldn't finish the sentence. It was too appalling. She swiped her hand over her cheek. It felt dirty.

She didn't want to think about it, but the scene replayed in her mind. Greyson had rung to request a bowl of salt and vinegar potato chips. When she brought it, she found him standing in the middle of the room singing "Here Comes the Sun." If you could call it singing. It sounded like the devil himself caterwauling. Greyson had taken the bowl from her, tossed the chips in the air and hurled the bowl down the length of the room. Then he gave her a big hug and a kiss on the cheek. The nerve! She wiped a tear of affront from her eye. She had a good mind to sue him for sexual harassment.

Birdie had been having such a fine life since the Screamer Attack and especially since Mr. Earl smashed his tailbone. Now Mr. Earl was happy, and no good could come from that.

Greyson tossed the Percocet. He needed to be on top of his game, and his coccyx no longer throbbed. Suddenly, without any effort on his part, he had a second chance to be BOM. While it was not enough to make him believe in God again, it did reinforce his belief in his own divinity. He was born to be BOM, and now the universe was stepping in to make it so.

He was furious, however, that Slinky had called the Organ, and now they were crawling all over the place. But there was nothing to do about that now.

Carlos should have kicked them out. He was now the acting BOM. That was not a situation that could be allowed to last for any length of time. The man was too popular, too photogenic, and too damn ethnic. He would seem a clever choice in the eyes of the president.

Unless he fucked up.

Such a fuckup should not be too difficult to arrange. This was not a war-hardened Alberta, who knew how to reinforce her flanks. This was a man who had drafted leisurely behind his mentor for years. Alberta had blocked the headwinds, and now Carlos had no idea what he was in for.

How to make an acting BOM fuck up? Usually, one could take advantage of his massive ego and associated blind spots. But Carlos didn't have a massive ego. He was a level-headed team player. How in fucking rolling donuts did somebody like that get so far in life? The man came out of nowhere, had no Mines pedigree, no connections, no damn anything but native ability and an ethnicity that checked all the right boxes. This was the sort of person who got ahead in the Mines these days, and it made Greyson furious. He paced the length of his office and stopped before the new whiteboard. He winced at the memory of breaking the old one. He couldn't afford to let his temper get the best of him again. He took five slow breaths and then he took up a red marker and wrote "BLINDSIDE" on the board.

Blindsiding an unpopular BOM was a hallowed tradition in the Mines. He just needed some good dirt to strategically leak to the press. Sure, Carlos appeared to be squeaky clean, but Greyson reasoned that anything—absolutely anything—could be made to look like dirt.

✦ ✦ ✦

The next day, when Greyson arrived at his Hale Plaza office, he found a dozen red roses on his desk. "What the hell?" he said under his breath. He poked his head out the door and called to Karen. "Where did these come from?"

A red flush spread over her face. "I brought them. You're going to be the next Boss of Mines. I know it. This calls for a celebration."

Greyson frowned. "No celebration until it's a done deal. I have things to do. Hold my calls." He shut the door. He got Carlos's personnel file from his safe and began to thumb through it. He tsk-tsked at the non-Ivy League college transcript. For the most part, nobody in the Mines cared where you went to school, but Greyson would never believe that As from a place like UCLA were equal to Cs earned at Princeton. He ran his finger down the list of classes Carlos had taken, looking for something questionable like "Marxist-Leninist Theory" or "Survey of Erotica." But no, Carlos had stuck to boring stuff like "Economic Development of Latin America." He'd passed his background checks without issue, scored well on aptitude tests, and completed the career prep course with nothing but good comments from his instructors. Greyson read through dozens of glowing performance appraisal reports looking for "however" clauses, but they were few and anodyne. He took special care with the appraisals written by Alberta, but there was nothing he could work with.

The next step was TRASHINT. Greyson had sent out the order to his favorite dumpster diver yesterday. The man should have something soon.

What could he do in the meantime? Greyson thought a minute, then hit the intercom button. "Karen, send someone down to the gym to get Harry Murphy. Chop-chop."

Harry arrived ten minutes later, still wearing his Mines logo gym clothes and perspiring profusely from taking the stairs two at a time. He was tall, sinewy, and balding, with a combover glued down by some industrial-strength hair product that resisted sweat. His recent tour as station boss in a small Eastern European country had ended, and he was awaiting his next assignment. Meanwhile, he spent his headquarters time in the gym using the weight machines periodically but mostly loitering near the leg press with a towel around his neck, checking out the younger female employees.

"Hello, Harry," Greyson said. "How's your daughter? What's her name, Katie?"

"Olivia," Harry said, "and she's good."

"Staying out of trouble?"

Harry reddened. "She learned her lesson." During his last tour, Olivia was caught hacking into her school's computer system. Harry and daughter were both on the verge of being declared personae non gratae when Greyson stepped in and fixed things.

"She learned her lesson," Harry repeated.

"I need her to unlearn it," Greyson said. "You owe me."

Hamid prayed under his breath as he loaded his truck. He prayed in the evenings on a worn silk rug. He prayed in his dreams, and Allah rewarded him with burning visions. He was ready.

Tomorrow, senior officials of the intelligence community would meet for their monthly lunch in the executive dining room of Hale Plaza. Hamid would deliver the food this afternoon. He wasn't scheduled to be at Hale Plaza during the meeting, but it didn't matter. It would be a short detour from his route. His deliveries were not so regular that the guards would notice an unscheduled stop. He would pull the truck into the spot behind the bushes, get out, and run toward paradise.

Hamid didn't feel the weight of the boxes and crates. He was sure he could lift his feet off the ground and float. Then he noticed something wrong. He checked his list and did a quick inventory of the boxes. Where were the items for the meeting of senior officials? Where were the scallops, the steaks, the shrimp? Where was the whipping cream for their desserts?

"There's been a mistake," he said to his supervisor. "The things for the big lunch are missing."

"Lunch is canceled," the man said. "Didn't you hear? Boss of Mines dropped dead at her desk. Nobody knows why. We'll have to wait for the autopsy. Can't wait to hear what killed this one. Damned if they don't drop like flies."

The disappointment brought tears to Hamid's eyes. How dare she die? Killing her should have been his honor. He felt deflated and weak. He barely had the strength to finish his workday. He went home and prostrated himself on his prayer rug, but his mind was empty, and his prayers had dried up.

25

Rabbit Hole

I exhausted my rich vocabulary of swear words when I read the email from Senator Brand. She wanted to see me as soon as possible to discuss my progress. I hadn't heard from her in weeks and now she summoned me? I thumped my forehead. Of course she wanted to see me. My superiors had undoubtedly failed to adequately answer her questions about Alberta's death, so she wanted to pump me for info. I called a meeting with Vernon to strategize.

When I arrived at the motor pool, I found him with a young man who unfolded himself from his chair to tower over me by a good foot and a half.

"This is Andy Dalton," Vernon said. "He's the financial analyst I was telling you about."

I reached up to shake his hand.

"Andy found out a few things about Constance Brand."

"She's dirty, dirty, dirty." Andy smiled with delight.

"Dirty how?" I asked.

"Insider trading," he said, "and she isn't the only one."

Vernon cut in. "It seems that Dashiell Aspling got his job by handing out stock tips on both sides of the Congressional aisle like Halloween candy. A few big names made some big bucks."

"As we suspected," I said. "Capitol Hill must be sweating out the investigation."

"Yeah," Dalton said, "the word from on high is to focus resources on Aspling's relationship with Kreative Industrial Sunlight Solutions. No straying onto 'irrelevant tangents.'"

"Like how he got his job?" I said.

"Exactly," Dalton said. "I know some people who do oppo research for Congressional candidates. They've been steered away from the subject, too."

"Good grief, is every member of Congress involved?" I asked.

"Only the most powerful," Dalton said. "And on both sides, there are people who would like to take them down, but they don't have the ammunition yet. So, yes, the sweat is flowing."

"I hate domestic political shit," I said. "Give me terrorists any day of the week."

Dalton chuckled. I could see why he and Vernon were friends. They both relished the nastier elements of their jobs.

"Are you really enjoying this?" I asked.

He shrugged. "Mud wrestling is fun."

I considered the implications. "So, Brand and a few others are guilty of insider trading, which led to an unqualified idiot being put in a post he should have never occupied, which led to a terrorist attack. But did any of them have more direct involvement in the attack? Or is that only Westerly?"

"My guess is it's only Westerly, but good question," Vernon said.

"And now we have a BOM dead under mysterious circumstances. What do I say to Brand in this meeting tomorrow?" I asked.

"As little as possible," Vernon said.

"Maybe she's worried about what I've uncovered," I said. "I have to make her think I've gone down the wrong rabbit hole."

Vernon nodded. "Play like you're following her instructions to the letter. Give her some dirt on Greyson Earl. There's talk that he not only had motive to kill Alberta, but the connections necessary to get the poison. Early in his career, he recruited an asset high in the Russian government who may be even higher up by now." His face brightened. "You'll have to go in your Jennifer persona. You want her to think you're following all the rules."

I groaned. He was right. I would have to break out the prosthetics and wig and get Joseph to drive me.

Joseph was still showing up at our house every morning in case I should need a ride. Indeed, he'd been arriving earlier and earlier. As for Mom, I had heard her in the kitchen at 4:00 a.m. singing "I feel pretty." I stuck my nose out from under my comforter and detected the smell of ham baking in the oven. She was fixing the special-occasion breakfast usually reserved for Christmas and Easter morning—Smithfield ham, beaten biscuits, scrambled eggs, and fried apples. Crap, she was going to be pissed when she found out I needed Joseph to drive me. Couldn't be helped. I'd never find a parking spot on the Hill. Besides, Brand's window overlooked the spot where government drivers drop off their passengers. I had to give the appearance of following her instructions to the letter.

I showered and dressed, buttoning my blouse and jacket over a deflated bra. My fake boobs and prosthetics were in my desk drawer at work. I waited as long as possible before I had to go down and interrupt breakfast.

I found Mom and Joseph in the kitchen doing dishes and laughing. Mom washing, Joseph drying. They looked so natural and happy together that I felt terrible about what I had to do.

"Good morning," I said.

They looked up, surprised, as if they had forgotten that I lived in the house, too.

"Good morning, Maddie," Joseph said a little too heartily.

"Good morning, Jellybean," Mom said. "I'll fix you some ham biscuits."

"I don't have time. I hate to do this, I really do, but I'm going to Capitol Hill this morning and I need a driver."

Joseph, professional that he was, allowed only a bare shadow of annoyance to cross his face before he smiled and said, "That's what I'm here for."

My mother had less control over her face. I recognized that expression. I got the feeling that she was about to address me by my first, middle, and last names and ask me to sit my butt down on that stool in the corner where I could think about what I'd done. She turned away for a moment, pretending to do something in the sink.

When we got into the car, I insisted on sitting up front with Joseph. "I can hear better. Besides, I cannot do the VIP thing. I've had it with VIPs."

"Most of them aren't so bad," he said, "as long as you don't make eye contact."

"Hmmm. Eye contact. That's probably my mistake. I can't lower my eyes. D.C. is a zoo. I can't resist staring at the exotic animals, and VIPs are exotic animals. A high percentage of them are abnormal. Some dangerously so."

"You do make things hard for yourself," Joseph said.

"We have to go to headquarters first," I told him. "I have to put on my Jennifer stuff. It's in my office."

We rode in silence for a while; then Joseph said, "Your mother is an amazing woman."

"You're going to tell me that I don't appreciate her enough," I said.

"You don't, but I understand that Gladys might be a bit too much for you at this stage of your life."

"'A bit?' I opened my underwear drawer yesterday and found my panties rolled into burritos and fitted into an organizer."

He laughed. "But wasn't it nice to have someone to care about you when you were recovering?"

"Yes," I admitted.

"I got a bad case of pneumonia last year. I could barely drag my sorry ass to the kitchen to feed myself. I thought I couldn't miss Lucy any more than I already did, but being sick and alone? That was the worst."

"I'm sorry, Joseph. That sounds awful."

"I took care of Lucy when she was sick," Joseph said, "and that was the biggest privilege of my life. I miss taking care of someone, too. A good marriage is a blessing."

"You know, I would be delighted if you married my mother," I said.

Joseph took his eyes away from traffic for a second to give me a side glance. "Really? It's too early to ask, but things are moving in that direction."

"Really?"

"She told me you weren't happy about her last marriage."

"That's because she married Harry Esterhaus, my faux-human ex-boss. It must have been temporary insanity. I approve of you, however."

"Do you think she would accept a proposal?" Joseph asked.

"Mom bought a big freezer for my basement so she could fill it with casseroles. I went down there last week looking for ice cream, and the thing was full of canapés. I think it's for your wedding reception. Mom has always been into advance planning."

Joseph couldn't keep the grin off his face.

When I walked into Brand's office, she was standing by the window, gazing out. It struck me as the pose of a professional poseur.

She turned and said, "Is that really you, Maddie?"

"I'm afraid so."

"I wondered who that woman was who doesn't know to ride in the back of a government car."

"I like to see where I'm going." I was tempted to add that the distinguished driver was going to be my new daddy. Brand sat down at her desk and waved me into a chair. She glanced at a document, turned it face down, and clasped her hands over it.

"So, you can hear now?" she said.

"As long as you don't talk fast."

"First, I have to offer condolences." Brand's voice went syrupy. "What a horrible thing for Alberta to die so suddenly. And nobody has a clue as to what really happened?"

"The rumor mill is going wild," I said.

A shift of well-lacquered hair indicated that her ears were perking up. "Is there any talk of foreign involvement?"

"Yes, but Alberta had plenty of enemies in the Mines, too."

"Oh?"

"Greyson, for one, made no secret of his feelings."

"I thought, well there was talk that they—"

"She dumped him the day she became BOM."

"Really?" An eager look came into Brand's face, but she suppressed it. "Well, that's interesting, but we should get back to your assignment. What are your findings thus far?"

I summarized everything analysts and investigators knew about the attack. Then I told her about finding Greyson burning documents in his office, but I let her think that those documents were destroyed. I didn't mention beaning him with a flashlight, although I doubt she would have disapproved.

She mulled this over. "Greyson again. Well, you can't put this in the report unless you find more solid evidence but retiring him would be the safest course. The committee has received complaints of sexual harassment. Yes, that will be my recommendation to the president." Brand paused; then she said, "I want you to find out more about what Greyson was doing. Focus on that aspect." She gave me a big smile, and our meeting was over.

I almost expected her to say, "Good girl, you've found an excellent rabbit hole; now dive into it.

I'd been working on my report all morning, trying to lay out the whys and wherefores behind the Screamer Attack. I had maligned previous commission reports for sticking with the superficial and never breaking the surface, but now I understood. Once you take that dive, where do you stop? How deep do you go? Soon you are flailing, over your head, and struggling to breathe.

In the past, drafters have dealt with this by sticking faithfully to their brief. Find out what went wrong in the Intelligence Community. A younger Maddie, more concerned with career and people pleasing, would have dashed off a highly acceptable report in no time. Bureaucratic barriers and clashing agency cultures? I could write a book. Inadequate vetting of government contractors? Another book.

Yet I could also write a book on the many good, intelligent, and ethical people working their asses off. People who shouldn't bear the entire burden of blame.

This older, sadder Maddie was no longer capable of sticking to her brief. She asked questions that pulled her into quicksand. "Why didn't they do their job?" is followed by "Was the job even doable?" Followed by "Why wasn't the job doable?"

American exceptionalism and American foreign policy. Time and time again, the big pinecones send us in to impose our vision on people we don't bother to get to know. They say it's in the name of freedom, but the motivations are murkier than that. The billions poured into "nation-building" go into the coffers of contractors who leave places worse than they found them. The big pinecones break crockery all over the world, and then they expect little people with glue sticks and a mountain of shards to keep the consequences at bay.

Greed was a key driver in the Screamer Attack. A few key elected officials, who fully believed themselves to be good and patriotic citizens, thought it wouldn't hurt to enrich themselves at the expense of good government. So much money to be made for this one decision! Maybe Dashiell was what the Mines needed. He talked a good game. Why not? Everybody does it.

Opportunism. A terrorist attack against our country spurs a hot outpouring of raw grief and rage. As a leader, you can try to lower the temperature, or you can whip up that feeling and harness it to your agenda.

Old grudges—personal, institutional, and just plain bizarre. Revenge for a dead bird. Old grudges trump good governance time and time again.

I could go back forever to trace the causes of this terror attack. Back to fragile egos warped by common cruelties. What kind of back story did Gordy have to turn out the way he did? What about Fahad?

I wrote out a ridiculous final sentence in my head—"and in conclusion, we need more kindness and honesty and less greed in the world." Ridiculous. True. Utterly unhelpful.

Then there was that other question, "What were we not allowed to look at?"

We alchemists are inundated with more information than we can handle. We can't help but be grateful that certain subjects are walled off by law, custom, and unspoken agreement. We don't have eyes in the back of our heads. The way to get ahead and to get along is to look where we are told to look.

But the threat always comes from the blind spots, because that's what threats do.

And we are not allowed to look at any role the United States or U.S. citizens might have played. Now that goes back to the National Security Act of 1947. The idea behind it was solid—the drafters of that act did not want to create an all-powerful intelligence agency. Putting a fence around the operational side is one thing. Putting a fence around thought and analysis is another.

Then another phrase popped into my head— "Write like there are no rules."

So, I wrote until I arrived at the final paragraph, the one that honesty forced me to write, the one that described the day they installed the lights in my office, and I handed that light back instead of having the smithies take it apart. I abandoned the stilted language of bureaucracy for the final sentence. "So, if you want to blame me, have at it, but that will do absolutely nothing to stop the next attack."

I asked Vernon and Justine to read the draft and comment. We met in Vernon's motor pool office. While they read, I took a walk around the compound.

Work was underway to repair and replace broken windows. I stopped by the boxes of glass stacked on the sidewalks around the building and read what was printed on the side. According to the box, this was laminated glass designed to mitigate the effects of a blast. I didn't trust it. I approached a supervisor and introduced myself as Katherine Jones. "I'm executive assistant to Salvador Nardovino. I'd like a demonstration of the glass."

The man frowned at me. I showed him my blue Mines tag. Mines tags have no names, only a photo, a color-coded border, and classification level and clearance codes. My tag showed that I had high-level clearances. In addition, I had one of the special tags that allowed me unfettered access to this enormous crime scene. Not many of those tags had been issued. Still, the man looked skeptical.

"I didn't hear anything about giving anybody a demonstration," he said.

"Do you want me to drag Mr. Nardovino down here and tell him you've been uncooperative," I said, "or do you want to break one pane of glass for me." I rolled up my sleeve and showed him the angry red scar on my arm. "I got this injury in the attack because somebody didn't check to make sure they were installing the right kind of glass in this building. I'm asking you to break one pane of glass and I'm not leaving until you do."

The man glared at me. I glared back. Finally, he yelled to an assistant, "Mike, bring a sledgehammer and one of the smaller windows."

I waited while they propped the window up against the building.

"Have at it," the supervisor said.

Mike gave the window four heavy blows. A thick web of cracks radiated from the point of impact, but the glass remained in one piece.

"Run your hand over it," the supervisor said.

I did. No sharp edges. This was the real thing. My mind went back to all the bloody footprints that led away from the building that day, to the silver flash of needles stitching flesh, to the gash in my own arm that laid open layers of skin, fat, and muscle. "Thank you," I said and then I held out my hand first to the supervisor and then to Mike. "I'll sleep better."

When I returned to the motor pool, Vernon looked up from his reading and said, "This is going to land like a crap in the pool. Not only are they going to fire you from the Mines; they'll never hire you on contract."

"I don't want contract work," I said.

"That's crazy, unless you are independently wealthy and never mentioned it to me."

"Well, maybe I'm independently wealthy."

"You live in a 20-foot-wide starter townhouse with builder-grade everything," Vernon pointed out. "If you're hiding wealth, you're hiding it well."

"Sometimes you have to walk away from money," I said.

"And food, clothing, and medical care?" Justine said.

"The Mines won't fire me," I said. "The Mines will never read what is in this report. Constance Brand will read it and burn it."

"Then she'll put out a hit on you." Vernon raised one eyebrow toward the shiny dome of his head. "You didn't write this to have no one read it."

"No," I admitted, "but I don't know what I'm going to do with it."

I met with my most trusted advisor that night. "So, Abu Bunny, what do I do with my report?"

He cuddled against my body and closed his eyes. He didn't like it when I kept the light on so late. I should turn it off and try to get some sleep, but the question would not leave me alone. Why did I bother to write the damn thing if there was nothing to do with it?

I could hand it to Constance Brand. She would bury it, but she probably wouldn't have me fired for fear I would go public.

I could hand it to Slinky, but would that do anything? He was physically courageous, but bureaucratically spineless.

I could hand it to the press and blow up my career and maybe end up in jail or impoverished by lawyer's fees. Also, I took an oath not to do that sort of thing and I take oaths seriously.

I had to give my report to someone who would think about it and learn from it. Did that describe anyone inside the Beltway?

Carlos.

26

Crash

Greyson paced, still mourning the lost sound of his footsteps. He had to content himself with the vibration of his feet as they hit the floor. He had purchased shoes with heavier, harder soles to enhance the feeling, but it was a poor substitute. At least the ringing in his ears had dulled, and he hadn't experienced an episode of phantom screamers in weeks. He was ready to move against Mr. Boring Normal Pretty Dimples Carlos.

All the ammunition he had gathered, however, turned out to be duds. Empty pill bottles found in Carlos's trash raised the possibility of exotic illness, but the "Charlie" Hernandez on the label turned out to be the family cat. Questioning of Carlos's neighbors revealed that a rolled-up carpet had been removed from the house. Greyson rubbed his hands with glee and put his most trusted people on the job. They located the carpet at a local landfill. No body was found inside. A thorough analysis concluded that the only substances on the carpet were bloody dog excrement, dark chocolate, marzipan, and pistachios. Not a trace of human blood.

Another late-night raid on the trash cans revealed only that the Hernandez family ate a lot of takeout, preferred high-fiber, low-sugar breakfast cereals, and thoughtfully bagged the used cat litter before putting it in the can.

Olivia hacked into the Hernandez bank accounts only to discover that the family lived within their means and paid off their credit card balance every month. "Oh, come on," Greyson had said upon hearing this news. "Nobody does that. Do these people have no aspirations? No taste? No imagination?" He spat, then rang Birdie to clean it up before it spotted his floor.

If anyone had dug into Greyson's trash, financial dealings, and family background, they would have found enough dirt to cover a football field to a depth of two feet. He had assumed that everyone was like that, but, apparently, no. A bilious wave of disappointment rippled through his digestive system. He rang for Birdie again.

"Tums," he said when she appeared.

"Please and thank you, ma'am," Birdie muttered as she turned away. "Nobody ever taught you manners? What did you learn in them fancy schools?" She returned a few moments later with a family-size bottle of the Gas Relief Chewy Bites in assorted fruit flavors. She sniffed the air. "I see I'm too late to prevent the farts. Worst-smelling gas of any man I ever met. Evil innards, that's what it is."

Greyson scowled. "Birdie, I can see you talking. What have I told you about talking when I can't hear what you're saying? I know it's something impertinent."

"Well I'm just going to put a look on my face like I'm sorry as I can be and pretend to apologize," Birdie said, "so I can get out of here before you float another air biscuit and I pass out dead." She left the room.

Greyson popped a half dozen Tums and chewed.

If there was no dirt, then what could be made to look like dirt?

The Hernandez family had a nanny for their children. She was a legal immigrant—that was the first thing Greyson had checked. She was also pretty. Surely, she could be bribed or coerced into making a charge of sexual harassment against Carlos. He would have Olivia investigate her background.

The next morning, when Greyson arrived at work, Karen handed him a note that said, "The Acting 'BOM' wants to see you in his office now." She always put BOM in quotes and rolled her eyes at any mention of Carlos. She was Team Greyson's most loyal cheerleader.

Greyson seethed at the idea that this little man could order him around like he was a summer intern. As he walked the length of the hall, he punched his hip with his fist and worked to get his face under control.

Carlos was a man who smiled a lot, but he was not smiling this morning. He seemed pained and embarrassed. He waved Greyson to a chair and handed him a note which began with the dreaded phrase "We serve at the pleasure of the president."

BLINDSIDE. The word scrawled itself in red across his field of view, obscuring the text of the note. He blinked several times before he could take in the next words. "The president has asked for your immediate resignation. I'm sorry, Greyson. I don't know why. You will, of course, receive the Distinguished Intelligence Medal, which you have certainly earned with your dedicated—"

Greyson crumpled the note without reading it to the end. Carlos extended his hand, but Greyson tossed the paper to the floor and left without acknowledging his boss.

Returning to his office, Greyson told Karen, "Type out a letter of resignation—a single sentence will do—then bring it in for me to sign."

A flush spread up Karen's neck and across her cheeks. She screamed "No!" and pushed her chair from her desk with such violence that she almost flipped over backwards. She flailed, and Greyson grabbed the chair and yanked it back into vertical. "Just do it." Greyson disappeared into his office, slamming the door.

Karen had tears in her eyes as she typed the wretched letter. She ripped it from the printer and delivered it to Greyson without looking at him. Back at her desk, she laid a stuffed Elmo face down and stabbed him in the back with a pair of scissors.

Birdie was enjoying a foot soak when she heard the door slam. What was Mr. Earl doing back home at this hour? She quickly lifted her feet out of the Calphalon roaster she used as a foot spa. It held the heat well, and she so enjoyed the idea of marinating her bunions in the same pot she used to make Greyson's favorite herb-crusted rack of lamb. She dumped the water in the sink, put the pot in the dish drainer without bothering to rinse it out first, and slipped on her house shoes.

"Birdie," Greyson bellowed from the foyer.

She fingered the cross at her neck and muttered, "Lord Jesus make me strong."

Then came a crash so loud it could only be the big glass nudie sculpture that stood on a pedestal by the door. Well, she had never liked that obscene thing. Birdie grabbed a broom and headed for the foyer.

She smelled the alcohol from across the room. She found Mr. Earl drunk as a skunk and leaning heavily into the corner where the sculpture had stood. The pedestal was on its side, and broken red glass covered the floor and glittered in the morning sun.

"A sea of glass mingled with fire," Birdie said. "Well ain't you just the beast straight out of Revelations?"

Greyson started to cry and then he vomited a stream of noxious liquid.

"There, there," Birdie said. "I hate to see a grown man blubber like a baby." She picked her way through the glass and vomit and took Greyson by the arm. "Come on; we'll get you cleaned up. Put you in that nice, fluffy robe you stole from the Hilton. A man who can afford to buy a hundred robes and you steal one? Me, I never had two nickels to rub together, and I never stole anything my whole life. Disgraceful. Why did you have to go and make such an unholy mess? I'm going to call your AA sponsor. I'm not going to let you go back to being the mean sot you used to be."

Greyson sobbed louder.

Birdie almost felt sorry for him as she steered him into the bathroom. "Tell you what. Tonight, I'll make you your favorite herb-crusted rack of lamb. Won't that be nice?"

27

Boom

The jet stream crimped, dropping a cold mass of Canadian air onto the sweaty mid-Atlantic. The result was a luxury, goose-down duvet of fog that muted the sound of car horns.

It did not take much weather to snarl traffic in Northern Virginia. The region had two troublesome species of drivers: the few who over-compensated for conditions by going too slow, and the many who believed that no mere weather had the right to make them adjust their speed, following distance, or propensity to cut off other drivers. The results were depressingly predictable. The collisions began before dawn and stained transportation arteries red with brake lights.

The fog let little sun through to the angel bears decorating the windows of Hale Plaza. They looked down on the Secret Service preparations with sappy smiles. The gloom didn't matter; they had already soaked up enough light to change the chemical composition of the gel that filled their wings and halos. An explosion within forty yards would set them off in a chain reaction that would bring down the side of the building.

✦ ✦ ✦

Hamid repeated the figure under his breath—forty yards. He didn't trust much that Gordy said, but he had taken to heart the direction that he must get within forty yards of the building or there wouldn't be enough damage to count. Forty yards or failure.

After the disappointment of Alberta's death, Hamid had once again prepared himself to die, but this time his mind was not as quiet, and his hands and legs were not as steady. His heart would leap and flutter for no reason. He broke into sweats. H couldn't eat. He wasn't ready, but he had to move forward. It would have been better if he could have driven directly to Hale Plaza, but timing was everything. The thing had to be done shortly after eleven o'clock, during the swearing-in. Because his shift began before dawn, that meant that he would have hours to drive around wearing his suicide vest under a windbreaker and sweating profusely.

The presence of the vice president would heighten security. Would they even allow his lorry into the complex? Over the preceding months, he had taken pains to cultivate the guards at the gate. He learned their names, smiled at them, gave them boxes of treats which he bought himself at the grocery store so as not to mess up his inventory and draw suspicion. They bent the rules enough to accept his gifts, but he doubted they would bend them this far. Then, yesterday, his supervisor had said, "I got a call from Hale Plaza. The new BOM made a special request for tiramisu for his ceremony, so make sure it's on the truck." That would be his excuse for entering the complex. When he made the afternoon delivery the day before the ceremony, he deliberately left the boxes off the truck.

"Forty yards," he said to himself. He had measured the distance out on the track. Then he paced it off wherever he went. When he made his deliveries at Hale Plaza, he measured the distance in his mind, starting at the door and moving forty yards into the parking lot.

The fog made Hamid feel hidden and protected. He hoped it would not lift before eleven o'clock. He imagined rising with the cloud to paradise.

Hamid did not see the brake lights of the car in front of him. He heard the crash, and a car appeared almost in his lap. He hit the brakes and wrenched the wheel toward the median. The truck came to rest with its nose pressed up against a Bradford pear tree. Hamid's hand gently touched his vest. He heard three more collisions as other drivers failed to react quickly enough. Someone bumped his truck. He had to get out of there before the police arrived.

Rubbernecking had slowed the oncoming lane of traffic. Hamid saw an opening and pulled his truck into it. Horns sounded. He did a quick Y turn hitting only another Bradford pear, then accelerated into the lane. He took the first turn off the road and drove through residential streets until he had left the accident scene behind.

Carlos Hernandez had a longer commute than most senior officials. His desire for a big yard for his kids to play in had pushed him out to Manassas. Now he sat on Route 66 with his car engine turned off, listening to sirens and watching blue strobe lights flash up ahead. He had started out earlier than usual to get a head start on a crowded schedule, but now it appeared that he would be stuck here for some time. He called to warn Tessa to watch the traffic advisories before setting out for the ceremony.

Carlos wasn't looking forward to it. He hated events arranged by the Mines Office of Protocol. They had none of the elements of a real party—no music, dancing, spicy food, or alcohol. No piñata. Carlos smiled to think how the presence of a piñata in the shape of, say, a brutal dictator, would liven up the proceedings. But no, Mines celebrations were all about empty, unctuous speeches, heavy blue curtains and flags, and endless grip-and-grin sessions for the photographer. His facial muscles twitched.

In the interest of consolidating official events, Carlos had directed that his swearing-in serve multiple purposes. After the vice president left, Carlos would present a Distinguished Intelligence Medal to the former Boss of Black Mines, Greyson Earl, as well as a half-dozen lesser medals to various high-level recipients.

Carlos had even arranged a medal for Maddie James. She must have been shocked when Protocol informed her of the decision. She had come into his office convinced that she was making a career-ending move by handing him the paper she had written. Her face was white as she explained the arrangement she had made Senator Brand.

Carlos knew enough about inside-the-Beltway machinations that he was not surprised. What did surprise him was the content of the report. No passive voice or high-flown language. The subject of every sentence was clearly identified. Senator Harrison Westerly. His cockatoo, Dirksen. Gordy Grant. Lyle Voth. Even Constance Brand herself. Carlos's own mentor, Alberta Bennet-Mason—no wonder she had sent him on so many trips. Less important than these individuals, however, was what she had said in the final section of the report about how the country got itself into these situations in the first place. She even covered the role of scapegoating in weakening the response to a terrorist event. It was all true, and it was all political dynamite. He knew the reception it would get if it ever went public. It would be called unpatriotic and worse. The public much preferred the simple, black-and-white, us-against-them conclusions that got us into trouble in the first place.

The paper answered many of Carlos's nagging questions. It raised a spate of issues he would have to deal with, but it would prevent him from being blindsided as so many of his predecessors had been.

What to do with it? It was clear what the people named in the report would have done. They would have covered it up. And look where it got them. Carlos wasn't like them. He took this job in the full knowledge that doing it properly might mean that his tenure was short. That was fine with him. There was life outside the Mines. He had Maddie delete the questionable adjectives and make two copies of the report. He sent one to the president and one to the Department of Justice. Then he directed her to come up with an unclassified version of the conclusions fit for public consumption. It would be up to the president to decide what would go public, but Carlos would be ready in case the decision was made. He doubted the thing would ever see the light of day unless it leaked, but at least a few people who should read it would read it. And it would ruin their day. That was the best he could hope for.

The car in front of him moved. Carlos started his engine. He was looking forward to one thing at this ceremony—tiramisu. It was his favorite dessert. He had felt sheepish asking Caterico to serve it. He did not approve of high officials who got too caught up in the perks of office, but when his secretary asked if there was anything special he wanted to add to the menu at the reception, his sweet tooth overruled his modesty. "Tiramisu," he had said. "It was my favorite thing about my tour in Rome."

A medal? Out of the blue? I was still trying to process this bizarre turn of events. I had plenty of time for processing because traffic on the Toll Road had come to a stop. I glanced over at the extremely tacky but thoughtfully made object on my passenger seat. It was a wooden treasure chest from a craft store. I had spray painted it gold and glued a Mines seal coaster on the top. It made me smile.

Protocol said I could invite five guests to the awards reception. I chose Mom, Joseph, Vernon, Justine, and Vivi. Mom was thrilled, although I had a hard time explaining to her why I was getting a medal.

Forty-five minutes later, I pulled my car into a parking space by the motor pool. Vernon and I were driving together to the ceremony because of the parking shortage at Hale Plaza. I might as well hang out here until time to leave. Vernon made reasonably good coffee, and he had stocked the freezer section of the fridge with frozen toaster waffles. I hadn't eaten breakfast before leaving home. I'd been on my way into the kitchen when I saw Joseph on his knees in front of my mother holding a small black velvet box. I backed out. No way was I interrupting that.

Vernon had pretended to be happy that I was getting a medal, but his nose was clearly out of joint. He ought to get some credit for uncovering Gordy's sins. I put him in for a performance award, but it had yet to be approved, and I didn't want to tell him about it in case it didn't go through. Then I thought of the perfect way to cheer him up in the meantime. I tucked the gold treasure chest box under my arm and headed for the break room.

I found Vernon with his feet up on the table, reading the *Post*.

"What is that thing?" Vernon pointed to the box.

"Your award," I said. "It's not a medal, but I think you'll like this better than a medal."

Vernon frowned. "What the hell?"

"Open it." I shoved the box into his hands.

Vernon's face remained grumpy as he undid the clasp, but he broke into a grin as soon as he saw the contents.

"Your boobs!" He took out one of the falsies and gave it a squeeze.

"Please," I said. "Do that later when I'm not here to see it."

Joseph was not supposed to pick his own passengers, but he broke the rules so that he could provide Gladys with a fitting ride to the ceremony. He made her get in the back of the government car. "You are not only a Very Important Person," he told her. "You are my Most Important Passenger."

Gladys glowed. She settled herself into the back seat. She'd spent years chauffeuring Maddie to dance lessons, lacrosse matches, and a host of other extracurricular activities. It felt strange and wonderful to be in the back of this government car driven by this most handsome, special man. The fog gave the atmosphere a magical feel, like time had stopped, and the moment would go on forever. The last of the shame and hurt from her brief marriage to Harry Esterhaus dissolved. Gladys couldn't stop smiling and admiring her new ring.

"I'm going to hire a stretch limo for our wedding day," she said. "Then we can both ride in the back."

"Damn," Joseph said, "I have always wanted to drive a stretch."

Justine had almost finished packing up her office. She had gotten the editing job and would be moving to a tiny cubicle next week. Tomorrow she would use the small stock of sick leave she had accumulated to get her pesky gallbladder removed. No more applesauce and nausea.

Justine didn't mind giving up her office and her proximity to very important people. After weeks of anxiety, the thought of an anonymous gray cubicle was comforting. It would be like crawling under a nice, safe rock. She could be bored during the day and spend nights and weekends writing about terror rather than living it.

She kept one eye on the clock. She did not want to be late for the awards reception. As an introvert, she dreaded it. As a writer, she couldn't pass up the opportunity to observe the ritual. It occurred to her that such a ceremony could be the scene of a terrorist attack. Since she couldn't safely eat or drink anything, her hands would be free to take notes. Her mood lifted. Despite being the gentlest of creatures, Justine absolutely loved blowing things up on the page.

The fog began to dissipate as we drove to Hale Plaza. Vernon insisted on driving us in his ridiculous big truck with its oversized tires. I hated it, but it did provide a better view than my Prius. We were taking the side streets to avoid traffic backups. It wasn't much faster though because of all the four-way stops in this neighborhood. A traffic feature that relies on courtesy and rule-following was a poor choice for Northern Virginia. Vernon had to throw on his brakes to avoid getting pancaked by a Caterico truck that didn't pause at the stop sign. Fortunately, it wasn't going fast.

As we waited to enter the complex, I assessed its vulnerability to terrorist attack. "Look, I can see a Secret Service guy over there and a security guard there, but there's a gap right by this corner of the building. It's a blind spot. Someone should be standing right there." We made a turn onto the road that went by the side of the building, and I noticed a guard with a long hose out in the parking lot. "What is he doing?" I asked.

"Cleaning goose shit," Vernon said. "They have a guy on permanent poop duty." He pointed to a gaggle of Canada geese hanging out by a clump of bushes on the edge of the parking lot. "And there are your fecal terrorists."

"When we get inside, I'm going to have a talk with the idiot in charge of security."

Vernon shook his head. "No, Maddie. You'll piss him off and get us thrown out."

"My biggest regrets in life are the times I chose not to piss people off."

Vernon sighed. "Fine, but if we miss out on those little crab cakes they serve in the executive dining room, I'll never forgive you."

I didn't have to go full Maddie on the Secret Service guy directing operations. He seemed grateful that I had alerted him to a gap in perimeter security. I stood and watched while he radioed the officer on poop duty and sent him around to watch the north corner of the building.

Greyson didn't want a fucking medal, and he certainly didn't want to take it from the tiny hands of Carlos Hernandez, who was not fit to lick his boots. He would go to the wretched ceremony, however. He would position his six-foot-seven body next to Carlos, who barely topped five foot eight. He wanted the photograph. He wanted everyone to compare the giant they could have had with the runt they ended up with. They would be sorry. That Greyson fully believed people would be sorry was a measure of how far he had drifted from reality.

The problem wasn't alcohol. After breaking the Persephone statue in the front hallway, he had suffered a murderous hangover that scared him back to sobriety. Then that wretched Birdie had flushed his remaining Percocet. He would have killed her but for the thought that he wouldn't have anyone to clean up the carnage.

Then Greyson lit on the solution that so many great men before him had chosen. He would write a book. He even had a title in mind—Spymaster Son of Spymaster. It would be a devastating account of how the Mines had declined since its glory days thanks to stifling Congressional oversight, political correctness, and lack of imagination. It would tell the story of the man who could have made the Mines great again, if only he had been given the chance. Maybe he could hire Alberta's novelist, Justine, to do the actual work of writing, which didn't appeal to him. The book would have a thick section of photographs in the middle depicting his life. Baby Greyson on his mother's lap in a peacock chair in Manila. Six-year-old Greyson astride a lion his father had shot on the Kenyan savanna. Teenage Greyson outside a brothel in Thailand surrounded by lovely, tiny women. And so on. Each photograph would build the image of a legend, a giant. Then, the last photo would be the one taken today with Mr. Boring Normal Pretty Dimples. Carlos would have a foolish frozen smile on his face, while Greyson would wear a look of dignified regret—not regret for himself but regret for the Mines. Greyson stopped in the men's room to check himself in the mirror to make sure his tie was straight. He licked a finger and worked the streak of gray in his eyebrow into a devil point.

I'd never been in the executive dining room of Hale Plaza. It was huge, big enough to do occasional duty as a conference room and awards suite. Today white-clothed tables had been pushed to one wall and set up for a buffet of finger foods, including those crab cakes Vernon loved. A bank of folding chairs filled the center of the room. Reserved signs marked the two front rows.

As a medal recipient, protocol directed me to sit on the end of the second row, so I wouldn't have to step over people on my way up to the lectern. My guests sat a few rows back. The horsemen were the last to settle. They milled about in front of the flags and deep blue curtains, as VIPs like to do. Greyson glared at the lectern. When everyone finally sat down, I removed my hearing aids. I had heard one too many cheesy award ceremony speeches. I would put them back in before my name was called. I was sitting behind tall people, so I didn't have the best view of the speakers. I occupied myself by looking out the floor-to-ceiling windows.

I saw a Caterico truck two streets away and wondered whether it was the same one that ran the four-way stop and almost hit us. I was relieved when it didn't turn toward Hale Plaza but continued south. Later, as the vice president stepped up to the lectern, I saw it again in the same place, coming from the same direction. He must have circled the building. That was weird. I kept my eyes on the intersection. The truck continued south again.

At this hour, Hamid should have been delivering dairy products to a facility in Vienna. Instead, he was circling Hale Plaza. On the next pass, he would turn onto the road that led directly to the entrance. He kept an eye on his watch. The ceremony was about to begin. The guests should be assembled. The vice president would be there. His heart raced. If he could get within forty yards of the building, he might kill the vice president of the United States.

Again, Hamid fretted about the extra security. He pulled to the side of the road. He would offer the security guards a special treat. He went around to the back of the truck and opened it. The cold felt good on his sweaty face. He tore into a cardboard box and removed a smaller box of ice cream bars, the kind covered in thick, dark chocolate and almonds.

At the gate, he handed the box out the window with a smile.

The guard took it. "Thanks, but you're going to have to delay your delivery until after the ceremony."

Hamid poured out the story he had prepared about forgetting to unload the new BOM's tiramisu and how he might lose his job if it didn't arrive in time.

The guard radioed his supervisor, who sent a message up to the executive dining room.

✦✦✦

When I saw the truck make the turn toward Hale Plaza, I got up and went to the nearest security guard. He frowned and told me to sit down. The vice president was administering the oath to Carlos.

I pointed to the truck sitting at the gate. "Radio down and tell them not to let that truck onto the compound."

"Go back to your seat," he said. "They won't let it in during a ceremony."

Very Important People frowned at us.

"I will not go back to my seat," I said loud enough to attract the attention of the room.

A member of the vice president's security detail came over to see if I was posing a threat. "Is there a problem?"

Then Carlos himself came over, leaving the vice president standing at the lectern. "What's up, Maddie?"

"Radio down and tell them not to let that truck on the compound. It's been circling the building."

"Do it," Carlos said to the guard.

He pulled his radio out and connected to the front gate. "Don't let the Caterico truck in."

He listened to the answer from the other end, and said, "It's okay. He's bringing your tiramisu. The chef okayed it."

The truck began to move through the gate.

"Jesus fucking Christ," I said. As the Secret Service agent grabbed the radio to countermand the chef's order, I ran to the stairwell and down three flights, somehow staying on my feet. Carlos was right behind me. I burst out the emergency exit on the first floor, setting off an alarm. I had no idea what I was doing. I ran toward the threat.

Hamid steered the truck on his usual route around the outer edge of the parking lot. He was ashamed to find himself shaking. He needed to be steady and run fast. Under the heavy vest, his torso was slick with sweat and itched. His lungs felt constricted, and breathing came hard. He drove to where trees partially obscured the view of the truck from the building. Hamid burst out of the cab and ran for an imaginary finish line forty yards from the building. Then he saw a woman running straight for him with a man right behind her. More men were coming from the front entrance with weapons raised. A gun fired. The bullet missed him, but he set his foot down on something slick and his legs went out from under him. As he hit the pavement, his thumb involuntarily pressed the detonator.

Hamid was seventy yards away from the building when he exploded. The bears did not detonate. The one person inside the building who could have set them off did not.

28

Oz Revisited

Hello, yellow brick road. I'm dreaming and I know it, but I can't wake up.

I look down at shoes glistening with blood, not rubies. My feet skip along, leaving droplets like pomegranate seeds on butter yellow brick. Abu Bunny and a deaf tabby scamper at my side. Flying monkeys—dense as starlings—blot the sun. I run, and the yellow brick sinks into the ground and becomes a crazy staircase with uneven steps, loose bricks, and shoes everywhere tripping me up. Sometimes my feet leave the steps, and I fall for several flights. Then I touch down again and keep running. I hear footsteps behind me. I know escape must be at the bottom, but the stairway doesn't end. Its geometry grows irrational, spiraling, branching, and turning upside down. Someone tackles me. The air fills with red smoke and falling paper. The stairway contracts, trapping me between walls of yellow brick. I scream and try to free myself.

Boom.

This is where I should wake up, but I don't. I sit bleeding in a pile of yellow brick as the smoke dissipates. When it has cleared, I see an unexploded bomb ten feet away, still ticking.

The nurses patted my shoulder as they tightened the restraints that kept me from flailing. I had been dreaming, but it was more than dreaming. A sense of urgency made it impossible to be still. "Not everything exploded!" I screamed.

Mom's face appeared, and then the Doodlebug with her message, "It's over."

"No, it's not," I said. I couldn't remember what it was that wasn't over. I had no memory of the attack, but I knew I had things to do. I tried again to get out of bed, but straps, dressings, and pain held me down.

"Quit trying to get up!" Mom wrote. "You'll tear your stitches." She spent the next hour on the Doodlebug summarizing what had happened at Hale Plaza, but nothing stirred my memory. The day was a blank. I didn't remember waking up, driving to work, or anything about the executive dining room. It was as if I had never been there. I did not remember the explosion. I was relieved to find that Carlos and I were the only injuries. He had tackled me right before the explosion. He would recover, although the fate of his left arm was still in doubt. Only the bomber died.

"Everyone is fine and dandy," my mother wrote. "And you're a hero!"

But nothing was fine and dandy, least of all me.

+ + +

In the coming months, my wounds healed, but my unease grew. My hearing returned, but memory of the Hale Plaza attack did not. When I came back to work, they assigned me to an innocuous job reviewing papers. It was a low-stress, low-difficulty assignment that should have been easy, but was not. I came to work with a satchel full of "issues" that made it hard for me to function. Issues that filled my colleagues, my mother, and my managers with concern.

I had migraines preceded by optic displays. My vision tunneled in from the periphery until I was completely blind for nearly an hour at a time. The darkness came quickly, leaving me stranded in hallways, groping around with an expression on my face that frightened people.

Mad Maddie grew madder. Management accused me of "randomly flipping off people in the cafeteria." False. There was nothing random about it.

The fog in my brain would not dissipate. Sometimes I drew a blank on the most familiar names, including the name of my immediate boss, who didn't appreciate being pointed at and called, "You, whoever the fuck you are."

I woke up screaming on three nights out of seven. I have amazing vocal cords. That is how my neighbors got involved.

Time got away from me. I couldn't keep the chronology of my life events straight. They moved back and forth in my memory and bumped up against each other. Amid some routine activity, a long-ago image would leap to the foreground with a vividness that jarred me out of the here and now and left me floundering in the what the fuck.

The black hole in my memory persisted, swallowing a terrorist attack that damn near killed me. I listened to many versions of what happened, but I couldn't judge which was closest to the truth. None sounded right.

In sum, I grew stranger and more annoying than I had ever been, and that is saying something. Vivi fussed over me. Vernon twirled a finger at his temple. Other people gave me the side-eye, slipped into stairwells to avoid me, and reported me to Medical. Finally, I got called into the BOM's office.

Carlos looked well, even though he had endured the same explosion that had turned me into walking mush. He didn't have the full use of his left arm, but otherwise he appeared whole, sane, and on top of his game. He smiled as he waved me to the sofa and sat down next to me.

"How are you doing, Maddie?" Carlos spoke to me gently, the way you would approach a feral cat.

"I suspect that you've already heard how I'm doing."

He nodded. "Reports have reached my desk. I want to offer you a short, therapeutic sabbatical—courtesy of the Mines."

I glared at him. "You don't want me to be here for the MOC hearings on the Hale Plaza attack."

A smile played at Carlos's lips. "Maddie, how do you think things would go if you appeared on the Hill in your current state? Be honest."

"I would probably do something inappropriate," I admitted.

"Wildly inappropriate," Carlos said, "and it would be all over the Internet, and you would never live it down."

"Okay," I said, "you're right. It would be a mistake for me to show up at the hearings, but I can't leave the Mines now. I have things to do. It's not over."

"It's over," Carlos said.

"Then who killed Alberta?" I asked.

"Leave that to the Organ."

"Constance Brand hasn't been arrested yet."

"The Justice Department is working on it. When they're ready, they'll move. Meanwhile, you need a break for your own health and sanity."

"No."

Carlos was a nice guy, but he wasn't a pushover. He looked me in the eye and said sternly, "This is not a suggestion; it is a condition of your continued employment. It's for everyone's good and especially yours. And it's just until you get your feet back on solid ground."

«29»

Maddie Zentangled

I had four weeks to sort myself. Four weeks of meditation, yoga, and healthy food. No alcohol. No caffeine other than green tea, which tasted like it was dipped straight from a frog pond. Limited sugar. I did have gummy bears hidden under my bed along with other contraband, but I had to ration it out. They didn't let me bring my car.

I had a handler, Elaine, a retiree on contract who used to run Special Employee Services, a unit created to work with miners gone weird. Elaine brought me to this mountaintop. It's an actual normal person retreat and not a Mines facility. We wear tags with our names rather than our clearance level. Doors are left unlocked and open. People don't cover their reading material or worry about being overheard. It's bizarre. Unprotected. I can't get used to it.

On my first morning, fifty people, mainly women, sat on grass and stone terraces set into the mountainside. We bundled up because it was early in the season. April, I think. The leaves had yet to stretch out and offer cover. The mountain felt exposed. My brain threatened to swell up and float out of my skull. Small sounds got lost in the rush of wind. Every branch and stalk swayed.

The view was spectacular, but, after decades in a cubicle, I found the space alarming. I felt something watching me from the woods. Despite my zafu, or ass cushion, I couldn't get comfortable. A petty demon in my lumbar region fired shooting pains up my spine. Don, the knot in my left shoulder, acted up. Don Knot and I have been together since the African embassy bombings. It's a terrible relationship, but apparently divorce is not an option. Don couldn't handle relaxation. He freaked out and radiated pain.

The meditation guide spoke in a syrupy monotone. She was a wiry, preternaturally flexible woman in a green hoodie and flow pants. I mentally nicknamed her Gumby. A small gong sat at her side. I prayed that she would thwonk it to signal the end of this session. Instead, she initiated an interminable round of alternate nostril breathing.

Urgency bubbled in my veins. I lost control and shrieked, "Somebody do something!"

I got the stink eye from Gumby. Elaine leaned over, squeezed my knee, and whispered, "Maddie, take a walk. I'll meet up with you at lunch."

I ran, leaving my zafu behind.

What was happening in the world? I had no idea. They had turned off the Wi-Fi because we were supposed to be on "digital detox." Anything could have been happening. War, terrorist attack, natural disaster. They might have been talking about me in the MOC hearings. Anything.

One of the staff told me about a spot where I might be able to use the signal from a nearby café. I hauled my aching body twenty feet up into a maple that leaned out over the east slope of the mountain. Below, I could see the Wi-Fi antenna on the roof of Bear Wallow Cafe. I had to call Vivi to find out what was going on in the world.

I held my phone out in various positions, but the signal was weak. Finally, I gave up, tucked it into the waistband of my shorts, and started to climb down. From the corner of my eye, I saw something large and dark and discovered why everything on the mountain was named after bears. The bear was thirty feet away. Oh, crap, it was two bears. Crap, crap, crap. Three bears.

I wasn't safe in the tree, but it would have been less safe to climb down. I froze. The bears were downwind. I hadn't brushed my teeth after a breakfast of oatmeal. Three bears and me with porridge breath. Shit.

I was going to die.

The bears paused to sniff a boulder. I eased myself back onto the branch I had been sitting on. Tension grew and I was afraid I would scream. I wished I had acquired some meditation skills.

Elaine thinks I suffer from monkey mind, but she's wrong. Monkey mind is capricious, restless, and all over the place. That's not me. I suffer from asshole mind, which is deliberate, constant, and focused on bad events, bad guys, or bad bureaucracy. It will not focus on my breathing.

A whimper escaped from my throat. I remembered the bears and glanced toward the rock. Nothing. I scanned the slope and finally saw them moving downhill.

I came to trust Elaine. She wasn't judgmental. She'd survived her years in the Mines with more peace and humor than most. I watched the breeze play with strands of her long, white hair as we sat in rocking chairs on the deck on a painfully bright, clear morning.

"After the Screamer Attack, I lost the plot and never found it again," I told her. "I found parts of it, but not enough to stop the next attack." I ran a thumb over the souvenir of the Hale Plaza attack, a thick ridge of keloid tissue on the side of my head. "I need to remember before I can move forward. Where do I even start?"

"Start by not obsessing," Elaine said. "Focus on this mountain and this moment. Let the memory come in its own time. You're not on a deadline up here."

"But there's always a deadline," I said. "If you don't figure things out before you reach the line, people die." I moved my fingers down to the bumpy, white ridge on my forearm. "You know, I tried to attend Shelby's funeral after the Screamer Attack even though I was still in bad shape. I got as far as crawling to the closet. I pulled out all my black shoes, but my vision was so blurry I couldn't find two that matched. I wanted to go because I had questions to ask him. Part of my brain knew he was dead, but another part thought I could walk up to the casket, pop the lid, and conduct a debriefing. That's how crazy I was then, and it's nothing compared to how crazy I am now."

Elaine's face showed no reaction. "What did you want to ask Shelby?"

"What did the horsemen know and when did they know it? Why didn't they tell people like me? Why were we the enemy?"

It was week two of digital detox. The leaves were further out. The wind was not as fierce. I was afraid to go into the woods because of the bears, so I walked the path that circled the lodges, cafeteria, and craft studios. I was trying to chill out, but I found myself ranting. I kicked leaves off the path and startled squirrels.

I obsessed over loose ends—the perpetrators who dropped off the radar, the odd behavior of certain people in our own government, the unknown sources of funding. I sped up to get ahead of the anxiety.

The money questions dogged me. Who paid to build that factory in Manchester? Dashiell's money went for bribes to legislators.

Westerly was not as rich as he appeared. Who paid? Why was this information never found? How did it connect to the Hale Plaza Attack?

I pumped my fist and made faces. I started singing the money song from *Cabaret*. Other walkers hurried past. Someone fetched Elaine. She emerged from the main lodge and approached me cautiously. "Maddie, are you all right?"

"Really, I'm fine."

"You're agitated."

"Agitated is my natural state. Don't worry unless I look calm. That means I'm dead."

"I have an idea," Elaine said. "Sitting on a cushion doesn't work for you so let's try walking meditation."

"That won't work either."

"Let's try," Elaine said.

It took forever for her to talk me through the first step. I tried to follow instructions. I focused on my center of balance, shifted my weight from heel to toe, felt the movement of every muscle and the twinges from old foot damage.

"Relax," Elaine said. "You look like you're in pain. Don't make it difficult. Walking is the most natural thing in the world."

But it wasn't. I couldn't remember how to do it. My foot cramped, my body jerked, and my head swam. I pitched forward.

Elaine looked down at me. "I thought you used to dance ballet."

"Not in slow motion." I got up and brushed the dirt off. "I need to move. Not think about moving. Move." I took off down the path. Elaine didn't try to follow.

The wind died, and a thick fog settled on Hidden Bear Mountain, whiting out the distances. It was not as thick as the fog in my mind.

"What's your biggest source of anxiety at the moment?" Elaine asked as we headed back to the lodges after breakfast.

"My head doesn't work like it used to."

"You'll learn to compensate," Elaine said. "The brain can rewire itself. Give your brain and yourself time to recover."

"Time is running out. Things don't add up. There are things we should know by now, but we don't because someone or something is throwing a wrench in the works. They gave me the job of finding out why; then they made sure I couldn't."

"Who made sure you couldn't?"

"The big pine cones."

"Big pine cones?"

"The muckety-mucks. The powers that be, whatever you want to call them."

The healthy food was getting to me. I speared a square coated in an oily-looking sauce and gave the server a questioning look.

"Teriyaki tempeh," he said, "but I call it 'Cubes in Lube.'"

I dropped my fork.

Our server, Nelson, was tall and thickly tattooed. He sported a waist-length white beard, which he clubbed like a British sailor's ponytail during food service. He had a soft mountain accent.

"You don't eat this, do you?" I asked him.

He laughed. "Hell no. I pack my lunch when you yoga people are here."

"I'm not a real yoga person," I say. "I was coerced into being here."

Later, as I circled the mountaintop, I spotted him taking in the empty trashcans. I stopped and struck up a conversation. I discovered that Nelson was in a long-term relationship with George, the cook, who hated the low-fat menus. They held a yearly pig roast with pies and cakes for dessert.

Nelson shoved the trashcans into a wooden shed, slammed the door, and padlocked it. I was about to ask why he needed to lock up empty trashcans, but then I knew why.

"Bears," I said.

He chuckled. "Yep, they can chew up the cans pretty bad." His tone was affectionate.

The next morning, as Nelson cleared the breakfast plates, he winked and slipped me something wrapped in a napkin. I slid it into a pocket and excused myself. I hurried outside, ducked behind a bush, and unwrapped the napkin to find three large peanut butter chocolate chunk cookies. I almost fainted.

I timed my walks to run into Nelson when he took in the cans. We would talk for a few minutes before he slipped me some napkin-wrapped treat. He told me that this place was built by a man who got rich quarrying stone from the local mountains and used his money to create what he called a religious retreat.

"You say that like it was something else," I said.

"They were KKK. Burned the crosses right on the other end of the parking lot." He pointed. "Right where that big tree stands. Most of them weren't local. They were rich men from all over."

I shuddered. Where could you go and not find a thick vein of hatred just beneath the surface?

"They lost the place during the Depression," Nelson said. "It's been through a few hands. Been rebuilt. These latest owners, the Eastmans, started the Hebrew Specialty Company. Made their money selling hotdogs."

The coincidence sent a chill up my spine. The Hebrew Specialty Company made the hotdogs sold at Burton Oil Park, the ones that terrorists laced with cyanide and handed to several children just as RC planes dropped smoke bombs on the crowd.

"What's wrong?" Nelson said. "It looks like you seen a ghost."

"Some days, all I see are ghosts," I said.

In my next session with Elaine, I brought up the KKK roots of Hidden Bear Mountain.

"Yes," she said, "Beth Eastman burned sage for days when she moved in. There are old photos in the library."

"Where?"

"There's a big album on the table in the back corner next to the display of local pottery. It covers the history of this place from white hoods to flow pants."

After lunch, I made my way to the back of the library, pulled up a stool, and turned to the first page of the massive book. It was an image of this mountaintop after clearcutting—all stumps and debris. I paged through the construction of the first frame buildings, to the dedication ceremony, to the eerie image of a burning cross right where Nelson said it would be.

I turned pages and watched the trees grow back, saw white frame buildings replaced by rustic-looking lodges. The ground where hooded figures stood was paved for parking. The gatherings grew gentler—artists, writers, religious groups, environmentalists, yoga retreats.

The place had been rededicated to higher ideals, but I felt the thrum of threat. The photos of antisemitic graffiti recently left on the long drive up the mountain were part of the anxiety, but not the main part. I said a quiet apology to the bears for thinking that they were the scariest things here.

Don Knot sent a wave of pain down my arm. I recognized the feeling. Forgotten Vein Anxiety. Blind Side Heebie-Jeebies. Out of Left Field Willies. The downside of living inside of categories and wiring diagrams and artificial divisions. The thing that doesn't fit, doesn't follow your rules, will explode.

If only threats would stay in their assigned categories. I closed the album. Those photos weren't history, and we had not turned the page. I felt a connection where there shouldn't be one. I felt the ground beneath my feet shift and begin to liquefy. My vision faded from the edges. I stumbled back to my room, closed the curtains, and dove under the covers.

The second day of my migraine coincided with the arrival of a new group on Hidden Bear Mountain. The yoga people didn't fill the dormitories, so management had booked the Highland Heritage Society for the next week. I sat on the deck and watched them unload long black bags. Too short to be rifle bags, I decided.

Rifles would have been quieter.

The next morning, I was under the covers trying to avoid light when I heard something that sounded like cows being slaughtered. Bagpipes. I was no longer the least zen person on the mountain. The yoga retreaters were losing it. I could hear agitated voices outside.

Things got ugly at dinner. The yoga people occupied tables on the south side of the cafeteria. The Highland Heritage Society took the north side. Instead of the regular hum of conversation in the room, it was whispering and side-eye. Then, into the demilitarized zone down the middle of the room, the servers rolled carts full of dessert— tiramisu.

The Highland Heritage Society had evidently chosen the "no restrictions" menu. As they sat lapping up their mascarpone, the murmuring among the yoga people grew angry. One woman knocked over her glass of tea and stomped from the room.

Later that night, Elaine came in wild-eyed and frazzled. "I just broke up a fight between two women in their late seventies. One of them pulled out a fistful of hair." She collapsed into a chair. "Tomorrow I'm going to drive into town. I'll get a king-size bottle of extra-strength migraine pills and ear plugs for everyone. And a heating pad for Don Knot. Hang in there. One of the staff has volunteered to take the bagpipe people on a wildflower hike tomorrow. Maybe she can lead them off a cliff."

Things finally got quiet after midnight. I fell asleep and started to dream.

> *I'm back in the ruined headquarters building watching Greyson burn. Not papers, a cross anchored in a cement-filled trashcan. Alberta appears from an inner office with her regular human head attached to the body of an enormous goose. Greyson hisses at her. Alberta plucks a feather from her tail and uses it to poke at Greyson until she has backed him into a corner.*

> *"Sit still!" she says, "while I tell you a story." Alberta pulls a large picture book from under her wing, opens it, and reads the title: "The Pet Scapegoat." Greyson-kitty snarls. Alberta pulls out a whip and lashes him. A window opens in the wall behind Alberta. Outside I see the Mines auditorium, the Bubble, expanding like an actual bubble.*

> *"Look!" I yell. "Look at what's happening!"*

> *"Once upon a time," Alberta reads, "there was a nasty little goat who caused all the problems in the world."*

*I watch the Bubble expand until its shell grows thin
enough to reveal the auditorium seats inside. They
are filled with people. No, not people, cows.*

"Look out!" I yell.

*"Everything bad was caused by that one little goat,"
she continues.*

The Bubble explodes, and the cows bawl.

The Highland Heritage Society was up. I wondered if I could find another explosion to render me completely deaf.

The mountain made me cry. I'm not usually a crier, except for the one sob fest I allow myself after each terrorist attack. Now the tears flowed free and at odd moments. I would be staring at the view, or sitting down to a meal, or walking around the path and suddenly, without warning, my face was wet. Elaine said the mountain does that to some people. "The things you've pushed away catch up to you here." When I asked her what to do about it, she said, "Just cry."

I was too restless to stay inside at night. The weather turned warm, and the lodges grew stuffy. The bagpipes people left, replaced by astronomers. I didn't worry about the bears anymore. The bagpipes had driven them deep into the forest. I did the circular walk after the sun went down and watched the stars come out so much brighter than they did at home. The air was cool and sweet with the smell of some unknown spring blossom.

I walked slowly. Some parts of the path were lit by the lights from the lodges, but others were dark. I was fine with the darkness, the rustle of leaves, the mournful sound of owls. Not everything had to be turned into a threat.

✦ ✦ ✦

I woke at 4:00 a.m. to the honking of geese, but there were no geese on Hidden Bear Mountain. This gaggle swam in my head bumping into fake boobs, American flags, crab cakes, and tiramisu. For forty minutes I blinked into the darkness as the images shivered, rearranged themselves, and finally coalesced into memory. I directed my gaze at a sleeping Elaine, trying to shake her awake with telekinesis.

Shortly after six, she opened her eyes and detected my laser focus. "Good grief, Maddie, what is it?"

"I remember the day of the attack."

"Hold that thought." When she returned from the bathroom, she wrapped herself in a fluffy robe and sat cross-legged on my bed. "What do you remember?"

"The fog. The security guard hosing goose poop. The Executive Dining Room. Blue curtains and flags. The Caterico truck coming through the gate. I remember running down the stairs and coming out in the parking lot. Then it all goes black."

I began to tremble, and Elaine took my hand. "It was an awful thing to go through."

I shook my head. "It's not that it was awful; it's that remembering it doesn't give me the answers I was hoping for. It's not over."

The Other Bear Drops

I t is the beginning of our last week on the mountain. They relaxed the rules so we could prepare to re-enter society. They encouraged us to hike down to Bear Wallow Cafe to catch up on social media, contact our pet sitters, and arrange to return home.

I sat at a live-edge wood bar with a mug of good coffee, a slice of peanut pie, my phone, and four blessed bars indicating an actual, working Wi-Fi signal. I had the expected backlog of messages from Mom, a few pics from Vivi of Abu Bunny, and a completely unexpected bunch of messages from Vernon.

I need to talk to you.

I need to talk to you ASAP.

What the fuck, Maddie? Call me.

Shit. Fan. Collision. CALL ME!

Fourteen messages in all, each one more urgent than the last. I put the phone down and finished my coffee and pie. I steeled myself for whatever fuckery I was about to encounter. I picked up my phone and punched in Vernon's number.

"Finally!" he said by way of greeting.

"What's up?"

"Mines Idiot Oversight Committee."

"I take it the hearings aren't going well?"

"Guess where they're directing the heat?"

"At the guilty?" I said.

"Very funny. Strangely enough, there is no mention of Senator Harrison Westerly, or even Gordy Grant, or the way Dashiell Aspling got his job, or any of the people responsible for getting Dashiell his job. You know who they're coming down on instead?"

I didn't want to know.

"Vivi."

"Vivi!" I shouted.

"UK-based groups were part of her account. She didn't connect the dots."

"Only because somebody deleted the most important dots. They're mentioning her by name?"

"They called her in to testify, and it went south. You know Vivi—too willing to accept blame. She got flustered. She cried. The press is blowing it into a mammoth shit show."

"She must be in introvert hell right now. We have to do something."

"We have to leak something," Vernon said, and I knew what he was referring to.

"You can't. We're not high enough on the food chain to risk leaking anything without going to jail. Besides, I keep my promises, oaths, and agreements. There must be another way to turn attention to the actual guilty parties."

"Unless we can get Harrison Westerly to confess, I don't see how."

"Did you ever figure out where he is?"

"No.

"Thelma didn't know?"

After a long pause, Vernon said, "There was an incident with Thelma. She took something I said wrong or something. Anyway, she made it clear I'm to keep my distance."

"Why didn't you tell me? I'll fix it. I'll call and tell her you're not as sleazy as you look. So, keep your eyes on her face. I'm sure she can find where Westerly is. She has more sources than the Black Mines."

The next afternoon, I race walked around the mountain path making emphatic hand gestures and trying to think of something I could do. As I passed the gazebo, I saw a familiar truck coming up the winding driveway.

It couldn't be. But it was. It was Vernon Keene, hundreds of miles south and west of where he belonged. He waved and honked to get my attention, as if I wouldn't notice his oversized truck with its oversized tires and "MORM&4U" license plate. The first few years I knew him, I thought he was Mormon, until he told me the plate meant "More man for you."

Vernon pulled off the road, parking on top of a patch of lady slippers.

"Get off the flowers!" I yelled.

He ignored me and cut the motor.

"What are you doing here?"

He jumped out of the truck wearing camo. "I needed to consult, and I didn't want to do this over the phone," he says. "Nice country. Thought I might get some hunting in as long as I'm down here."

"Don't shoot the bears," I said. "I'm coming to terms with them."

He shook his head. "This time of year, all I can shoot is groundhogs, nutria, coyotes. It's target practice, at least."

We sat down in the gazebo. Vernon gave me a searching look. "So, are you ... less weird than you were?"

"I am as weird as ever and proud of it. Why are you here?"

"Thelma found Westerly's location. Now you need to make him 'fess up."

"Me? What? How?"

"You," Vernon says, "because you have a way with marginal personalities like Dashiell's ditsy wife. And because Westerly is on the next mountain."

"What?"

Vernon points south. "His family's summer home is right over there. Do you believe it? It's like providence is tossing the ball in your court."

"From what I hear his brain is functioning even worse than mine."

"You two will get along great. I'll be hunting, but I'll check my phone. Text me on your progress."

Standing on the top tier of the amphitheater, looking south with borrowed binoculars, I could see Harrison Westerly's place, a grand amalgam of cabin, fort, and castle cantilevered over the hillside. Everybody knows everybody else in mountain communities, so I asked Nelson about it.

"The Westerlys have been here forever. My sister is his nurse."

I slapped my forehead and cursed myself for not questioning Nelson more thoroughly about his family. It's only polite.

Nelson continued. "She used to work in a nursing home down the mountain, but after the senator retired, she got hired to look after him."

"How is he doing?"

"He has his days. He's in and out, like old people get. He mainly talks to his bird."

"I thought the bird died."

"This is a new one. Its name is Orrin, but he calls it Dirksen."

Nelson drove me to the Westerly place and dropped me at the foot of the driveway. He'd armed me with pockets full of the dry, fibrous, gluten-free mini muffins served in the cafeteria, as well as grapes and pine nuts. These were the parrot's favorite treats. Nelson warned me about the bird and about his sister Nancy. "She scares some people," he said. "She's protective, so don't upset the senator."

When Nancy opened the door, I looked up at her towering, buzz-cut, tattooed figure and blurted out, "You look exactly like Nelson."

"I know," she said. "Well come on in. I don't know why I let Nelson talk me into this, but he says you're good people." She frowned at me. "So behave like it. Don't rile the senator and don't piss off the bird."

"I brought muffins," I said meekly.

"Don't give any to the senator," Nancy said, "or he'll choke." She led me through a house that was as strange, in its way, as Dashiell Aspling's home office. The Westerly family blew a lot of money on taxidermy. Deer gazed from the walls, while smaller creatures lurked below.

"Oh my fucking god," I said as I almost tripped over a stuffed badger. "Rich people are weird."

"Honey, you don't know the half of it," Nancy said.

The place needed cleaning. Cobwebs stretched between antlers and dust covered high-end examples of local crafts. Everything was labeled, as if this were a museum. At some point, a professional decorator had been involved, but a lesser aesthetic had taken over. A gaudy ceramic Jesus lamp sat next to a beautiful raku vase. A spectacular blown glass bowl was filled with candy wrappers and used tissues. A fleece Confederate flag throw was tossed over a leather Eames chair in the corner.

A big white bird sat on the back of that chair, so still he could be stuffed. He screamed, and I almost jumped out of my skin. Then I noticed the wrinkled, shrunken face buried in fleece. I barely recognized Senator Westerly.

"I made him put his hearing aids in for your visit," Nancy said. She addressed the senator in a loud voice. "There's a lady here to see you. Be nice. You, too, bird." She left us alone.

I took a muffin out of my pocket and approached cautiously. "Hello?"

"Hello," the bird replied, and then repeated the word several times. Westerly said nothing. He looked frightened.

"Well, aren't you a pretty bird, Orrin?" I said in my most ingratiating voice. I stretched out my hand. "Want a treat?"

Orrin cocked his head. The bare, wrinkled patch around his eye gave him a wise look. "Treat?" he said. His crest lifted, fluffed, and flattened again.

I edged close enough for him to take the muffin from my hand. His beak was huge, but he snagged the muffin with a delicate touch, leaving me all of my fingers. Orrin transferred the muffin to one talon and proceeded to take small bites, dropping crumbs onto the fleece. He kept a wary eye on me.

"Dirksen!" The senator said loudly. "His name is Dirksen! Everybody gets it wrong."

"Okay. Thanks for correcting me. Dirksen it is. He's beautiful."

"You'll never see a more magnificent example of a bare-eyed cockatoo. He's smart, too."

"I can see that," I said. I had urgent questions for the senator, but I was willing to flatter the bird as long as necessary to soften him up.

"He loves me," the senator said. "I don't know how he'll manage when I die. There's a lady who's going to take him, but it won't be the same."

The catch in his voice triggered an unexpected wave of sympathy. He was once one of the most powerful men in the country, but now he was failing, frightened, and living in a world he didn't recognize. I tried to reassure him. "That lady will love him so much. How could she not? He's a rock star."

The senator nodded. "He is a rock star."

Orrin dropped the remaining fragment of muffin. The senator reached for it. I grabbed it first, remembering Nancy's warning. Orrin raised his crest. "Treat?" he said.

I gave him a grape from my pocket. He took it and began to hollow it out with surgical precision.

"Who are you?" the senator asked. "I know you from somewhere."

"My name is Maddie James."

The name rang an alarm bell. The senator's eyes got big. "Mines?"

"Yes, I'm from the Mines. I testified before your committee."

"Goose chaser?" he asks.

"Yes, that's what the press called me after you questioned me." Annoyed at the memory of that embarrassing nickname, I pushed too far. "I came to ask you about the Screamer Attack."

"The what?"

"The Screamer Attack on the Mines."

The senator shrank into the fleece. "I don't know anything about that."

"You paid for it. But it wasn't all your money. You got the money somewhere else. I need to know where. I was injured in that attack." I show the ugly scar on my arm.

Westerly disappeared completely under the fleece.

"Treat?" said the bird.

I offered another muffin.

The senator's head reappeared, and he bellowed, "Leave, now!"

Nancy came running and coldly escorted me out.

I lowered my eyes to avoid Nelson's look of reproach. Nancy must have given him hell for sending over an idiot to upset the senator. I thought I'd lost my chance, but that afternoon, Nelson flagged me down from my walk.

"The senator wants to see you," he said.

"I'll need more muffins," I said.

Nancy glared at me when she opened the door. "I'll tell you again, and this time, listen. Do not rile the senator." She led me back to the fleece-covered chair.

Orrin recognized me and screamed, "Treat!"

I pulled a muffin out of my pocket and offered it up. Westerly's head slowly emerged from the fleece.

"I did it," he croaked. Tears ran down his fissured cheeks. "I was angry, but I didn't mean to hurt anybody. I told the man to phone in a warning first. Then I got my new Dirksen, and I wasn't angry anymore. I told him to cancel the attack, but he didn't. He didn't warn anybody." The senator's eyes fixed on my scarred arm. "I'm sorry. I did things I didn't know how to undo." His voice lowered to a whisper. "Now I'm going to Hell." He shrank back into the fleece.

I took a long breath. "May I sit down?"

The senator nodded. "I was angry. Now I'm ... confused."

"I'm confused a lot, too," I said. "I got a concussion. Then another concussion. Sometimes I wake up and I don't know where in my life I am."

"Yes!" Westerly said. "That's exactly it. Sometimes I think I'm still powerful and angry. But I can't remember why."

I pulled up a hand-carved rocker. "Tell me how it happened," I said gently.

His narrative jumped wildly in time and place. He spoke at length about the murder of his son. He was talking about the original Dirksen.

"They killed him," he said with a sob in his voice. "The Mines. The damn Mines. You people. That's why I ...." He shut his eyes and went quiet.

"What?" I prompted.

"I didn't mean to hurt your arm." The senator stared at my scar. I folded my arms to cover it.

"I know you didn't. Just tell me who you worked with. Was it Gordy Grant?"

The senator started at the name. "He made it sound like it was my idea, but it was his idea. An attack. But he said he would phone in a warning. Then the screamers would shake the building down. But there were lots of people in the building. They got hurt and the building didn't fall. I didn't mean to ..." His voice trailed off.

"It wasn't your money that paid for the attack, was it?" I said. "At least not all of it."

The senator shook his head. "I was having cash flow issues. I got investment advice from that little bald man that eventually helped, but at the time, I was short."

"Little bald man?"

"Dashiell Hammett."

"You mean Dashiell Aspling? The Boss of Mines?"

The senator nodded. "He really wanted to be a spy."

"He gave you insider information that allowed you to make your money back?"

The senator's eyes shifted downward. "It was a suggestion. I wouldn't call it insider information."

"You pushed Dashiell to hire Kreative Industrial Sunlight Solutions to change out all the lights in the Mines?"

He nodded. "It was Gordy's idea."

"The money that was funneled to Manchester. Where did it come from?"

The senator looked down and said softly, "My social club."

"What's the name of your social club?"

"I don't like to say."

"You need to say if you ever want to be forgiven for your role in the attack. What was the name of your group?" I asked.

The words come slowly. "Brotherhood of the Blood Drop Cross."

I had heard of them. "They're right-wing extremists," I said.

"The left wingers are the extremists," he muttered. "The brothers are good people."

"Good people who funded a terrorist attack?"

This point seemed to confuse the senator. "I thought I ...." His lower lip began to tremble. "I thought I knew things. There were things I was sure about, but I don't know anymore."

"Yeah, I used to think I knew stuff, too." I watched Orrin preen as I tried to process what Westerly was telling me. "Gordy was also a member of the Brotherhood?"

"He was my cut-up."

"You mean cutout? How did you know Gordy? How did you know he was sympathetic to your cause?"

The senator frowned in confusion.

I tried to jog his memory. "Did you meet him in your office? Was he there to give you a briefing?"

"I never let him come to my office."

"Then where did you meet him?"

The senator chewed on something. Maybe memories. Finally, he raised a finger. "Black Barn! Yes, that's it."

"You met in a black barn?" I say. "Out in the country?"

"Near the metro stop."

"What metro stop?"

"In Virginia."

"Orange line? Blue line? Yellow line?"

"One of those."

"And it was a barn? A black barn?" The only kind of barn I could think of near a metro stop was a Dress Barn, and I couldn't see the senator and Gordy having a tête-à-tête between racks of polyester blouses.

"Not as clean as I like. I never ate anything."

"Was it a restaurant?"

"Greasy spoon. Gordy liked it. He always ordered black bean soup and fries. He dipped the fries in the soup. Disgusting."

I knew the place. "The Black Bean," I said. "It's a Cuban restaurant called the Black Bean."

"I'm sure it was Black Barn," the senator said.

"It has booths with coral benches and lime-green Formica tables?"

"Well, yes, but I'm sure it's called the Black Barn."

"No, it's the Black Bean, after the soup. It's their specialty."

The senator grumbled under his breath. He did not like being contradicted. He started to withdraw into the fleece throw.

"No," I said. "You're right. It's the Black Barn." The name didn't matter. "So how did you come to meet him? Why were you both at the Black Barn at the same time?"

"Somebody gave me his contact info."

"Who?"

The senator sighed. "Sofa."

"Sofa?"

Westerly pointed to a nearby sofa. His voice trailed off; then his face lit up. "Davenport. He's the Big Brother."

"Davenport gave you Gordy's contact information?"

The senator let out a snort of impatience. "That's what I said. Are you slow?"

"Yes," I said. "I'm slow. You said you introduced Gordy to the Brotherhood of Blood, but then you said the head of the Brotherhood gave you Gordy's contact information. Which way was it?"

"Well, both. Davenport hadn't met Gordy, but he'd heard about him. The Brotherhood wanted to recruit someone from the Organ, and I needed a cut-up to keep me up to date on Brotherhood activities."

"Who told Davenport about Gordy?"

"I don't know. Davenport knew lots of things about people in government. More than me. I don't know how. I asked him once, and he got mad and said, "I have graphite in my pencil. That's all I'm going to say."

"Graphite in his pencil? Do you have any idea what he meant?"

The senator shook his head mournfully. "I don't know. I'm tired. I used to be mad; now I'm tired, sad. I'm going to Hell. There's no way to atone."

"You can confess. You can make sure that the Brotherhood never pulls off another terrorist attack."

"They wouldn't do that," he said, but I could tell from his voice that he knew they would.

I pulled my rocker closer and looked into his eyes. "If you want atonement—peace—you have to work for it. You can't sit up here and hope nothing else bad happens. You have to talk to the Organ and testify against the Brotherhood."

"My reputation ..." The senator's voice trails off. "The public outcry ..."

"Will not be as hot as Hell," I said with emphasis on the H word, which pushed all the senator's buttons.

"I don't want to go to Hell." Westerly's voice broke, but then he said, "I don't want to go to jail either."

"You won't go to jail. You can cut a deal, use your lawyers to delay, all the things that powerful people do to avoid consequences."

The senator brightened. "You're right. I know how to do those things." His face clouded. "But what about God?" He started to cry, and I joined him, because the tears came too easily these days. I held his hand as we blubbered over the wrong steps we had taken. Orrin joined in with an eerily good imitation of the senator's mewling sobs. The man must have cried a lot.

I met Vernon that afternoon at the entrance to the retreat. I eyed his hunting rifle as I climbed into the truck. "Did you kill anything?" I asked.

"Groundhog," Vernon said. "Got him with my right front tire. I wasn't even trying."

We drove to the nearest overlook on the Blue Ridge Parkway and sat on a low stone wall with a view of Table Rock Mountain. I repeated my conversation with the senator. When I got to the part about the Brotherhood, Vernon let out a whistle.

"Damn. What an alliance. Looks like we're about to spend quality time with our counterparts on the domestic side. They can probably find the evidence to round up the Brotherhood even without Westerly's input, but it would certainly expedite the process, not to mention ensuring convictions. But that connection doesn't explain everything."

I shook my head. "It doesn't explain Alberta's death or how a likely Russian-made poison made it onto a deck of Mines logo playing cards. Do you think it could be Greyson? Does that mean the events aren't connected? That the timing was a coincidence?" I thought back to my conversation with the senator. "Westerly said that Davenport knew a lot about people in the government."

"Didn't Westerly wonder about that?"

"He did ask. All Davenport said was 'I have graphite in my pencil.'"

"What is that supposed to mean?" Vernon said. "I mean, I know what the phrase 'lead in my pencil' means, but how does it make sense in that context?"

"We're getting this filtered through Harrison Westerly. Who knows what was actually said?"

Vernon paused to consider. "Suppose those are Davenport's exact words. What does that say about him?"

"That he's either being hyper correct about what's in a pencil or he's not a native speaker of English."

Vernon muttered "graphite" and "pencil." Then he came out with a foreign phrase—" У меня в карандаше грифель."

"I keep forgetting you were a Russia analyst. Say that again?" I made him repeat the phrase several times. "Okay, just say the word that starts with a K sound."

"Карандаш. Ka-ran-dash."

Again, I had him repeat the word. The rhythm of it sounded familiar. Finally, I yelled, "Karen Dasch!"

"What?"

"Greyson's secretary's name is Karen Dasch."

"That woman who looks like a toad? A Russian agent? I never knew her last name. She's been with him forever." Vernon jumped to his feet and issued a stream of profanity foul enough to impress even me. "That would explain—" he stopped, spread his arms wide, and stared up to the heavens. "That would explain so much. Is she still working in the Mines?"

"I think so." Darkness crept in at the periphery of my vision. I shielded my eyes with a hand to shut out the light. "It's not over. We've circled back to the Cold War. Our whole careers have been one long, slow circle. Every sleazebag imaginable is connected to every other sleazebag imaginable, and the only guiding principle is chaos."

Vernon intoned, "What rough beast slouches towards Nottingham?"

"Bethlehem."

"What?"

"Slouches toward Bethlehem, not Nottingham," I said. "It's not a poem about Robin Hood."

Vernon grew huffy. "I'm sure it's Nottingham. I had to memorize it in high school English. I even made a diorama of Sherwood Forest with Styrofoam and sticks."

"You didn't ace that class, did you?" I asked.

Karen Dasch now worked on the first floor of Hale Plaza. It was quite a comedown after being Greyson's secretary, but she chose this job for its location. She was alone in the office. Everyone else was at a three-hour training course. She had volunteered to stay back to answer the phones. She let them ring, however, as her eyes moved from the clock to the three angel bears sitting in her window. She had placed a trash can full of combustibles below the window and disabled the sprinklers in the vault. Soon she would touch the Mines logo cigarette lighter in her hand to the trashcan and throw in the bears. The explosion would create a chain reaction up the side of the building. Not as devastating as it would have been in combination with the explosion from the suicide vest, but it was the best she could do.

She should have set the bears off on the day Hamid blew up. That was the backup plan in case Hamid didn't get close enough. Her nerve failed, and the operation fizzled. Davenport was furious.

Months later, the bears still sat in the window, soaking up the sun. The explosive inside would be easily detectible to the bomb-sniffing dogs now. The dogs never went through the vaulted offices, but they would go over every box when the occupants of Hale Plaza moved back to the Old Headquarters Building next week. Tomorrow was packing day.

Karen had been under heavy pressure from Davenport to set the bears off. She delayed because she didn't want to die. She hoped to find a way to set them off remotely, but that would increase the chances that the operation would fail, and she would still die. Davenport made it plain that this was the punishment for failure. And it would be a hard death.

The ingratitude! She had assassinated a Boss of Mines. But Davenport considered this a failure, too, because it didn't put Greyson Earl in the BOM's desk with Karen right outside his door.

It would have to be today.

Karen planned to detonate the explosions at nine o'clock, but at two minutes 'til, she moved it to nine thirty. Since then, she'd been hating herself for her cowardice. She would not delay again. She secured the vault door so that nothing would interrupt the operation, but as the time drew near, she heard someone working the combination. Karen got to her feet and rushed toward the trashcan as a security guard and several armed 110 agents burst through the door. She tried to flick the lighter, but her hands shook. Other hands shoved her against a cabinet, cuffed her, and hustled her out of the building.

Epilogue

Deacon Davenport, real name Vasiliy Komarov, shed his mutton chops, thick glasses, and bolo tie and fled the country the same day that Karen Dasch—AKA Katarina Morozova—was arrested. He left his blood brothers to face prosecution alone. Apparently, he was the only one in the Brotherhood connected to Russian intelligence. He had been sent to the United States to deepen divisions in the country. Mission accomplished.

Westerly fessed up to the 110, struck a plea deal, and went to his eternal reward shortly thereafter—whatever that reward might be.

Orrin, AKA Dirksen, landed softly in a new home where he had other cockatoo friends.

Investigators determined that Greyson had no knowledge of Karen's connection to Russian intelligence and no role in Alberta's death, but he was left looking like a fool. He dropped plans to write a book and moved to a small tropical island. Rumor has it that he spends his time sitting on a peacock chair on his front porch, drinking rum and lobbing coconuts at anyone who dares approach his house. Birdie has a tan for the first time in her life.

The Mines damage assessment report is likely to run to several volumes.

Shannon Aspling gave birth to a healthy boy, and Stella, AKA Twerkin', had four healthy kittens. Shannon is keeping them all. She ended the relationship with her lawyer, who is allergic to cats.

Meanwhile, the Esteemed Legislative Body is too busy with its own problems to dismantle the Mines. Authorities are still trying to track down the witting and unwitting connections between Russian agents, American extremists, foreign extremists, and legislators. The link chart must look like an Olympic game of pick-up sticks. The ethics investigations are running into the wee hours. A wave of retirements, starting with Constance Brand, hit the senior legislative ranks. Reforms to prevent lawmakers from profiting from insider information are being seriously discussed. Seriously, it's in committee and everything. I'm sure it will happen.

Carlos is quietly working to set things right in the Mines and keep us out of the news. He is the most popular BOM in living memory.

Only Vernon knows about my role in getting Westerly to come clean, so I don't have to testify before any committees. Reporters don't call me or Vivi. We are blissfully forgotten.

With the help of daily meditation, my mind has cleared enough for me to return to work. Yes, I said meditation. I finally sat my butt down and got serious. It helped. What can I say? I was wrong about the woo woo stuff.

My brain is not the same, but that's all right. I'm learning how to use it differently. A wonky brain can be uniquely useful in wonky times. I let other people do the fast-breaking stuff. I look for insights elsewhere. I still write papers that piss people off, which is as close as Maddie gets to a happily ever after.

Glossary of Terms

alchemist. A slang term for analyst in the Mines.

Auger. Electronic terrorism database.

Base, the. The English translation of al'Qaida.

Black Mines. The operational sector of the Mines responsible for clandestine intelligence gathering.

BLIP. To judge as Below the Level of Interest of the Policymaker.

bomb dissector (BD). Counterterrorism specialist.

Boss of Mines (BOM). The presidentially appointed director of the Mines.

BOM Tunnel. The corridor in the Mines where portraits of former BOMs hang.

canary crew. A special team set up to handle a particular terrorist threat.

Central Counterterrorism Supersector (CCSS). The unit responsible for following terrorist threats.

Daily Threat Roster (DTR). A listing of current threats.

Drones. Administrative personnel.

DoneIntel. Published and disseminated intelligence.

Ear, the. Familiar name for the National Audio Collection Agency.

Evil Empire. The Soviet Union.

Esteemed Legislative Body (ELB). Congress.

face boss. Line manager.

grouper. Foreign asset, agent.

hadiths. A narrative record of the sayings of Muhammad.

Heartland Defense. A new agency of government set up after the Strikes to defend the homeland from a dearth of agencies responsible for defending the homeland.

Internal Investigative Organ (IIO, in the Mines known simply as "the Organ"). The agency responsible for domestic law enforcement.

Main Shaft. The executive wing of the Mines, headed by the Boss of Mines.

Mines. The agency responsible for gathering and assessing foreign intelligence for the president.

Mines Fine Arts and Historical Preservation Committee (MFAHPC, pronounced emfahpsee). More powerful than the name suggests, the MFAHPC includes influential senior officials and retirees.

National Audio Collection Agency (known in the Mines as "the Ear"). The agency responsible for the collection of audio intelligence from satellites, wiretaps, etc.

New Shafts Building (NSB). Built in the 1980s, it lies to the west of the Old Shafts Building at Mines Headquarters.

Old Shafts Building (OSB). The original headquarters building of the Mines.

Paper Mines. The administrative sector of the Mines.

Pentagon Council of the Wise (PentCOW). A temporary unit set up in the Pentagon to take intelligence rejected by the Mines and turn it into casus belli.

President's Intelligence Update (PIU). Daily "newspaper" of the most critical intelligence for the president and a few top officials.

rockslide. An unfortunate public incident involving the Mines.

slag. The daily inflow of intelligence cables, intercepts,

diplomatic reports, etc.

subshaft. A small work unit focusing on a specific subject area.

Safety and Security Sector (sss). A unit in the Mines responsible for grounds security and developing and enforcing information security procedures.

sharper. Operations officer or, less politely, spy.

Smithery. The sector of the Mines focusing on technology.

smithies. Technical experts who make spy gadgetry.

Special Employee Services (ses). A unit within the Mines responsible for helping employees deal with personal and psychological problems, as well as substance abuse.

Strikes, the. The 2001 attack on the World Trade Center and Pentagon.

TRASHINT. Dumpster-derived intelligence.

White Mines. The analytical sector of the Mines.